The *Dean* of
CLINTON COUNTY

The *Dean* of
CLINTON COUNTY

A Baseball Novel

Doug Feldmann

Acclaim Press
MORLEY, MISSOURI

Acclaim Press
TM
— Your Next Great Book —

P.O. Box 238
Morley, MO 63767
(573) 472-9800
www.acclaimpress.com

Book & Cover Design: Frene Melton

ISBN: 978-1-948901-88-8 | 1-948901-88-9
Library of Congress Control Number: 2021937310

First Printing: 2022
Printed in the United States of America
10 9 8 7 6 5 4 3 2 1

This publication was produced using available information.
The publisher regrets it cannot assume responsibility for errors or omissions.

A NOTE TO THE READER

The content, characters, and events within this novel are a mixture of fact and fiction. The actions of real individuals in this novel are not designed to cast any of them in a positive or negative light but are merely intended to advance the story.

ACKNOWLEDGMENTS

A few words of thanks. . . .

. . . . to Gus Kuczka, my uncle, who grew up a mere 150 yards from the Beckemeyer coal mine. His insight into the town's history has been invaluable.

. . . . to Brad Lokitz, my cousin, who provided important historical data for the story.

. . . . to the late G. H. Fleming, a wonderful writer who put together the first book on the Gas House Gang I ever read—*The Dizziest Season*, a compilation of the colorful newspaper articles of the great baseball campaign of 1934.

. . . . to Robert Gregory, whose 1992 book *Diz* inspired me long ago to conduct further research into the Cardinals of the 1930s.

. . . . to Tim O'Neil from the *St. Louis Post-Dispatch*, whose retrospective articles have helped to create part of the historical context for this story.

. . . . to J. Dallas Helton, a former student of mine, for assistance in translating German entries.

. . . . to Gary Schwab, another former student of mine and perpetual student of Southern Illinois history.

. . . . to Doug Sikes and Charlie Francis at Acclaim Press, whose professionalism and expertise added greatly to this project.

And last, and most of all, to my wife Angie, the expert writer in our home, who helps me with plot, conflict, point of view—and life in general every day.

DEDICATION

For my grandfather John, the coal miner; for my father John, the ballplayer; and for my son John, who carries their legacy. The amalgamation of these men produced the protagonist in this story.

I would be true, for there are those who trust me;

I would be pure, for there are those who care;

I would be strong, for there is much to suffer;

And I would be brave, for there is much to dare.

—Howard A. Walter

The *Dean* of
CLINTON COUNTY

A Baseball Novel

CHAPTER ONE

The soothing Florida sun dipped slowly over the trees of Anna Maria Island late in the afternoon of January 17, 1934. Rolling west in their Model B Ford toward the majestic blue of the Gulf of Mexico were Jay and Patricia Dean, aged twenty-four and twenty-eight respectively, brimming with excitement as their goal was just a few blocks away.

On the edge of Bradenton, they turned off the main road. Weaving slowly through a scenic neighborhood on streets lined with sandy shoulders, they came upon their destination—7815 Senrab Drive. Atop the driveway was a three-bedroom stucco house, adorned with a grand archway entrance and a backyard nestling up against the first touches of the gulf waters in Palma Sola Bay. The property had just become their new winter retreat, complementing the suite they rented during the warmer months at the Forest Park Hotel in St. Louis. Having rented a place in downtown Bradenton for the past month, the happy couple had just celebrated Jay's birthday a day earlier with a sumptuous dinner at the Terrace Hotel up in Tampa.

With the cozy haven far removed from the bone-chilling winters of the Midwest, the corners of their eyes met as they smiled in satisfaction. To Jay, part of a nomadic cotton-picking family from Arkansas and Oklahoma, those cold, rugged northern winters always served as a reminder of the stark poverty from which he had come.

By this time, Jay was known to most folks as "Dizzy," a pejorative nickname issued to him in San Antonio in 1928 by his drill sergeant during a brief stay in the United States Army. Now, six years later, he was an established professional baseball pitcher for the St. Louis Cardinals. The precocious Dean appeared on his way to becoming one of the best the game had ever seen, leading the National League in striking out batters in each of his first two full seasons in 1932 and 1933. With his rapid success in pro ball, Dizzy had been finally able to provide a stable income for himself and Pat, despite working for the penny-pinching Cardinals' president and owner Sam Breadon. His success also enabled him to alleviate some of the struggles of the rest of the family and their sharecropping lives—including his widowed father Albert, his mentally-disabled brother Elmer, and his brother Paul, another aspiring pitcher who, in the past year, had been the number one hurler for the Cardinals' top farm team. Dizzy's newfound prosperity had come just ahead of the phenomenon that would later be called the Dust Bowl and that would drive many sharecroppers, as well as those who owned the land on which they labored, to ruin.

All the hardships, however, seemed a million miles away in the Sunshine State. "Dizzy and his wife have been here since December 22," a snooping reporter in Bradenton for the *St. Louis Star-Times* revealed to the folks back home. "Dean has been hunting, fishing, playing golf, and otherwise living the life of a winter visitor." Pat had started dating him back in 1930 while working in a shoe store in Houston during one of Dizzy's minor league stops. It was here where the brash Dean—convinced he would soon be a star—began telling local merchants to just put his cashless purchases "on Mr. Rickey's tab," in reference to one of Breadon's office employees.

Now entering his third big-league season, Dean received a fine raise to place his salary at $7,500 for the year—a 150 percent increase over his $3,000 rate from his first two seasons. Building a nest egg, Dizzy operated a gas station in downtown Bradenton for further income as he was suddenly doing better than most of his contemporaries during the Great Depression. "A career in baseball is much less attractive now than in other years," Westbrook Pegler would write that spring in the *New York World-Telegram*. "Wages have been revised sharply downward, and club owners have no players' union to contend with. The individual athlete, as always, is obliged to take it or leave it, except that this year he is obliged to take much less—or leave it."

Their belongings having been moved into their new home, Diz, with an entire month to enjoy before the Cardinals' grueling spring training workouts would begin at the ballpark in town, made a short drive back down Manatee Avenue to the Bradenton Country Club. Settling over his golf ball, he suddenly straightened up and let out a laugh. "Won't be no wolves howlin' at our door this winter," he proudly told his friends about his comfortable bankroll.

Slowly reaching his club back in dramatic fashion, he whipped a shot with his wooden cleek down the middle of the fairway with another proud laugh as he snatched his tee from the ground on the sun-splashed morning.

That same morning, the same sun simultaneously struggled to burn through the rugged Midwestern winter that Diz and Pat had left behind, managing a mere 28 degrees in a remote place forty-five miles east of St. Louis in Beckemeyer, Illinois. On Randolph Street sat a three-room, one-level house with flaking white paint, where twenty-two-year-old John Laufketter forced his lean six-foot-three frame off a mattress that had no sheet or blanket. Aware that he was a year and a half younger than Dizzy Dean, John nonetheless felt decades older with a body that ached with nearly every movement. Trying to ignore the pain, John instinctively shook himself from his slumber within a minute or two of five o'clock every morning, the beginning of his daily routine that was never altered, except on Sundays when a couple of extra hours of sleep was possible before Mass at St. Anthony's.

With the wind screaming incessantly against the unhinged front door along the west wall of the house, John tried to tiptoe silently toward the kitchen so as not to disturb the other people who lived in the house, including not only his wife Rose and their seven-month-old son Joseph but also Rose's father and mother. Slithering down the hallway he was able to see, even indoors and in the semi-darkness, his breath was puffing out in front of him.

Boiling what was left of some diluted coffee, John stoked the fire in the potbelly stove and peeked into the icebox for anything that might remain. The Laufketters were fortunate to have kept the appliance running to extend their food supply a bit longer, as many of their neighbors had been forced to shut off their electrical service in recent months. Besides canning some vegetables from the backyard garden, the residents of Beckemeyer had little ability to store food beyond a day or two (John personally did not care to eat anything from the garden, as he always thought there was a peculiar smell to the vegetables grown in the lots on Randolph Street, unlike the delicious ones he recalled from his boyhood home on the other side of Beckemeyer). More for sustenance than leisure, families around Clinton County had taken to hunting and fishing frequently since the crash while many had returned to antiquated coal oil lanterns for basic lighting.

With the deepening of what was being termed as the four-year-old "Great Depression," Clinton County mirrored the misery of the region, nation, and world as sources of income had also been in short supply as the family farms surrounding Beckemeyer had been particularly decimated from plummeting corn and soybean prices. To make matters worse, several horrific dust storms had swept through the country and into Southern Illinois—a series of thick, ruinous, black blizzards that had originated in South Dakota two months earlier. The beginnings of the assault arrived in a wall of dirt, 350 million tons in weight and climbing nearly 10,000 feet in the air.

After the Beckemeyer coal mine was shut down, John had been able to maintain part-time employment at the shaft in Breese, four miles to the west. With no form of transportation available, John and his Beckemeyer neighbors lucky enough to have spots in the Breese mine began their walking commute by 5:30 in the morning. The Beckemeyer mine, the latest of a string of Clinton County mines to have recently been idled, first opened in 1894, the same year an adjoining zinc smelter had begun operations on Harper Street near the Laufketter residence on the east side of town. The mine butted up against the north side of the railroad tracks, making it easy for the product to be loaded into waiting cars. Across Harper Street to the west of the mine and smelter stood Ed Roach's Tavern, where after a quick, futile rinse in the washhouse, many of the miners took their paychecks when the closing whistle blew, in an attempt to self-medicate their fatigued, damaged, and discouraged bodies. With the danger of collapse or explosions at every turn, every worker wandered into the job thinking each day may be his last.

On the outer edges of Roach's lot, the so-called coal camps were visible, a collection of makeshift tents where miners working only temporarily in town would sleep for the night, while paying rent to the mining company for the primitive sleeping space.

Despite the conditions, John paid little attention to the pitfalls of the occupation. To him, working in the mine was simply what the local men did, whether the Becky mine had work or if they had to make the forty-five-minute walk over to Breese, a trip made in fair weather or foul.

Work is an honor, John often thought to himself, genuinely but involuntarily.

After a glance into all corners of the icebox revealed there was nothing to eat, John's stomach emitted a rumble. Again, he paid little mind. He knew the feeling of going hungry for days at a time, even during the brief time he was away at college. Since it was a Wednesday, John figured he might be able to dash over to the soup line on Walnut Street in Breese during the lunch hour and be back in time to resume his shift.

Still inching along as quietly as possible, John made his way across the kitchen to a basin that was half-full of pungent water from the well in the backyard. He stooped over it and began washing his face.

Suddenly, his left hand shot quickly over his mouth to muffle his loud groan. An instant flash of agonizing, familiar pain streaked up the right side of his back, electrifying his shoulder.

The ailment had worsened in recent months, with the spasms now occurring as often as several times a day. He knew the exact moment the injury had happened; it was six short years ago while he was still a teenager. The intensity and perils of working in the mine had exacerbated his suffering even further, but he had no choice. There was no extra money for anyone in the family to see a doctor, except for the baby.

Straightening himself up from the basin with another grimace, John saw the calendar on the wall of the kitchen. The pain, as well as *how* he had injured himself, was a constant reminder that, despite being a young man, John was already growing old. As if beset with a crippling, degenerative disease, his time on earth was outpacing the actual years as they passed.

Stumbling outside into the frigid dawn, John paid no notice when the windbeaten screen door slammed loudly behind him, the damaged bolts loosening a bit further. Despite the chilly air plunging deep into his lungs, John was in no hurry to retrieve his work outfit from the clothesline. Even after the usual Saturday washing a few nights ago and his limited hours of work, his pants and shirt already had new stains. In the early light, the garments hung upon the line like stiff, condemned men, having received only an inadequate freshening overnight in the cold breeze. Though it was winter, dirt and grime from the Dust Bowl seemed to always linger in the air. *Nothing good comes from the weather*, John scoffed as he gazed off in the distance.

Still, besides seeing Rose upon returning home, it was John's favorite time of the day. It was a moment when the pain departed, when he was able to close his eyes and imbibe everything he loved about Beckemeyer since his childhood, like it had been for his father . . . the peace and solemnity of the rural landscape, where a man's work was his salvation.

John straightened himself again with another grunt. Wincing after a sip of the bitter coffee, he saw through a neighbor's yard the tracks of the Baltimore and Ohio Railroad, the very tracks his father helped lay, which sat two blocks north of his home. A coal train was approaching from the west, its lumbering engine coughing exhaust upward through the crisp early morning. Although he had watched the locomotive approach a thousand times, John stopped and stared as he always did. For him, it was yet another comforting element of Beckemeyer as he loved hearing the growing volume . . . *click-CLANK, click-CLANK, click-CLANK*. . . .

A year ago, the train would have been slowing down for a stop at the Beckemeyer mine. But now it rolled through town unabated, as John's father came to his mind. His head drooped, swallowing a lump of sudden sadness as he stepped quietly back inside.

Passing down the hallway one final time, he was grateful to notice the house had warmed slightly since he had stoked the fire. He whispered to Rose as she turned over in her sleep.

"See you tonight. Love you."

Slipping out the door, John crossed the tracks and turned left onto the shoulder of US Route 50 for his shivering walk to Breese. A handful of his neighbors were already on their way, although John noticed there were fewer of them recently, and of those who remained, fewer still were clutching lunch pails. They walked with a lifeless, arm-dangling gait, almost as apparitions, facing straight ahead with expressionless countenances and never looking off to the side.

From among the march, he heard a friendly voice.

"Hey, Johnny!" his neighbor Gus yelled from across Route 50, as John made his way over to the north side of the road. "Did you hear about Dean's new contract?"

Gus, like John, had always shown the greatest loyalty not only to Beckemeyer but also to the baseball team in St. Louis. "Over seven grand just to pitch," Gus proclaimed, not waiting for an answer. "Frisch'll have those boys ready, I'm telling you."

"Yeah," John affirmed quietly as he circled his right shoulder. It was an old habit that occasionally surfaced when someone mentioned baseball, but it also caused a small stinger of the familiar pain to shoot through his body once again. "That's a lot of scratch," John offered in the way of conversation, "but he's worth every penny of it."

Gus nodded in complete agreement. He continued with another question.

"You think he'll ever be as good as 'The Meal Ticket'?" he asked about the famous New York pitcher Carl Hubbell, who had lived up to his nickname the past autumn. In October, Hubbell had led his teammates to much-needed bonus money with their 1933 World Series title over the Washington Senators.

John again shrugged in minimal acknowledgment, his mind not on baseball but on how many hours he might get this week. As they continued their slow trek westward, Breese eventually came into view. Soon in the distance, they spotted the entrance of the mine—the dusty, dangerous meal ticket for a lucky few from Beckemeyer.

CHAPTER TWO

Alphonse Laufketter was part of a new wave of German immigrants who had come to St. Louis in the late nineteenth century, landing on the banks of the Mississippi River as a sixteen-year-old during the early afternoon hours of May 8, 1884, within minutes of a son being born to John and Martha Truman on the other side of Missouri. Two months earlier, "Alphie" and his uncle had left their hometown of Paderborn, Germany, with the half-hearted blessing of Alphie's father Wolfgang. Wolfgang had regularly preached the importance of loyalty to home, and until young Alphie revealed his hunger for adventure on the distant, mystical soil of America, Wolfgang had believed his son would follow in his footsteps in becoming a skilled machinist.

Upon disembarking a steamship at the foot of Spruce Street, Alphie and his uncle ventured a short distance northward along the shore. They ultimately found work in a small German-owned beer brewery on Destrehan, just a stone's throw upstream from the city's fabulous new bridge. But Alphie sought out more new territory and soon left his uncle behind to begin roaming the eastern bank of the river in Illinois. Due to his good nature and reliable work ethic, he found steady income in railroad construction and maintenance, quickly picking up on the many facets of the job as he happily went about his labor every day. He enjoyed seeing the new places the work offered him each morning and felt privileged to be contributing to the building of his adopted home country.

"Arbeiten ist eine Ehre . . . Arbeiten ist eine Ehre!" he proclaimed about the honor of hard work to the few toiling alongside who could understand him, words he had heard every day from his tireless father as Alphie smiled in thinking of him. *"Arbeiten gut und mit Stolz,"* he was quick to add—noting that one should also have pride in work done well.

During a five-week job on the railroad outside of Granite City, a local schoolteacher living along the tracks offered to tutor Alphie in English during the evenings for ten cents a session. The teacher gave Alphie the idea to drop the "o" from the German spelling of his surname, suggesting it might be easier for Americans to pronounce. He did so and incessantly practiced writing "Laufketter" instead of the traditional "Laufkoetter" that he had brought over from Germany.

When a long day ended, many of the railroad workers often took their pay and headed straight for the makeshift taverns lining the shore on both sides of river—rough, brawling places where teeth and sometimes eyeballs were pushed outside with the broom in the morning. But Alphie preferred to save his money carefully and stayed out of such places; he never permitted himself to waste anything, foregoing a boarding room to instead live in a large tent with three other laborers who were also miserly. Alphie liked to assert that he could live on a dollar a week if it ever became necessary.

After putting his strength, dependability, and upbeat disposition on display for almost three years on the railroad, Alphie was told in 1889 by his foreman that he was receiving a nominal promotion to gandy dancer, one who identified and completed repairs on existing tracks while following behind the construction crew. He wished to take time to meet people in the different places where the crew would work, which included stops in Freeburg, O'Fallon, Mascoutah, and other towns as they ventured farther into Illinois.

Alphie became especially fond of the people in the New Baden area, and finally, in 1904, he found himself fixing his final rails outside a newly formed mining community in central Clinton County known as Buxton. The town's name was officially changed shortly thereafter on July 27, 1905, to honor August Beckemeyer, one of the founders. With a strong German enclave and encircled by lush, rolling farmland that reminded him of the territory surrounding Paderborn, Alphie's heart was seized. His work on the tracks brought him to a home in his new land.

Standing majestically at the southwestern edge of Beckemeyer was the new St. Anthony's Catholic Church, built in the summer of 1905 after a great hailstorm had struck the area and destroyed the windows of St. Dominic's Church just west of town. Construction of St. Anthony's had been completed under the moonlight by local farmers after toiling in their fields each day, and the church soon became the religious and social cornerstone of the community. Within a year, the summer parish picnic was launched in what would become annual tradition each July, as residents eagerly filled their plates with large helpings of fresh fried chicken, ripe watermelon, green beans, corn, and other vegetables, all washed down with tall glasses of ice-cold lemonade and followed by strudel, pies, and cakes for dessert. Catching up on local news, they carried their food to comfortable spots under the shade trees.

It was here at St. Anthony's very first picnic in 1906 where Alphie, now thirty-eight, met Leah Erlhaus, a twenty-six-year-old woman whose family had assisted with the construction of the church and owned a small farm on Beckemeyer's southwestern border with Bartelso. Leah, at five-foot-six, was a few inches shorter than Alphie. While engaging and having several local suitors, she had put off marriage to help with the farm duties at home. The beautiful Leah had magnificent jet-black hair, which was straight and always brushed beautifully, appearing to glisten at Alphie each time he saw her.

At the picnic, Leah was helping her mother tend to the pie table when Alphie bashfully approached to introduce himself. Soothed by Leah's warmth, he was most happy to accept the slice of apple cobbler that she herself had baked.

Before long, they could hardly wait to see each other. At least once a week for the remainder of the summer, Alphie ran from the crew's worksite at quitting time to where the rail line met Bartelso Road, which formed the western boundary of Beckemeyer. He then turned south and kept running until he encountered Leah, who rode her bicycle from the family farm. On weekends, she would ride all the way to Beckemeyer and meet Alphie for evening strolls around town, a cool, refreshing diversion from the sweltering Southern Illinois summer heat. While fatigued from his ten or eleven hours on the rails each day, Alphie nonetheless looked forward to the encounters; he spoke of them with great anticipation to his fellow workers, always with a small smile visible in the corner of his mouth.

To win the favor of Leah's father, Alphie had to make trips to Bartelso as well, calling on her at the Erlhaus farm. While suspicious of Alphie's thick accent and minimal earthly belongings, Mr. Erlhaus ultimately consented that the couple be married as Alphie's honesty, work ethic, and frugality carried the day.

The wedding took place at St. Anthony's on April 6, 1907, putting an abrupt end to Alphie's practice of living in tent camps with other itinerant railroad workers. He knew it was time to settle down in one spot for the first time since leaving Germany a full twenty-three years earlier.

With assurance from the railroad bosses that he could work solely in the immediate vicinity for the foreseeable future, Alphie nervously took out a small mortgage loan from the Beckemeyer branch of the Farmers and Merchants Bank (an experience made more comfortable for him when the loan officer was able to converse in German). The money enabled Alphie to complement his sizable cash down payment from his savings to purchase a fine four-bedroom house on Lincoln Street near the tracks on Beckemeyer's west side; and while not happy owing anyone *any* amount of money, Alphie was nonetheless proud he now had a piece of America to call his own. The front porch offered a clear view of St. Anthony's and its festival grounds just two blocks away, where Alphie could always recall meeting the love of his life. After spending nearly each moment in America on the move, he found that the sudden stability suited him. With the church always in view, Alphie and Leah spent hours after Mass on Sunday afternoons chatting on their front porch, ultimately wandering to the backyard later in the day to tend to their beloved garden. They used every available square foot to grow peppers, tomatoes, blackberries, basil, and onions.

With his reputation for fairness and honesty becoming known throughout Beckemeyer, businessmen occasionally approached Alphie with various financial opportunities, such as investments in land, livestock, and commodities. Alphie always politely declined them, partly out of mistrust and fear of being swindled and mostly out of the fear of losing the loyalty of the railroad and its steady paycheck. Another person alerted Alphie to the booming coal business that was quickly taking over the area with the potential for him to take home a salary of sixty dollars a month while allowing him to be closer to home. The job would also permit Alphie to be around more German speakers, the man told him, as the mines were mostly manned by European immigrants.

Yet, he declined. His allegiance to the railroad was so complete that, over the course of his career, Alphie would cross a picket line on three separate occasions, choosing to go to work instead of joining his striking colleagues. He never wanted his regular support of the family to ever be interrupted, even at the expense of friendships.

On September 17, 1911, that family expanded, as he and Leah welcomed their son John.

As soon as he was able to walk, John loved following his father wherever Alphie went around the house. If Alphie was fixing something, the boy was right there by his side, and while it would have been quicker and easier for Alphie to complete the task alone, he never shooed John away. Instead, he welcomed the company and encouraged his son's interest.

"Ach, Johnny," Alphie would say to get his attention when a new job had to be done. "Work *ist eine Ehre!"* he would add with a wide grin.

By the time John was twelve, he had already learned how to replace spark plugs in a small motor, do basic carpentry, and even patch a leaky roof, during the latter of which he had clung lovingly to his father's back as they headed up and down the ladder.

Alphie regularly stopped short with tasks and left one piece of the work unfinished; with another grin, he threw up his hands in feigned bewilderment. Folding his arms and looking at his son, he challenged John to figure out the remaining part of the job. Leah followed the same practice with chores inside the house. John was amazed at how his father seemed able to fix anything, and when he asked his father the secret to his success, Alphie responded that he had listened to *his* father.

John also loved to share in the one solitary activity Alphie always strove to complete—reading the newspaper or, at least, as well as he could. One of the daily St. Louis papers was available in Beckemeyer, costing two cents and dropped off in large bundles at the town's train station. The two particularly looked forward to their routine on Sundays, a day when the stories in the paper were expanded and often accompanied by pictures. After church, they spread out the paper on the living room floor, and young John would point to the pictures and identify the contents. If guests visited the Laufketter home, Alphie would proudly instruct John to read passages aloud from the most recent copy.

It was during John's youngest years when Alphie and others around Beckemeyer were closely following newspaper accounts of the growing unrest in Germany and a mounting concern about relatives who remained in that part of the world.

At the outbreak of the Great War in 1914, nearly one-third of the St. Louis population either had been born in Germany or had at least one parent who had emigrated from there, with a similar percentage among those in Clinton County as well. As soon as hostilities were sparked, rallies were held by German Americans in St. Louis to show support for both their old and new homelands. An example of this fervor was an event held at Turner Hall on Chouteau Avenue just days after the war began, with German and American flags waved in the air while the band played polkas as well as "The Star-Spangled Banner."

Soon, however, sentiment turned against those who were referred to as "the Hun." Once the United States entered the conflict in 1917, first-year German courses were banned in St. Louis public schools, while advanced courses were phased out once matriculated students had completed their diplomas (under the guise of "a lack of enrollment"). The names of many businesses in the city, and even some city streets, were changed to remove German nomenclature. Certain St. Louis newspapers previously printed in both German and English versions would now only circulate the latter. "I am glad to see the agitation now sweeping the country antagonistic to German-language newspapers, sermons in German and German textbooks," pronounced former St. Louis mayor Rolla Wells in a fiery speech at the St. Louis Club in the spring of 1918 while rallying people to buy Liberty Bonds for the war effort. "Why should such a custom be permitted?"

But a more troubling story in the *St. Louis Post-Dispatch* from April 5, 1918 caught Alphie's eye. After skimming the contents, he gently shooed aside John, who had been curiously hanging on his shoulder. Alphie asked Leah to read the article to him in a private whisper, making sure he got every word.

The article told of a thirty-year-old coal miner named Robert Prager of Collinsville, a town sitting about thirty-five miles west of Beckemeyer on the river bluffs overlooking St. Louis. Prager had been born in Germany and worked at the Donk Coal Mine in Maryville. One day on the job, some of Prager's fellow miners became suspicious after overhearing him ask unusual questions about dynamite. It was well known in the mine that Prager had earlier tried to enlist in the United States Navy. Nonetheless, a rumor began to spread that Prager was a spy.

Within a few days, the gossip took root as Prager stopped going to his job, fearing something bad was about to occur. On the night of April 4, he was out walking near Collinsville's city hall when he was spotted by one of the miners. Knowing he was being followed, Prager attempted to hide. But the man—and soon, a converging mob of ten others—caught up with him. They dragged the kicking Prager to a tree west of town. One of them pulled a pencil and a piece of paper from his pocket, permitting Prager to write a final note to his family back in Germany. They then lynched him.

Two months later in a trial at the Madison County Courthouse in Edwardsville, all eleven men were acquitted of the crime before an hour had passed in the trial. Emerging from the courthouse with arms raised triumphantly, the men were greeted by well-wishers and even a makeshift band that struck up a patriotic tune to celebrate the result.

After learning of the story, the distraught Alphie decided not to speak any more German on the worksite at the railroad. With no confidence in his English, he thus kept to himself, determined to simply let his reliability conquer any doubts that anyone might have about his loyalty to his new country.

In time, the war ended, and much of the angry sentiment toward Germans subsided. The 1920s dawned with life returning to a pleasant rhythm as attention shifted from front-page news to happier pursuits. Life was especially good where the Laufketters found themselves on the west side of Beckemeyer, where the houses were slightly nicer than those on the east side. The children played outside for long hours. The adults took walks. And the magnificent focal point of the whole community, St. Anthony's, stood there as well.

And, most noticeably, the air was cleaner.

As one ventured eastward and crossed Louis Street, the north-south meridian that dissected Beckemeyer in half, a different landscape was clear, as geology itself had created a cultural divide in the town.

With the coal mine and the adjacent zinc smelter churning around the clock with few interruptions, a filthy haze always hovered over the east side of the community. While men from all parts of town *worked* there, none ever chose to have his family *live* there if an affordable place was found elsewhere. Louis Street was as far east in Beckemeyer as most from the west side ever wished to travel, with the fortunate few owning automobiles traveling past the dirty section on their way to Carlyle or farther yet to Centralia to do their shopping out of town.

Nothing in the eastern half could escape the constant soot that drifted from the mine. The perpetual, strangulating black fog was intensified by train engines that belched salvos of smoke as well, always standing ready to ship the freshly mined coal off to unknown destinations. When the trains started up, east side residents knew everything was soon to be blanketed in a defiled, discolored mess. Women frantically gathered clothes from the wash line while corralling their children indoors, in the very same manner they would when a deadly storm during the Dust Bowl was about to approach.

By the early 1920s, a rumor was circulating around town that toxic chemicals from the zinc smelter were beginning to seep into the wells of the east side's water supply. But no one dared complain for fear of the plant being shut down, as the existence of the mine and smelter was necessary for the town's survival. Aside from employment, the only thing the east side seemed to have going for it was the baseball field, sitting just south of the industrial area.

On Louis Street stood the cultural epicenter of town. George's Tavern, operated by Henry "Beans" Garcia, served sandwiches day and night, in addition to plate lunches, and was a place where local news could be acquired quicker than any newspaper. When school was out during the summer months and the rest of his chores at home were complete, John could often be seen hurrying to George's near the end of the afternoon, asked by Alphie to bring cold draft beer back home. Balancing two buckets over his shoulders on a stick, John arrived back on Lincoln Street with an appreciative smile and pat on the head from his father, who noticed one bucket had apparently lost some liquid during the trip.

When Prohibition halted the sale of alcohol starting on January 17, 1920, Alphie returned to the craft he had learned during his teenage years on the Mississippi—that of brewing beer himself. He read of amusing stories in the newspaper of others trying to circumvent the Volstead Act, such as fancy folks in St. Louis holding lavish yet covert parties at upscale spots, such as the Chase Park Plaza and Forest Park Hotel.

With no beer to haul home from George's once Prohibition hit Beckemeyer, the remainder of John's summer days as a teenager were filled with playing baseball, fishing, and meandering around nearby Shoal Creek. He and his friends were too young to work in the mine, at the smelter, or on the railroads, and the only farming was done by families on the periphery of town. With little else to do, John and his friends would sometimes sneak away to play basketball in Carlyle as the school building possessed a brand-new hardwood gym floor. The shiny wooden surface was much to the boys' preference compared to the dirt basketball grounds on which they had to play in Beckemeyer, even though John's absence would also anger Leah when he was late for supper.

The Beckemeyer baseball field, however, was the most regular daily destination for John and his friends. It was in a small park on the town's eastern boundary at Murray Street, less than a quarter mile south of the coal mine and smelter. It had been constructed on a plowed-under cornfield by Garcia and his associate, Anton "Putt" Skrobul, the latter borrowing a tractor from a local farmer to get the job done.

On Sunday afternoons from mid-May through mid-September, the grounds also served as the home field of the Beckemeyer Eagles of the Clinton County Baseball League, of which Garcia was the president and Skrobul was the team manager. Ten towns in the county had teams in the league, each with a maximum roster of sixteen players. In addition to Beckemeyer, participating towns included Carlyle, Hoffman, Bartelso, Germantown, Aviston, Breese, Trenton, New Baden, and Albers. Most of the clubs attempted to practice two nights a week in preparation for the weekly games, if enough men could get away from their jobs in time. Fierce rivalries emanated from the Sunday contests, which always evolved into full-fledged community events. Fans by the literal truckload, hanging off the back ends of jalopies, flatbeds, coal train cars, and by any other means necessary, traveled loyally behind their team after church each Sunday morning. Well in advance of the one o'clock games (with occasional doubleheaders scheduled as well), the fans always arrived at the park early to find the best places to sit and spread out their blankets. Across the league an assortment of ages dotted the rosters, ranging from the late teens to early fifties. Playing for another other town in the League other than one's own was unthinkable—and illegal, anyway, under the CCL rules.

Each game and each season comprised an intense struggle for local pride, and the children became entangled in this pride as well. For in addition to dreaming of one day playing for the great, mystical, unseen St. Louis Cardinals, only known from newspaper stories and the occasional broadcast of a game on the radio, John and his buddies equally longed for their first goal in turning eighteen and, thus, becoming eligible to represent Beckemeyer in the league.

CHAPTER THREE

Lugging their equipment along with them, John and his friends from Beckemeyer's west side spent their morning journey to the baseball field happily, snatching apples along the way from the tree in Joan Mazeka's yard (with her consent), talking about their latest adventures of taking catfish out of the creek, and bragging of their impending athletic exploits in the coming afternoon.

Among the group was John's best buddy of all, Bobby Durstmiller, a year ahead of him at St. Anthony's School and the best ballplayer John was sure he would ever see. Bobby was always the last one to join the growing group as it made its way to the field, as he lived closest to the park on Scoville Street on the east side. Along the way, John and Bobby loved to discuss their favorite Cardinal players; John's choice was pitcher Jesse Haines while Bobby's idol was the hard-hitting first baseman Jim Bottomley.

While John was more interested in doing the pitching, Bobby scanned the selection of bats the guys brought along to the field, looking for his weapon of choice. Most of the sticks had been handcrafted by the boys' fathers from materials and tools at home. John had to rely upon others for his own equipment as Alphie, though handy, was not sure how to make baseball gear.

"Man, I love to hit," Bobby often said while arriving at the field with a swagger, tossing a few bats aside before locating one he liked. Grasping it with both hands and holding the war club in front of him, he peered at the barrel ominously with his head tilted back as if planning destruction. Waving it slowly and regally, he strutted toward home plate, well before the other boys had even stepped onto the field. They would play for hours, losing all track of time playing a nine-inning game, resetting the score to 0–0, and starting all over again until their faces were sunburned when heading home for dinner.

As John grew throughout junior high school, he began to dominate the local and regional competition in baseball and basketball. Most of the formal instruction he received in both sports came from his teacher and coach at St. Anthony's, Father Karl Schweighart. Alphie had wanted little to do with sports, largely considering it a waste of time that could be spent at work or with family. Still, he was fascinated with the obsession Americans held with baseball and even tried it himself when the railroad workers summoned an impromptu game during a break. He did not mind his son playing if all chores were finished. And knowing that John was a zealous fan of the Cardinals, Alphie got a team pennant for him from one of his coworkers and hung it carefully for John in his bedroom. In the fall of John's eighth grade year, the Cardinals won their first World Series title in triumphing over the mighty New York Yankees and their immortal slugger Babe Ruth. John and his friends were glued to every pitch, listening in on a Philco radio at George's behind a throng of grown men who crowded around the set.

John soon became a star athlete at Breese High School, a three-grade secondary institution on North Second Street that opened a year prior to his freshman term. By the start of his junior year in the autumn of 1927, John stood nearly six-foot-three and possessed considerable strength despite a trim frame at 175 pounds, utilizing his long, rope-tight arms and legs to slither effectively around the basketball floor. When the Breese High basketball squad practiced after school, they were assisted by the girls' team so that full scrimmages could be held.

The first glimpse of John's athletic exploits outside of Beckemeyer occurred over Christmas 1928, when a three-day basketball tournament was held twenty miles to the east at Centralia High School and its huge, imposing gymnasium. Led by John, Breese waltzed through the first two days of the schedule to reach the championship game against the host school. Fighting against a talented Centralia team and its hostile home crowd, John gave birth to his legend in nearly breaking the single-game Illinois state scoring record. He ended the evening with 59 points, 5 shy of the mark, leading Breese over the heavily favored home team by a score of 77–68.

It was on the pitching mound of the spring-thawed baseball field, however, where John truly overwhelmed the opposition. Loosening his shoulders before every pitch by shrugging them a few times in a circular motion, John befuddled batters with lightning strike throws, making the ball look like an aspirin tablet as it reached home plate. In his junior year he struck out twenty hitters in a single game against Highland with the senior Durstmiller as his catcher. Around Beckemeyer, John always referred to his best friend Bobby possessively as "*his* catcher," not the *team's* catcher.

Unlike many high school pitchers from small towns, John did not rely solely on his fastball to conquer opposing batters. Other teams were stunned to find John had a full arsenal of pitches, including a devastating curveball and changeup, the latter of which John called his "dead fish," appearing to drop off a table at the last moment and causing the frustrated hitter to swing over it nearly every time. He was feared by *opposing* pitchers, as well, his smooth righthanded swing sending line drives whistling far into the outfield beyond the eye's reach as John's galloping frame rounded the bases to easy stand-up triples.

With plenty of organized baseball every day at school, John, Bobby, and the rest of the gang no longer played pickup games at the Beckemeyer field; instead, Saturdays and Sundays were now spent slurping glass bottles of Coca-Cola outside Diekamper's General Store. While most people got their food at Janet's Grocery on the next block, Diekamper's—situated prominently off the main drag of Louis Street in the center of town—was the place where everyone in Beckemeyer got everything else. Candy, clothing, hardware, small and large tools, cooking and heating oil, feed for cattle, ammunition, wedding gifts, and all else imaginable was available for purchase from the kindhearted Joe Diekamper. Times were good; people from all social classes and all professions came through the door, each with some spending money in his or her pocket. Virtually no one needed extra consideration, as the credit log on the shelf underneath Joe's cash register rarely had any entries and usually gathered dust.

One of Joe's regular customers was Genevieve Schutzenhofer, who often had her son Heinie in tow as she went about her errands in town. It was typical for Mrs. Schutzenhofer to make Heinie wait by Diekamper's back door while she completed her shopping inside. On one such visit, Mrs. Schutzenhofer met Joe at the register.

"Mr. Diekamper, I need a new pair of overalls for my Heinie."

"Well," Joe responded, "how big is your Heinie?"

"Come around to the back of the store and I'll show you."

John had the world by the tail. He loved baseball, and it continued to come easy to him. But at one point in his senior year, his coach felt he was taking the game for granted, and he warned John to take care of his pitching arm. The coach advised aspirin, salt baths, and regular running after games to maintain circulation and keep the wing healthy. While nodding and politely listening to the advice, John privately dismissed it. He could pitch every day, he figured, and nothing would happen to him.

On April 23, Breese High was playing its most distant road game of the season at Salem, twenty-five miles to the east. In the brisk, cold weather of springtime baseball in the Midwest, the teams were ordered by the umpire to hustle on and off the field in between innings. John was doing his part to expedite the contest, mowing down the Salem batters in his customary fashion and not paying any attention to the chill in the air. He begrudgingly wore a jacket in between innings as directed, but he tossed it aside whenever the coach was not looking.

With two out in the sixth inning and Breese ahead by a 4–0 score, John held a 2-2 count on a batter when he reached back for something extra on his fastball to get the final strike. As soon as he flung his arm forward, he felt a "snap" in his shoulder. A twinge of minor pain immediately followed, but John paid no mind.

He labored through the one final inning in the seventh to get Breese another win, pushing the team's record to a sparkling 15-2 for the season with four games left to go. As the team was halfway home on the bus, however, John was struck with such pain that he had to lay on the floor on his left side.

The following Saturday, Alphie took John to a physician in Carlyle, who determined he had strained his acromioclavicular joint in his shoulder, likely caused by the overuse of the pitching arm. The injury would heal properly, the doctor told John, if given ample rest; if not, the condition could become chronic and worsen.

John decided he would not tell the coach about the diagnosis; he would just fight through the pain and pitch in three of the four remaining games, giving way in the final contest of the year as it was the second game of a doubleheader, anyway.

He discovered that shrugging his shoulders between every inning (and sometimes every pitch) helped to loosen the joint a little bit, at least to the point where the soreness was temporarily tolerable.

He lost the first two games after the shoulder injury, by which time the crowds at Breese games had noticeably shrunken. At the midpoint of the season the stands had been full, including a sizable number of out-of-place, middle-aged men who wore straw hats and carried peculiar little briefcases around with them.

But now only fifteen to twenty spectators were present on the season's final day, mostly comprised of locals and some parents of the home players. With no postseason state tournament for high school baseball in Illinois at the time, the Breese schedule ended abruptly, though joyfully, with a shellacking of Keyesport in a doubleheader by scores of 5–0 and 6–2. In hurling the first game, John disposed of the Keyesport batters in just an hour and seven minutes, despite the increasing agony in his shoulder. Fortunately, his swing in the batter's box was unaffected by his injury, as he went five for five at the plate in the first contest to lead the offensive attack. The five hits had bolstered his batting average to an even .500 for the season with 27 hits in 54 times at bat.

As the team was having a bite to eat in between games, the coach pulled John aside and asked if he would like to sit out the second contest to ensure his average would remain at the .500 mark to close the year. John declined the offer, wanting to compete to the very end. He proceeded to go three for four in the second game, raising his final average to .517.

John was the last one to get on the bus to head back home. Before boarding he looked around, hoping that one of those men in the straw hats would be there to speak with him. None was.

In a moment's notice, his baseball career was over.

Another two weeks of classes remained between the Keyesport doubleheader to conclude the baseball schedule and his graduation from high school. While not stellar, his report card showed Bs and Cs, though handwriting became an arduous, painful task with the shoulder injury. John enjoyed those two weeks as much as possible, making sure to spend some quality time with each of his friends as Bobby had already left town the year prior.

As the fortnight quickly faded away, a lingering uncertainty had loomed in John's mind. Aside from hastily filling out a few college applications, the names of which he could not even remember, he had no plans after graduation, as the enchantment of the baseball season had taken his full attention. He had never pictured himself as "college material" in terms of intelligence and, thus, was never enthused about the application process, and as accomplished as he had been in athletics, no offers for college basketball, college baseball, or professional baseball had come his way. While some tried to assuage him by saying it was due to coming from a small town, John was convinced he was being passed over because of his injured shoulder.

Since the first day John had started pitching in high school, the Beckemeyer and Breese townspeople always whispered about some pro scout or another having a fixed an eye on him. A scout from the Detroit Tigers had corralled Bobby at the end of the previous spring and given him a good chunk of money to sign a contract with the organization. It came with the stipulation, however, that Bobby had to leave Beckemeyer immediately to begin playing in the Tigers minor league system before he had a chance to finish the credits for his diploma from Breese High.

But now, a year later, those same scouts did not materialize for John. A stark, cold reality shrouded over him. As he had stood on the pitcher's mound early in the season, he could see them behind the backstop, watching his every move. But as soon as he had hurt his arm, they had quickly vanished, melting off into the distance with the rest of the people who attended the games, never to be seen again. The scouts' gradual disappearance started convincing John, sore arm or not, that he was just a good *small-town* player, the same type of player the scouts had seen a thousand times, he figured.

Pitching for Beckemeyer in the Clinton County League was the only baseball to which John could now look forward. While this had been his first boyhood goal, its prospect was now a disappointing consolation prize. While John knew that amateur players, even those in the obscurity of the Clinton County League, could be signed to professional contracts at any given time, he also knew it was highly unlikely. The pro scouts were like the trains rolling through Beckemeyer, departing just as fast as they came.

More self-doubt began to settle inside. Maybe he would not fit in with the pro ball, anyway, John figured. Those men who rode trains from city to city as important wealthy people did were larger than life, seen only in sporadic newspaper photographs.

There were his father's wishes to consider. Alphie made it known to John that he preferred his son first seek the reliability of steady work instead of going after a college education. As Alphie also had made it clear he did not want John working on the railroad, John knew he was likely destined for the coal mine if nothing else panned out.

John had no objections with the prospect of a job in the mine once high school was finished. He knew it was hard, dangerous work, but he also knew this was simply *what Beckemeyer men did*. If hard, manual labor and the familiar comforts of Clinton County was good enough for his father, whom he held in such esteem, it was good enough for him.

But there was another emotional variable at work inside of John.

Into his teenage years, a strange and powerful intrigue had gripped him, a beckoning of mystical places described in his *McGuffey Reader* textbook at St. Anthony's. It caused him to long to see "the world" or even just nearby St. Louis for the first time, where his beloved Cardinals played and about which he had heard so many stories from his father. It was a curiosity that made him wonder further about why things were the way they were in the world. For despite his loyalty to Beckemeyer and to his parents, John also wanted to show his father that he had the same adventurous spirit and brave soul Alphie had possessed as a young man, a willingness to accept new challenges and adventures into the unknown.

On one of his last days of high school, with no baseball practices or games to be had, John again pondered such possibilities. He sat by the front window of the house, staring out into the western reaches of the town and into the soybean fields beyond, wondering what was out there.

His daydreaming ended. His eyes were drawn to the postman, who was slowing to a stop in front of the house.

As John started to walk out the front door, the postman glanced at him and pulled an envelope out of his bag, holding it up with a quick nod of his head. He handed it to John with a second nod and moved on down Lincoln Street. The letter was addressed to John himself.

Save for a rare delayed correspondence from a family member back in Germany, mail delivery of any kind was unusual for the household. There were never any outstanding bills making their way to the Laufketter door, as Alphie invariably paid them all on time, in person and in cash at the Farmers and Merchants Bank. John therefore figured the letter to contain something special.

He ran the tips of his fingers across the envelope, taking a moment to study the printing on the front. It had beautiful blue ink that read "Lindell Avenue, St. Louis" on the return address corner. Flipping it over, the envelope had an imposing seal across the back cover.

Looking back at the house, John remembered he was alone. He proceeded to open the envelope very carefully and slowly unfolded the brief letter, which was typed on the heaviest single sheet of paper he had ever held. He began reading.

3 May 1929

Master John Laufketter
c/o Mr. Alphonse Laufketter
RR #2 Beckemeyer
Carlyle, Illinois

Dear Master Laufketter:

After careful review of your application for admission, this letter herein represents a promissory note of remitted course tuition for your full-time enrollment at Saint Louis University for the fall and spring semesters of 1929–30, and which is renewable (pending performance) for subsequent academic terms. This offer is in return for successful completion of your studies each term and your participation on the University's intercollegiate basketball and/or baseball teams, for which you have been recommended by other parties. Living expenses beyond basic room and board are to be your responsibility. Please contact the Director of Activities by telephone, US mail, or cable within ten days for confirmation of your receipt.

Yours in Christ,

Reverend Joseph Cloud, SJ
President
Saint Louis University

Saint Louis University. John now recalled it was one of those applications that had passed through his hands. But who were the "other parties" who had sent in their recommendation of him?

It soon came clear. His benefactor had been Father Schweighart at St. Anthony's, who had extolled John's athletic abilities in detail to a parochial vicar he knew at the university. Father Schweighart had forever encouraged John to apply to different colleges, even as John groaned about the annoyance of having to do so, trying to mask his self-doubts about his own academic abilities.

Father Schweighart, however, had always believed that John was destined for great things, on the athletic field or off it, but probably both, he figured. He had continued to mentor and challenge John long after the student had departed the parish elementary grades for the public high school setting in Breese. "Jesus goes forth and prepares a special place for us, so that we may know the way," the priest had always assured his students at St. Anthony's in quoting the beginning of the beginning of the Gospel of John 14, encouraging them to trust in the Lord's plan for them.

But even with the exciting opportunity to continue his career in athletics as well as schooling, it was still difficult for John to envision himself leaving Southern Illinois altogether, let alone Beckemeyer or even Clinton County, as the loyalty of home once again cut deep within him. He decided that he needed to discuss this feeling with his pastor. Father Schweighart dismissed his trepidation, even by poking a little fun at him, suggesting it was an innocent cover-up for John's lack of planning beyond his high school days. "It's fine to be loyal to one's home, John," the priest said. "But the Lord also wishes for us to venture forth to the outside world and take our talents to others, to share the gifts He has bestowed upon us and spread His word to those unknown."

It was all the reinforcement John needed to hear. Nonetheless, he kept the letter a secret from his mother and father for two days, unsure how he would approach them. He was uncertain of what their reaction would be; would they be upset at his desire to leave the family and the area? Or would they encourage him, like Father Schweighart had told him, to go visit the outside world as Alphie, his own father, himself had done?

On the third evening after receiving the letter, John entered the kitchen to find his mother at the small table where the family meals were held. Alphie was in his usual position the living room, sitting in his chair with his back to the window, smacking his lips at his pipe as he stared across the room in thought with his eyes half closed.

John asked his father to come to the kitchen. He sat down in between his parents, pulled the letter out of his pocket, and handed it to his mother. Leah started glancing it over.

Within a few seconds, she was unable to contain her delight, revealing a smile that she quickly covered with her hand. Dimming the smile slightly out of respect to await Alphie's reaction, she then passed the note to her husband as she and John awaited Alphie's assessment of its contents once he understood them.

Alphie needed Leah's help with some of the more complex words but soon fully comprehended the magnitude of the letter's meaning. He gently placed the paper onto the table, drew a deep breath, and looked up at his son.

"*Nein*, Johnny," he said. Alphie imagined the overall venture being too expensive, even with the tuition paid.

John was prepared for the response and was not at all surprised with the curt, unqualified answer. It was the direct approach that Alphie always used with anyone, regardless if he was speaking to a complete stranger or with his closest family members.

"Dad," John began in a defense he had practiced. "This is my chance to go someplace, to see the shores of the Mississippi as you once did. To educate myself further. To find the meaningful work of my life. . . ."

Alphie just stared at him quietly, and without expression, until the word *work* had caused him to raise his eyebrows momentarily. From that point on, he was unable to say no to his son again but was still unable to say yes.

"Dad," John tried again. "I want to reach for great things, even if I can't reach them. For at least one moment in the future, I want to be remembered for something I accomplished. Even if I come back to Beckemeyer later and have to work in the mine forever, I first want to leave my mark *someplace.*"

A few more endless silent moments passed.

The three people gazed lovingly at each other. Alphie finally burst forth with a wide smile and a quick laugh. John gave him a strong hug with one arm and a kiss to his mother on his other side.

He had convinced his father that it was indeed a good opportunity. But even with his blessing, Alphie nonetheless warned John that no extra monetary assistance would be available from the family. John understood and put in three months of hard work as a stock boy at Diekamper's in the summer of 1929, gaining every hour he could possibly acquire and even making extra deliveries for the store on the weekends. John had plenty to time to work, as there was no baseball he could play; he would not be eligible for the Clinton County League until the following summer, as he would not turn eighteen until September, which was just a couple of weeks after the CCL season would conclude.

On Saturday night, August 31, John stuffed his large army-style duffel bag full of all the clothes and personal items he could carry. He was leaving first thing in the morning but had one more thing to do before departing. After packing, he hustled the two blocks over to St. Anthony's, where he was hoping to find Father Schweighart one last time, looking to garner any last bits of advice.

As he turned the corner around the church, the lights in the rectory were off, so John checked the school building. The door was open. Once inside, he called out, but there was no answer. The classroom doors were locked as John looked through the window of each one as he passed down the hallway. At the very end was Father Schweighart's tiny "office," a small workspace afforded to him as principal of the school. It, too, was locked.

To take at least *something* with him, John glanced up at the inscription above the pastor's desk. It was a quote from the famous educator Horace Mann, a line John had seen every day at school as he passed by the office.

"Be ashamed to die before having won some victory for humanity."

He read the words thoughtfully one final time and headed back home to say goodbye to his parents.

CHAPTER FOUR

After walking around Beckemeyer in the pre-dusk hours on Sunday, September 1, 1929, John returned home and momentarily awoke his sleeping mother and father with a kiss. Walking out the front door, he stood at the intersection of the newly named highway of US Route 50 and Bartelso Road, swiveling in all directions to imbibe one last breath of the perpetual stillness and peace of his hometown.

During high school when turning over dilemmas in his mind, John had occasionally risen out of bed in the middle of night and, unbeknownst to Alphie and Leah, left the house and wandered around town. While doing so, he often stopped for several minutes to look at one of Beckemeyer's new streetlights. To him, the lights symbolized the town's move into the modern world. They seemed to be magically suspended in the air like frosted moons, which in late summer were sparkling with bugs swarming around each one. The electricity from the lights hummed in a strange, uneven symphony with the insects, the only audible sound except for another train approaching, still far off in the distance.

Now, as John looked down the Beckemeyer streets with the morning sun beginning to rise, the horizon showed nothing but farmland in all directions, and nothing visible beyond. He was slightly homesick already, even before leaving town. *Was this really a good idea?*

Suddenly, instead of thinking of the exciting, mystical lands about which he had read in school, he was reminded of stories from the same textbook of explorers who had started their quests gallantly but then perished on their so-called "adventures."

Snapping John from his dreaming once again, just as the mailman had done, was a growing cloud of dust billowing towards him. Along with it came a woeful noise, gradually deepening like a moose call in the wild.

It was his good friend Bobby Durstmiller, chugging along in his secondhand truck that always seemed to creak in protest when he yanked it out of first gear. He slowed to a stop beside John and peered at him through the open passenger window.

"So, you're still going," Bobby smirked as he shoved the door open. John raised both eyebrows to answer in the affirmative.

"Well, climb on in," Bobby continued. "Toss your bag in the back. If it's got some weight, it shouldn't fly off the top. I have got to get back here later this morning and deliver this dirt."

John threw his duffel bag upon the soil Bobby was carting and climbed into the cab, jerking forward in unison with the truck as Bobby launched it into motion once again. John hung his magical right arm out the window as he took one final stare at Beckemeyer, thinking it might be his last ever.

As they gathered speed heading west, the town and its prominent steeple of St. Anthony's soon faded from view as Breese began approaching. The towns in Clinton County were, almost without exception, four miles apart—as if they had been carefully placed in even measure on a cosmic baking sheet by the Great Confectioner above. Yet to John, the scene had become redundant.

"Got to be something more," John muttered to himself out the window.

"What was that?" Bobby asked, half listening while shuffling some papers beneath his seat with one hand.

"Nothing. Say, Bob, I need to ask you something. . . . What do you think Father S. means with that saying, 'Be ashamed to die before having won some victory for humanity'?"

Bobby was silent as if he did not hear him and even seemed a bit annoyed as he drew a deep sigh and glanced out his own window at nothing.

John rephrased his question. "What is it *we're supposed to do*? How do we know when we've found success?"

Bobby's eyes darted around the cab of the truck, as if now at least trying to give John an answer. He still had none.

John continued, "I guess it's just about laying all your cards on the table, I suppose. As long as you put yourself out there . . . make an effort . . . as long as you're not just another guy from the county."

Bobby just stared straight ahead, still silent.

A load of bitterness had overcome John's best friend in the past year, a bitterness growing more and more palpable with people who knew him around Beckemeyer. Over the last eleven months, Bobby indeed had laid every card he held on the table—and, in the end, the house had beat him.

A series of setbacks and failures in the strange, faraway, and unforgiving places of professional baseball's new farm system, as it was called, had reduced Bobby to an angry young man before his twentieth birthday. It all began with Branch Rickey, or so Bobby liked to claim about the origins of his disastrous year.

As one of his innovations with the Cardinals, Rickey had devised a network of understudy teams that were placed throughout the Midwest and beyond, teams charged with the role of supplying future players for the big-league club in St. Louis. The teams were stocked with raw but eager young men who would be trained in the Cardinals' way of baseball. For pennies on the dollar, Rickey figured, they could be cultivated internally to compete with the larger, more immediate investments the wealthier New York and Boston teams could make in established players. Notorious for fighting for every cent, Rickey would "go into the back of his office and open the safe to bring you a nickel's change," lamented one Cardinals player. "The cheapest, the shrewdest, and the most hard-hearted of men," added another. "If you went into Rickey's office to talk salary, and you left four hours later, taking a dime less than what you wanted coming in, he would consider that a victory." Preparing for that office visit required much acumen and planning. "Someone once laid down the basic rules for negotiating with Rickey," a sportswriter revealed. "Don't drink the night before, keep your mouth shut, and your hands in your pockets."

Soon after Rickey came up with his creation, other organizations immediately copied the idea and created their own farm teams, thus ultimately producing leagues in which the teams from different organizations could play against one another. To fill these teams, all the clubs began dispatching armies of scouts into every area of the United States, remote and urbanized, to mine new talent.

It had been just over a year earlier when a scout with the Detroit Tigers was impressed with Bobby's potential after having seen him perform as John's catcher at Breese High. The scout told him that the Tigers had employed several different unsatisfactory catchers in Detroit over the past few seasons and that the job was up for grabs to anyone who showed enough potential.

With Bobby's father unable to work for seven weeks that spring from a broken leg suffered in the coal mine, it was not difficult for the scout to convince Bobby to quickly sign a tantalizing contract. Bobby received an immediate payment of a $500 bonus, plus $75 a month and a place to live as the family was grateful for the money arriving at such an opportune time. Before he inked the deal with the Tigers, he asked the Detroit organization for only one condition—that he be permitted to remain in Beckemeyer for an extra month so that he could finish high school and make sure his family's situation was settled before he left town. The request was denied, and Bobby was directed to join the Tigers farm system immediately.

Among anyone in Beckemeyer, young or old, only Bobby loved baseball as much as John. Looking for any possible edge to improve his game, Bobby subjected himself to torturous physical training on the backroads of Clinton County, taking long, grueling conditioning runs on the dusty paths that connected the various towns. And with his long-dreamt opportunity of professional ball now before him, Bobby only increased the intensity of his workouts in the days leading up to his departure.

With nothing but his catcher's mitt, a gunny sack with a change of clothes, the train ticket provided by the Tigers, and three dollars in the pocket of his overalls, Bobby left Beckemeyer at 5:00 a.m. on June 2, 1928, hitchhiking toward St. Louis. With the help of a few early morning truckers, he made his way to the intersection of Market and Eighteenth Streets and walked into the massive Union Station terminal, which had recently become the busiest train station in the world.

The Detroit scout had promised to be there to see him off. Before stepping fully onto his assigned car, Bobby glanced around while hanging off the arm rail, waiting until the very last second for him. Not seeing the scout anywhere, Bobby had to leap onto the departing train as he settled in for his trip 650 miles south, where he would play for the organization's team in the Texas League, the Fort Worth Panthers. In his last contact, the scout informed Bobby he would be competing for the starting catcher's position at Fort Worth with a thirty-three-year-old veteran named Joe Cobb, whom the team had also just acquired.

Ten years earlier, Cobb had attained the personal goal he shared with Bobby and thousands of others, that of reaching the majors. After hitting .385 in the latter part of the 1917 season for Cumberland in the Blue Ridge League, Cobb made the big-league club in Detroit after a strong showing at the team's 1918 preseason workouts in Waxahachie, Texas. In the Tigers' third regular season game on April 25, three games into the 1918 season, Cobb was watching intently from the bench when he was summoned by manager Hughie Jennings in the bottom of the eighth inning to pinch-hit for Tigers pitcher Rudy Kallio with Detroit trailing 6–4.

Cobb fought off his excitement as he stood in the batter's box, waiting patiently for a good pitch. Trying to give himself the best chance to get on base, he watched four of five pitches from Cleveland pitcher Fritz Coumbe go wide of the strike zone. Upon the fourth pitched ball, Joe sprung from the box and bolted down to first base with a walk. But a moment later, he found himself stranded there. Lee Dressen was then retired to end the Tigers' threat, and Detroit was sent down in order in the ninth inning as well. After Joe batted in the eighth, Jennings decided to not have him remain in the game and play a defensive position and returned him to the bench.

Over the next three weeks, Joe yearned for his next chance to play. Even with Jennings's regulars fumbling to a 7-14 record to start the season for Detroit, Joe would not be permitted to appear in another big-league game. On May 17, his contract was sold by the Tigers to the St. Paul team in the American Association.

Disheartened in being returned to the minors, Cobb left baseball for three full years before giving the game one more shot in 1923. He came back from the hiatus better than ever, batting .320 in each of two seasons in the International League—the second of which he added 22 home runs to lead the Baltimore Orioles to the 1924 league crown with a remarkable 117-48 record. As the everyday catcher for the team, Joe tutored the young pitching staff, which included a promising local Maryland boy named Robert Grove, who had gained the nickname of "Lefty." Yet, despite Cobb's success, no team in the National or American League took an interest.

Now in 1928, Cobb found himself in North Texas, having come to town via another stop in Wichita Falls, which was the property of the Browns, the American League counterpart of the Cardinals in St. Louis.

As Bobby's train slowed to a stop in Fort Worth, he started to rise from his seat when he spotted a distinctive-looking man outside on the platform. The man, staring right at Bobby, was dressed in slacks and a nice jacket, though his outfit was worn with a small hole noticeable on the sleeve. He stood motionless with his hands in his pockets, holding an uncaring expression on his unshaven face as his eyes followed Bobby down the stairs of the train car.

"Joe Cobb. Welcome t' Fort Worth," the man grunted stoically in offering his hand. Bobby was surprised that, in his first encounter with a professional ballplayer, he was a couple inches taller than Cobb's 5'9" height. Cobb started walking away before Bobby could even answer him. "Follow me, and I'll get you to your boarding house."

Bobby looked around for the automobile that would take them through town to their destination. There was none.

"Better get used to the heat," Cobb snapped behind without looking at Bobby, sensing that the newbie was looking for a ride instead of a walk.

"It's fine," Bobby snapped back, annoyed with the cold reception he was getting. With night baseball only in the discussion stage for the Texas League in 1928, all games were still played under the hot Texas sun.

Bobby did not mind the heat at all. He considered Clinton County to be just as hot, and besides, he never thought of baseball, under any conditions, as being a chore. Having researched the team and the Texas League with recent copies of *The Sporting News* he had borrowed from a man in Beckemeyer, Bobby was excited to know he was joining a team that veteran manager John Atz had crafted into a source of local pride for Fort Worth, just like the teams in the local Clinton County League back home.

The two walked for over a mile after leaving the train station, with Bobby clutching his catcher's mitt and Cobb keeping his hands in his pockets, hardly even aware that Bobby was still behind him.

They finally reached the place where the rookie would be living, a large but decaying two-story structure on Calhoun Street on Fort Worth's north end, near the banks of the Trinity River with one of the city's junkyards sitting next door. The house, owned by a widow, already had three other first-year players for the Panthers living there. As Bobby swung his hand to knock on the door, he turned to see that Cobb was already long gone, halfway back down the block with no words of encouragement.

Turning to face the door once again, Bobby heard some shuffling inside the house. He knocked a second time; still, there was no answer. Pushing the door open, he peered in to see the widow only a few feet away in the kitchen, stirring a concoction in an oversized pot on the stove. Her wordless greeting was no warmer than Cobb's, consisting of a momentary glance that quickly returned to the pot.

Bobby went upstairs and examined the hallway, ultimately finding an unoccupied room that contained only a bed and a desk. He threw his bag into a corner and collapsed onto the secondhand cot, looking to the north out the window with no curtain. Already thinking of home, he wondered if his dad was okay. Bobby knew he now had to take care of himself. He drifted off to sleep while thinking of his first day at work at his first job the following day—a job in baseball and not in the mines, as had been his plan his entire life.

He awoke and discovered that, in Fort Worth, baseball was a cutthroat war. Until arriving in the Texas League, the sport to Bobby was an artful activity of throwing, hitting, and catching. Now it was no longer a game but a daily dogfight, and not only with the opposing teams but also even with one's own teammates, as each man was clawing for advancement through the minors with the goal of making the organization's big-league club.

Even the *crowds* in the Texas League, Bobby discovered, were hostile, and those on the field sometimes had to defend themselves with unusual means. This became clear to Bobby three days after his arrival in his first start in a game at San Antonio. As Bobby approached the plate at the start of the second inning for his initial professional at bat, the umpire bent over to dust off home plate. Tumbling out of the umpire's jacket was a Colt pistol, which he hastily grabbed and shoved back inside his coat. While Bobby recoiled at the sight, San Antonio's catcher, thirty-seven-year-old league veteran Frank Gibson, merely chuckled and squatted to begin play.

Bobby's initial chances to see the field were few and far between. While Bobby had been promised by the scout he would play regularly in Fort Worth, it was, nonetheless, Cobb who received the lion's share of the work at catcher as Bobby played in only four games in his first month with the team. While wishing to dip into Cobb's vast experience and knowledge, Bobby sensed the veteran wanted nothing to do with him. So, instead, the rookie sat at the opposite end of the bench, observing with interest Cobb's most minute routines. As the weeks passed, Bobby noticed that Cobb's movements were getting slower and slower, his battered body shriveling and his face wincing from the thousands of battles over the years. While Bobby was somewhat bitter that Cobb was taking playing time away from him, he simultaneously admired him; Cobb was still sticking it out in the "bush leagues," even with seemingly no shot in getting back to Detroit or anywhere else in baseball's magic kingdom of the major leagues.

But more than anything, Bobby wanted to play. He needed to play. And he spent his free time making certain he was ready when his time came.

Every night in his modest room, he made copious notes about pitchers around the league and about his own strengths and weaknesses, just as he and John had done back home. In the mornings, he began arriving early at the stadium in Fort Worth every day for extra work. After putting on his uniform and going over the opponents' hitters with Atz, Cobb, and the Panthers starting pitcher for that day's game, he would complete a long series of running and stretching exercises before batting practice and then worked with the other pitchers in the bullpen.

But after the game, when he got back to the boarding house around 7:00 or 7:30, the "down time" at night took over, which was even worse than not playing.

With little else to do, he struggled to keep his mind off his ailing father, his struggling family, and whatever else might be happening with life back in Beckemeyer. To pass the time, many of the other players (including the other three rookies with whom Bobby was living) liked to gamble and get their hands on black-market liquor, but Bobby resisted both things. He did little more than lie in his bed and stare at the ceiling. A great loneliness often overtook him during these moments in this place so unrecognizable, so unforgiving, and so far from home. Baseball itself was all he had.

Feeling he needed to bond with his teammates, Bobby ultimately decided to join some of the other players at a speakeasy near the ballpark where the proprietor, who was friendly to the team, usually gave the players free drinks. Bobby faked enthusiasm for alcohol in accepting a glass of whiskey on his first visit, finishing it in small sips over the course of the entire night.

After the Panthers secured an exciting 7–6 win the next day with four runs in the ninth inning in front of a large Saturday home crowd, Bobby's sips of whiskey went down in larger slurps. Although Bobby was still a second-string player, backslapping fans and local girls smiled at him and bought the next rounds as he decided it was okay to have one more.

It quickly grew into a nightly routine. Because of the late nights partying, Bobby stopped his practice of arriving early to work out at the ballpark, but in its place, he believed that a camaraderie was building between himself and his teammates. He was confident that loosening up with a drink or two was doing the trick as he found himself hitting a hot streak on the field, smacking ten hits in nineteen at bats in an early August stretch. Atz then inserted him as the team's starting catcher for five straight games as Cobb took his turn on the bench. The swagger and leadership Bobby displayed on the ball field in high school finally returned, a confidence that had allowed him and John to lead Breese High to victories past larger schools. He was acting like a veteran catcher, as even the coldness between himself and Cobb had finally warmed as the older player was happy to see the growth and emergence of his unlikely protégé.

Over the Labor Day weekend, the Houston Buffaloes came to Fort Worth to play a critical series against the Panthers in a battle for first place in the Texas League. The talented Buffaloes were one of Rickey's battalions in his widespread army of the Cardinals farm system. With the first game of the series tied 1–1 in the top of the eighth inning, Houston's dangerous hitter Red Worthington, who was near the top of the league batting charts with a .354 average, stood at the plate. With a runner on second, Worthington jumped on a fastball on the outer half of the plate and laced a sharp hit to right field. Bobby sprung up and readied himself, preparing for an imminent play at the plate.

In the corner of his eye, Bobby saw the base runner, Carey Selph, sprinting around third with the potential go-ahead run and knew a collision was likely going to take place. A beautiful, one-hop throw came in from Fort Worth's right fielder, the perfect kind of toss that seems to glide to the catcher in a comfortable slow-motion though traveling at a great velocity. The path of ball, however, took Bobby two steps up the third base line. He shifted himself accordingly, still bracing his body.

Bobby, however, underestimated the speed of the Houston runner. As the catcher lunged when the ball skipped on the grass, Selph plowed into Bobby's left knee. The baseball fell free from Bobby's mitt and Selph skidded across the plate as Bobby writhed on the ground in misery. Houston took the momentum with three more runs as the Buffaloes went on to a 5–1 victory, while Bobby finished the ninth inning clenching his teeth in unbearable pain.

With no full-time team trainer or physician, Panther players were expected to treat their own wounds unless a hospital visit was required. For the last two weeks of the season, Bobby pushed through the pain on his mangled knee. He could not decide between telling Atz that he was seriously injured and risk being banished to bench or playing the best he could.

He again thought of his ailing father back in Beckemeyer, whose position at the coal mine had now been permanently replaced because of his absence from his own injury. If a miner complained of a medical problem, Bobby knew, there were many other hungry workers who were happy to take his place.

He, therefore, decided to stay quiet and hide the pain from Atz. His self-medication took the form of longer nights out after games and more alcohol.

For the final weekend of the season, the Panthers went to Houston to face the Buffaloes once again, with the latter already having wrapped up the Texas League pennant. Hitless in his last twenty-three at bats and permitting five passed balls recently on defense, Bobby was nonetheless in the starting lineup once again for the Saturday game after the series opener the day prior.

Among the other St. Louis-bound Houston stars was twenty-five-year-old outfielder Homer Peel, already a six-year veteran of the minor leagues who had been up with the Cardinals for two games in 1927. Peel was a speedster on the bases, evidenced by his posting of 16 triples for the Buffaloes back in 1925. Peel got on base all day long against the Fort Worth pitchers and, in doing so, provided Bobby another lesson of the mercilessness of professional baseball.

The catcher could do little more than watch as Peel stole five bases on him in the afternoon, including a steal of home. The pitch had beaten Peel to the plate, but Bobby, working on essentially one leg, was unable to get the tag down in time. As Peel trotted back to the roaring Houston dugout, he laughed at Bobby over his shoulder as the catcher was unable to get himself to his feet without assistance from the umpire.

When the game was over and Houston had administered yet another thorough beating to the Panthers, Bobby slumped down in complete desperation in front of his locker.

Twenty minutes later, he was only halfway out of his uniform, having merely removed his undershirt and jersey. Suddenly, he was summoned into the manager's office.

As Bobby sat down in front of him, Atz was already sliding a slip of paper across his desk.

"What's this?" Bobby asked.

"That be a bus ticket," Atz said plainly. The manager, puffing on a cigarette, just stared at him.

"For treatment?" Bobby wondered, thinking he was being sent to a hospital for help with his knee.

"No, for *good*," Atz replied. "I'm afraid you've done all you can do here, son. You won't be asked to repay your bonus, so don't worry about that. Good luck."

With that, Atz wheeled around his chair and took another drag on the cigarette.

Bobby retreated to his locker in a daze, picked up his mitt, and wandered out of the ballpark, still in half of his uniform. He just starting walking, nowhere in particular, his eyes looking down at the dusty Texas streets and his mouth agape.

Joe Cobb would catch the final game of the 1928 season for Fort Worth on Sunday, September 23. The following spring, Cobb would be released again as his contract was sold by the Panthers to New Haven in the Eastern League. He never played a game for that club but instead was released a month later and sent back to Fort Worth and then later to the teams of Scranton, Wilkes-Barre, Harrisburg, and Hazelton in the New York-Pennsylvania League.

By 1931, Cobb had seen enough and finally retired. In addition to his one momentary five-minute appearance with the major leagues with the Detroit Tigers, Cobb had played 891 games in the minor leagues.

Bobby, meanwhile, had played in thirty-seven. Both of their careers were finished.

CHAPTER FIVE

As he drove John to St. Louis, Bobby remained silent behind the wheel of the truck and stared straight ahead, reaching Belleville and finally coasting down from the bluffs. John, hardly ever having been outside of Clinton County, let alone all the way to the city, looked upon the Mississippi River for the first time, the banks along which his father had worked for many years before his son was born.

On their way up the Eads Bridge, John and Bobby could see "Whiskey Shoot," an endless string of filthy, short buildings reeking of iniquity that lined the riverfront of East St. Louis on the Illinois side. Grim edifices came into view on the west bank in front of downtown St. Louis as well, with more such buildings stretching along the shoreline from the Eads all the way to the Municipal Bridge a couple miles to the south. John looked upon the maze of railroad tracks that strangled the area and wondered if his father had a hand in constructing them.

The route to Saint Louis University took them by Union Station, where the first trains of the day were starting to screech out of their platforms. It was here where Bobby first appeared to awaken from his catatonic state, looking off to the side. But, still, he said nothing.

They came to a stop a mile later at the corner of Grand and Lindell Avenue, directly in front of one of the entrances to SLU. "Do you think we're close to Sportsman's?" John asked about their potential proximity to the Cardinals ballpark. Bobby, like John, had never been to a Cardinals or Browns game, and while both knew the ballpark was at the corner of Grand and Dodier, they had no idea how far up Dodier lay.

"Probably," Bobby answered in a nonchalant manner as the truck halted in front of the university's administration building. "I don't want to run around looking for it, though. Gotta get back this morning." He reached around to the truck bed to grab John's bag and tossed it unceremoniously all the way over the truck onto the curb.

Yet, at that instant, Bobby felt his insensitivity. He paused to rest his arms and head on the steering wheel. He looked through the open passenger window at his friend, who was retrieving the bag from the sidewalk. Bobby got out, placed his arms on the hood, drew a deep breath, and then peered up Grand Avenue at the SLU campus and Sportsman's Park, presumably beyond as well.

"Johnny," he began slowly, "let me tell you something, and this is coming straight from the heart. . . ." He continued to stare blankly as if he had bottled up his forthcoming words over the past fifty miles after leaving Clinton County.

"This ain't Beckemeyer. The world is a dark place. I put everything I had into the only thing I loved—the game—and the game spit right back at me. The world spits out country boys like a bunch of used-up chew. It has no use for us."

John just looked at him. He had no response.

Then, Bobby suddenly got louder. He was still looking up Grand.

"The hell with the Tigers—the Cardinals—and this city! Peel and Selph too—they all stole it from me. Stole baseball. Shit, I did things right, worked hard, respected the game—and now look where I am. I wanted to come back to Beckemeyer more of a man than when I left—as *somebody*. And I came back *less*. Now, I'm not even just another guy from the county—I'm the guy who left and *failed*."

John still did not know what to say. He reached for the most comforting idea he could find.

"Bob, you're still the best catcher I've ever known. And you laid it all out there, gave it your all. Nobody can ever take that away from you."

"Yeah, fine," Bobby replied, calming slightly but still upset. "But what's out there for me now?"

John had no answer. He stepped around the truck and offered his hand. Bobby was able to force a minimal smile and accepted the shake as he got back inside the cab.

Wheeling around in a U-turn to get back east on Forest Park Parkway, he looked back one more time at John as he drove off.

"Don't say I didn't tell you so."

As Bobby's truck growled off toward Illinois, John stood awkwardly for several minutes at the corner of Grand and Lindell. Up the block, he saw the imposing marquee of the newly completed Fox Theatre staring back at him. He was frozen with uncertainty—not only about the long-term future but also simply the next five minutes.

He looked about himself in all directions, absorbing his first experience with the breakneck pace of urban life that was amplified with the morning rush. An unrelenting wave of humanity kept scurrying around him.

When John asked two different people for directions to the housing unit to which he had been assigned, they appeared not to hear him. He was finally able to corral a third, who informed John that the destination was a mere two blocks away. It was an apartment building on Spring Avenue, a street whose name sounded familiar to John despite the fact he had never previously been in the city.

The building—at five stories high, the tallest one John had ever entered—was the dormitory for the male freshman athletes of the Saint Louis University Billikens. While an occasional meal was provided in the small kitchen on the ground floor, John for the most part would be on his own for sustenance despite room and board having been mentioned in the letter he received from the SLU president. In the coming months, John sometimes went a day or more without eating due to having no income. He found a job setting pins at a local bowling alley for the sporadic moments when he was not in class, studying, or at sports practice; in return, he got a few bucks and a sandwich made for him by the short-order cook at the bar.

Despite the intensity and challenge of college-level instruction from the Jesuits, John held his own with his schoolwork. He was conscientious about his studies, carefully organizing his lecture notes and completing homework assignments immediately upon returning to his room, a habit he had begun at St. Anthony's school long ago. "You need to use your head for something other than a hat rack," he would often hear his father say. It was the way in which Alphie spoke English the best, using idioms and proverbs he had picked up from his coworkers on the railroad.

As the air cooled through the fall semester, John was anxious for basketball to begin, with baseball of course waiting in the spring. Home to the SLU basketball team was the West Pine Gym, a facility modest in size compared to other college basketball facilities but nonetheless reminding John of the largest arena in which he had played to date, the splendid high school gymnasium in Centralia, where he had played his greatest game. Practice began on Monday, October 28, 1929, as John was finally able to test his athletic skills against more advanced competition.

John had never been through such an arduous physical struggle as his first college basketball practice. The team worked for over three hours, as Head Coach Mike Nyikos had his players' tongues hanging out and their hands on their hips. Every dribbling, footwork, and defensive drill was followed up with a round of "gasser" sprints up and down the court. Nyikos had the team do very little shooting that first day, a regimen bemoaned by most of the team but appreciated by John as it gave his right shoulder, still a problem since his high school pitching injury six months earlier, a chance to acclimate to renewed activity.

John's muscles were so sore on Tuesday that he could not get out of bed, sleeping late to the point where he decided to skip his classes altogether and rest up for the second basketball practice at four o'clock. Still struggling to get moving at 3:30, he dressed quickly, headed downstairs, and galloped out of his building on his burning quad muscles.

Running for two blocks, John abruptly stopped when he turned from Spring onto Lindell, hearing a large group of people chattering as he approached the next corner. A crowd of some fifty or sixty people had gathered in front of a department store. The growing mass was congregated around a radio that stood on a riser at the edge of the sidewalk.

The body language of those listening made it clear. There was important news was coming from somewhere—locally, nationally, or perhaps even internationally.

Before even reaching the back edge of the crowd, John learned from a frantic passerby that, in New York, the stock market had plummeted. It had been falling steadily over the past several days but now had experienced a complete crash, with the Dow Jones Industrial Average losing nearly a quarter of its value since the previous Thursday.

Wandering for a couple of blocks with his mind drifting away from practice, John saw another mob converging upon the door of a nearby bank on Laclede Avenue. Everyone appeared to be in a mad rush to withdraw their savings, as news of the crash was now spreading like wildfire. Some professors at SLU dismissed their classes early amidst the chaos. John milled around the streets with other students, stepping out of the way of distraught businessmen who swayed in torment while gripping their hair.

John was largely unmoved by the scene, until he got the news from Clinton County a few days later.

Corn and soybean prices from the crash continued to fall rapidly as a bank panic among the farmers had hit Beckemeyer as well. Shortly thereafter, the Beckemeyer coal mine was idled, with production being halted immediately.

Concerned for his family, John's instinct was to pack his belongings, leave school, and return to the area, even though his college career had just begun. When hearing of the mine closure, he figured work on the railroads was soon to follow as well. He hurried his way to a public telephone at university union and was able to connect to his father. Alphie convinced John that his job with the railroad and the family's well-being were in no danger. With complete assurance from the man he trusted the most, John remained in St. Louis as his father had directed.

Throughout the rest of the fall semester, John tried to keep his mind on his business in the classroom and on the basketball floor. He could feel himself growing stronger daily, while knowing that each passing hour drew him closer to Christmas vacation when he could go back to Beckemeyer.

Scribbling some quick final thoughts on his last exam booklet late in the afternoon of Friday, December 20, John grabbed his duffel bag from under his desk and slung it on his shoulder. As he stepped out onto Grand Avenue, he discovered that a light snow was falling. The weather did not discourage him; he knew that, somehow, he would make his way home to Clinton County by nightfall. He started walking east toward the river and smiled to himself as he stuck his thumb in the air, remembering that his father always forbade him from hitchhiking, even though Alphie had often done it as a young man himself.

A truck driver picked him up within a few minutes. As he rode excitedly into Illinois, John figured he was making such good time that he might even arrive for dinner, which he had enjoyed only twice in the past week on campus. The driver was on his way to Indiana and dropped John off right in Beckemeyer on US 50.

Upon entering the house, he noticed right away that some things were missing, such as a few picture frames. The old daguerreotypes of family ancestors now hung unframed on the wall.

Leah was first to greet John, and Alphie quickly followed, grabbing his pipe from his mouth as the three embraced. He was a bit thinner than when John had left but looked generally well to his son.

The time at home went too quickly. As the stark, barren days of winter passed, hunger again often gnawed at John while at the university in January 1930. He tried to stretch the few precious dollars he earned at the bowling alley to give himself at least two solid meals per day, while many others in the city were also simultaneously rationing their intake. By the spring, over 35,000 able-bodied St. Louis laborers—nearly 20 percent of the workforce—would be without a job in the wake of the stock market crash. Particularly hard hit were St. Louis construction workers, as three-fifths of them were idle as building projects were halted with a lack of capital from the shuttered banks.

Basketball at SLU provided John a distraction from the growing despair, despite having to spend the entire season on the freshman team (during which he practiced with the varsity but did not appear in any games, as was university policy). With each passing week, the weather improved, and the ground thawed. John saw his fortunes brightening as the peeking green of the grass hinted that baseball season was soon to come.

One of the rare luxuries John enjoyed was the complimentary daily copy of the *St. Louis Post-Dispatch* newspaper on campus, available in the lobby of the main building. In addition to the entertainment and information it provided, the paper also served as a conduit between himself and his father, an artifact from their favorite shared activity long ago. As in his childhood, he turned immediately to the sports stories and the column of J. Roy Stockton, the beat writer who covered the Cardinals for the *Post-Dispatch*. While John was skimming the latest edition on a cold March afternoon, Stockton was reporting to his readers from sunny Bradenton, Florida, the new spring training home of the Cardinals after the team had spent three preseason years farther east at Avon Park.

As with basketball, John was relegated to practices and intrasquad games only in freshman baseball. Though ineligible to play, the freshmen were still required to dress for the games, largely to perform necessary menial services, such as hitting fungoes in pregame, chasing down foul balls, or warming up an outfielder in between innings.

The daily schedule prevented John from giving in to his temptation to venture up Grand Avenue to Sportsman's Park in April to finally see a big-league game for himself. With the Browns and Cardinals providing two major league teams for St. Louis, one or the other was always in town. But even when free for an afternoon, John put it off for another time, worried that such an expensive venture would threaten his ability to eat for perhaps an entire week.

In practice, John amazed the older players and the coaching staff with his abilities—so much so, in fact, that by early May, another form of temptation was getting the best of the SLU baseball coach, Vernon Lee.

In the final game of the season against Westminster College at SLU's home field in Forest Park, the university's athletic policy was surreptitiously undermined. Lee, having been overwhelmed with the skills John had displayed during team workouts, could wait no longer to see John in a game situation. The coach told the surprised freshman to be prepared.

With two out in the top of the eighth inning, Lee gave the home plate umpire a name the coach had illegibly scribbled onto the lineup card and inserted John into the game. With temperatures dipping into the forties and with SLU already losing badly by an 11–2 count, the umpire hardly cared who the new pitcher was; a quick out was all that was silently desired. Thus, he did not bother to check the substitute's name against the SLU roster. John strode to the mound wearing jersey number seventeen, under which there was no name in the game program.

At the start of the game two hours earlier, around twenty people watched from the stands on the chilly day; less than half that number now remained as John took the hill while shrugging his shoulders a couple of times to loosen them up, a habit he had performed since his injury in high school a year ago. Among those having already left were a few pro scouts who had stayed to observe only the first few innings, as scouts typically did.

A representative from the Cardinals, however, had remained. He had walked to his car at the end of the fourth inning to finish some paperwork and get a sip of lukewarm coffee. Wanting to get more information on a Westminster outfielder, however, he had returned to the field with SLU batting in the bottom of the seventh. Thinking he was familiar with the Billikens roster, the scout was confused by the appearance of the tall stranger entering in the top of the eighth.

John rocked back into his motion. On his first pitch, he unleashed a devastating overhand curveball that froze the surprised Westminster hitter, buckling his knees. The umpire, himself fooled by the pitch, was delayed in his reaction but ultimately hollered while flinging his right arm to indicate "strike one."

"Really?" the impressed scout said to himself.

In letting go of his second pitch, John winced and grunted in pain, issuing his first fastball. The catcher sat in stillness, not having to move a muscle as the perfectly placed shot popped into his mitt a millisecond later, just nipping the outside corner for strike two.

The Cardinals representative inched forward in his seat and scratched his chin as he stared out at the mound.

The third was a changeup that tricked the batter once again. But he was able to halt his swing just in time, as the pitch wound up just below the knees for a ball.

The fourth pitch was another fastball. This time, John's agonized groan was audible to everyone on the premises. The pitch was a powerful four-seamer, fired with so much velocity that it appeared to rise on its brief trip to the plate. The batter's swing began much too late and was completed when a simultaneous *BOOM* echoed off the catcher's mitt, the likes of which the Cardinals scout had never heard before.

The scout scanned his roster for a player with the number seventeen but only a sixteen and an eighteen were on the list. Looking back up, he stared at the young man for an extra moment as he and his teammates trotted off the field. The pitcher was quietly shaking hands with everyone, suggesting he was finished and would not pitch in the ninth inning. The scout looked over at Lee for a moment, left the field, and returned to his car.

At eight o'clock the following morning, the Cardinals scout was knocking on the door of Lee's office on campus, wanting to know the identity of the mysterious one-batter pitcher. In return for the information, the scout agreed not to reveal to anyone that a freshman had pitched in a regular season game, so long as the scout was granted exclusive access to the player in the future on behalf of the Cardinals.

Lee asked the scout to step out into the hallway. He looked down the corridor in both directions.

"His name is John Laufketter," the coach began, barely above a whisper. "He's from a very small town, but from what I understand, he essentially dominated everyone in his home area throughout his high school career. Strictly speaking, he's better than anyone else I have right now."

The Cardinals man, although having seen many other small-town pitchers, concurred.

"Well, he's got more live stuff than anyone I've seen this year," the scout admitted. "Or maybe last year also."

"We've got big plans for him next season," the coach added.

"I'll be back," the Cardinals man concluded, departing down the hallway.

The rhythm of the baseball season suited John more comfortably than had been the case over the winter, which helped his academic performance. His hard work resulted in an A- average for the spring semester of 1930, a vast improvement from the C average he had posted in the fall. His reading of the *Post-Dispatch* continued to be the one daily indulgence he permitted himself, with Stockton's articles keeping him up to date with the Cardinals. John particularly enjoyed reading about the exploits of the Cards' colorful, newly signed pitcher named Jay Dean, who, in his professional debut in May for the St. Joseph team in the Western League, had struck out ten Denver batters in gaining a ten-inning victory.

On the morning of May 11, John was in his room packing his duffel bag for the trip home. He was not leaving for three more days but was so excited to get back to Beckemeyer he had started planning early. He was looking forward to seeing his parents, seeing the familiar landscape of home, and seeing Bobby, whom, John was sure, was certainly over his bitterness toward baseball and would be John's catcher for Becky in the Clinton County League.

Suddenly his head snapped toward the open doorway as he heard the quick, soft steps of the landlady scurrying up the stairs. She entered without knocking. A cabled message had just arrived for John, the contents of which the lady, from her disposition, seemed to already know. The message was from John's mother.

A few hours earlier, the sixty-two-year-old Alphie had suffered a heart attack while working on the railroad near Carlyle.

Despite his age, Alphie had convinced his supervisors that he could still do his job and often outperformed men half his age laboring alongside him. Alphie's tenacity toward his employment reminded John of Jurgis Rudkus, the main character of the novel *The Jungle*, which John had been assigned to read in high school. While he toiled in the Chicago stockyards, Rudkus's immigrant family had faced perpetual difficulties, the solution for which Jurgis always remedied in one statement: "I'll work harder."

Work is an honor.

Nonetheless, the years of stressful, dangerous labor had finally caught up with Alphie. In the overnight hours of May 14, 1930, he found himself clinging precariously to life at St. Dominic Hospital in Breese.

John dropped the telegram. His eyes darting in the direction of his half-packed bag, he snatched it, left a few other belongings behind, and ran down the stairs of the apartment building and out onto Spring Avenue, turning east. With tears forming in his eyes, he began sprinting, the bag slipping from his shoulder as he dodged traffic at every intersection. He hardly stopped running until he met the river over three miles later.

Along the way, he passed the desperation of other peoples. He went by a throng at the corner of Twenty-Second and Locust, frantic souls who were clamoring for work at a government jobs office. Further down, he encountered another haggard group that had massed outside the newly formed Citizens Unemployment Relief Bureau as a serpentine line of needy had extended out from the lobby of the Southern Hotel at Fourth and Walnut.

Nearing the Mississippi, John looked south toward the Municipal Bridge and, underneath, saw hundreds, maybe thousands, swarmed around the Hooverville of makeshifts tents and shacks on Wharf Street. A mountainous heap of garbage formed a boundary at one end of the squalid camp, while at the other, a group of twenty or so raggedy-dressed women were busy canning vegetables and peaches at the Welcome Inn, a public feeding repository having just opened a month earlier. The women were paid for their work with allotments of the very food they were canning.

As John paused to catch his breath, he envisioned his mother as one of them. He then looked north and, upon seeing the railroad yards, sank to his knees and wept bitterly.

Forcing himself up to his feet, John made his way across the Eads Bridge. He sought a ride—not with a casually extended thumb but with a maniacal flailing of his arms. Taken by his evident grief, a driver skidded to a halt on the other side of the bridge in East St. Louis. John did not even look at the occupants as he barreled into the back seat, clutching his bag with both arms as he buried his chin into it. Next to him on either side were two small children, as the mother and father sat in the front. The man driving told John he could take him as far as O'Fallon before they would have to turn north and leave him behind. While John was grateful, the segment would still leave him twenty miles short of Breese.

John exited the car saying nothing, nodding his head to the driver as a thank you. He resumed his sprint, heading eastward alongside Route 50 and struggled to keep his balance when forced into the ditch by traffic. He stopped only to catch his breath when completely spent. Fortunately, a considerate trucker, whose name—Chris Mallory—John would never forget, spotted John outside of Trenton and beckoned him into his cab. Mallory took him the rest of the way, dropping John off right at the hospital in Breese.

After charging inside the front door, John got to the desk and asked for the room of Alphonse Laufketter. The receptionist looked up abruptly and then excused herself, leaving his question unanswered. In a panic, John began wandering through the halls of the three-story facility.

On the second floor, he found his mother. She was sitting quietly with her hands folded in her lap as he stood over her. "John, I know you tried, but you're too late," Leah scratched out softly. "Dad's gone. It happened about forty-five minutes ago."

A cold force swept through John. He slumped back against the wall, looked to the ceiling, and then fell into the seat next to her.

"What?—how?—"

"He had a severe aneurism," Leah explained. "He had been taking longer shifts on the line, even though his boss advised him not to."

"Why?"

"We don't have to worry about that now," his mother responded. "I'm just glad you're here."

Alphie's death was no less a shock to the community than it was to his family, as he was thought by all around Beckemeyer to be indestructible. Idled with the closure of the coal mine, a large majority of the Beckemeyer community was able to appear at Alphie's memorial service. He was laid to rest in St. Anthony's Cemetery, just a half mile from the church off Bartelso Road, right along the path where he and Leah had often met long ago. The family took some money out of the savings account for a stone to be carefully engraved. It read:

Alphonse Dieter Laufketter
1868–1930
The Most Honest Man We Ever Knew

The thought of enrolling for a second year of college was the furthest thing from John's mind. His duty now was to look after his mother and his home. He informed no one at SLU, not even his coaches, that he was not returning. With only the things he had hurriedly stuffed into his bag before leaving the city, he moved back into his room at the house on Lincoln Street in Beckemeyer.

John spent the first few weeks trying not to think of his father, but it was impossible. He loafed through the fields, fished in Shoal Creek, and hunted squirrels and rabbits in the woods. He thought about searching out Bobby but was hearing stories that Bobby had permanently moved somewhere in or around St. Louis and rarely returned to the area.

Thanks to the many skills Alphie had taught him, John was able to pass some of the time repairing things around the house for his mother. With little else to do, John decided he had better earn some money, but he found there were few jobs of any kind available around the county. Many of the Beckemeyer and Carlyle businesses owned by the fathers of his friends, where many of them had gone to work, had already closed their doors from the weak economy as John saw his classmates from Breese

High wandering the streets just like himself. The familiar businesses, such as the sawmill and shoe factory, had been places where, a year ago, John had figured he could easily get work before the SLU scholarship offer came along and sent him to college.

One place held a possibility of work, but it was a place where Alphie had never wanted his son to end up. John walked across town to the offices at the Beckemeyer coal mine, hoping to get a spot at one of the shafts in the area.

With the Beckemeyer mine having been closed indefinitely, the displaced laborers had scattered to find piecemeal hours in the locations that remained in operation around the county. Some mines had even closed in recent years when times were good. Carlyle had not drawn coal from its shaft since 1888; the West Breese Mine had shut down back on February 27, 1923, after over forty years of operation when its parent company, the Consolidated Coal Company of St. Louis, had deemed the facility as being no longer profitable.

Near the gate, he approached a trailer that served as the personnel center, took a deep breath, and pounded on the door. Answering the knock from within came an indifferent response. "Yeah, what?"

John opened the door to find a gruff, weathered, middle-aged man behind a desk, who did not look up when John entered. Beside him, two young women were facing the back wall while they stuffed folders into filing cabinets.

"Nothing at all," the man responded to John's inquiry for work.

Undaunted, John headed west toward the two nearby mines that were still functioning, the East Breese and North Breese locations. Despite no experience in this line of work, John was determined to become employed, bad economy or not.

When he arrived at the gate of the North location, however, his heart sank when he saw dozens of other men looking for a job, all with perfectly clean clothes like himself, suggesting no experience in the field. He was sent away empty-handed from the North mine and, later, from the East shaft as well.

But after four weeks of waiting, John got word in early June that, by a stroke of luck, he was wanted in the East Breese location. A laborer there had gotten into a heated argument with a foreman, leading to a fistfight that sent them tumbling through the compound. Without the slightest semblance of a hearing on the matter, the laborer was quickly fired after being deemed the instigator by management. The event opened a "full-time" spot in the shaft, which consisted of up to only a mere eighteen hours per week.

Work was tentative for *everyone* daily, however; at three o'clock every afternoon, workers and their families went outside to listen for the mine's whistle, indicating that the laborers were to show up for their seven o'clock shift the following morning. If there was no whistle, there was no work the next day.

The man in charge of hiring at the East Breese location was from Beckemeyer. When the man was out of work a year and a half earlier, his family of six had nothing and was near starvation. Leah had learned of their condition and cooked lifesaving meals for the family.

John was early on his first day and arrived at the mine at 6:40 in the morning, twenty minutes before his shift was to begin. The shaft went 430 feet straight down underground, where the miners dug through a coal seam nearly ten feet thick. On his first trip down the elevator, John, discovering he had claustrophobia, gritted his teeth and took deep breaths, but he found that the discomfort lessened with each ride.

The work was exhausting, painful, and suffocating. John had to prepare himself mentally for each day in the mine and did his best to go about his duties cheerfully. Although the occupation was far from ideal for most people, John considered every day that he was able to get hours to be some sort of small victory, some sort of a small step forward in his life and in that of his widowed mother. The Cardinals were barely over the .500 mark in the National League standings, but John was no longer paying attention. Baseball was a game. He had to work.

He was now driven with a sole purpose, determined to build a reputation for being a reliable workman like his father. A careless attitude toward his pitching arm had led to his injury; he vowed now to never take anything for granted ever again. Through hard work in the mine, he figured, he could somehow prove himself with this second chance.

Arbeiten ist eine Ehre.

Exhausted on most evenings after coming home, John usually played cards with his mother at the kitchen table or found refreshment in taking a stroll around town. As he walked the streets of Beckemeyer, previous summers popped into his mind, a time back when goals and dreams wafted easily through his head—and which was now an entire lifetime ago.

Maybe Bobby was right. Maybe us small-town guys are supposed to stay right here.

Despite the mine in Beckemeyer remaining closed throughout 1930, a perennial dosage of optimism arrived in the form of the favorite local summertime entertainment, the Clinton County Baseball League. In 1930, 21,369 people were living in Clinton County, and nearly all of them who were old enough to understand took a keen interest in the CCL standings.

Each Sunday when the Beckemeyer Eagles were at home, the fans returned home after Mass at St. Anthony's to change into more comfortable clothes, pack whatever food was available into their picnic baskets, and head out for the ballpark on the east end of town. With few trains now stopping in town and no coal being loaded onto the ones that did, the air around the baseball field was cleaner than normal.

As word circulated around Beckemeyer that John was back home, it was assumed he would begin pitching for the Eagles. The barbershop on Louis Street was full of excited talk of the summer's possibilities. If John took the mound, the locals figured—and if they also could get Bobby to catch for the team—the Eagles would be the CCL favorite for the season. Neither one had yet donned the Becky uniform, as in 1929 John had been too young while Bobby was in Texas playing professional ball. But since the start of the league schedule on May 25, neither Beans Garcia nor Putt Skrobul, who were once again running the team, had heard from the pair. Disappointed with the absence of the two potential stars, Beckemeyer residents still had dutifully taken their seats in the stands each Sunday.

Bobby, while sometimes boarding in a farmer's trailer outside of town, was believed to mostly be spending his time in St. Louis. And for the foreseeable future, John's only concern in the world was looking after his mother.

By the time the Germantown Reds came to Beckemeyer to play the Eagles on June 15, John had grown restless at home. When not working, he still devoted every single moment to his mother. Nonetheless, he was also feeling adulthood creep upon him, despite only his nineteenth birthday approaching in September. Wanting to become part of the community again, he decided to walk over to the field and watch the game, knowing he would likely be harangued by the townsfolk to get him to join the team.

Hoping to be less conspicuous if he arrived a little late, the one o'clock contest was already in the bottom of the second inning by the time John had woven his way on the streets through town from west to east, hearing loud bursts of cheers and groans along the way. Near the ballpark he slowed to a cautious, step-by-step advance, carefully staying out of sight of those in attendance.

When the third out was made, the Beckemeyer catcher emerged from the dugout to warm up the Eagles pitcher for the top of the third. John, still watching from a safe distance down the left field line, smiled to himself as he noticed the catcher's familiar gait. He watched Bobby bounding toward the plate through the dust, gabbing at people in the crowd in his proud, provocative way.

But in the next instant, John's smile faded. Taking a few more steps down the left field line and looking more closely, he discovered it was not Bobby after all, but someone else catching. John walked back home before Beckemeyer went to bat again.

Despite the disappointment, he wanted to become involved in things locally once again. The following morning as he left for the mine, John went to Garcia's home on the southern edge of town near the corner of Scoville and Fifth Streets, among the last row of houses brushing against the cornfields that stretched all the way to Bartelso. John passed Bobby's old house on the way, which appeared vacant. John asked Garcia about the possibility of joining the team. Naturally, he was most welcome.

While the work in the mine was getting more difficult, John was also getting more comfortable each day in being back in Beckemeyer, especially with the prospect of playing for the Eagles. He was convinced he was right where he needed to be.

CHAPTER SIX

Fighting through the nagging pain that regularly surfaced in his pitching shoulder, John got back into playing shape very quickly. The fact he had faced only one batter for SLU during the spring would pay dividends for Beckemeyer, as his otherwise well-rested arm would presumably permit him to throw as much and as often as the Eagles needed him.

Still only 18 years old, John's level of talent quickly separated him from nearly everyone else in the Clinton County League. Immediately, the Becky team began rocketing up the league charts, winning four in a row from the end of June to mid-July after the precocious hurler had joined up.

On Sunday morning, July 20, the Aviston Aces and their perfect 7-0 record invaded the Beckemeyer field to take on the second-place Eagles, who now stood at 5-2 after a 1-2 start without John in the lineup. As the noon hour approached, a squadron of jalopies creaked to a halt on Murray Street along the third base line, carrying the Aviston players and fans.

An overwhelming, stifling heat had already begun to envelop the area. Typically, Clinton County residents paid little mind to oppressive temperatures in the summer months, as its daily appearance was just as reliable as Diekamper opening the front door to his general store at seven o'clock sharp. But the weather in July 1930 had been markedly different. The recent blast of heat across the county had been coupled with a devastating drought that had battered the Heartland, threatening farm families in Southern Illinois with massive crop failures come autumn. As the Beckemeyer and Aviston teams took the field, record temperatures were hitting many parts of the nation including Washington, D.C., where an all-time high mark of 106 was endured. The following day on the 21st, the 110 degrees that swallowed Millsboro, Delaware, would set a record for that state. A week later on the 28th, Greensburg, Kentucky, would set a state record with a temperature of 114.

The players and fans of the Clinton County League dismissed the conditions as best they could, determined to perform their Sunday outdoor ritual. It was the day of the week that made all the toil in the fields and mines worth it, a chance to watch their hometown men scratch up the dirt with their cleats while doing battle with their neighbors. The top buttons on shirts and blouses were undone and sleeves were rolled up, as spectators took their seats in the stands. Stories and laughs from the past week passed the time until the first pitch. Out on the field, the players loosened up as they flopped about in thick flannel uniforms, accelerating the perspiration streaming off their necks. One could drink water ladled from a nearby tub for relief, but it was a badge of honor and toughness for a ballplayer to not taste it.

When the game began, Beckemeyer wasted no time reaching for the top spot in the CCL standings. In the bottom of the first inning after the first two men had made outs, John singled sharply to center field as the ball sizzled past the Aviston pitcher's ear.

Next up for the Eagles was big Clayton Wagoner, one of those farmers whose livelihood was imperiled with the extreme weather. Tall and sinewy, Wagoner was one of the league's top power hitters, and his talent had made him the subject of controversy since entering the league three seasons earlier. The fringe of Wagoner's scorched farmland formed a shared border between Beckemeyer and Breese, and the team from the latter had also coveted his services. Before the 1930 season began, Breese manager David Haake had finally filed a complaint with the league commissioner, claiming that Wagoner had conducted most of his personal business in Breese for the past two years and, therefore, should be on his roster. The request was denied.

As he walked to the plate as the cleanup hitter for the Eagles, Wagoner was chided with derisive comments from the Breese bench. "Famous for friendliness!" Wagoner laughed and hollered back as he took his stance.

He let the first pitch go by while John bolted for second base, stealing it successfully as the locals up sprung up out of their seats.

In deference to the imposing Wagoner, the Aviston third baseman retreated to the edge of the outfield grass in anticipation of a hard liner being hit his way. Noticing how far off the bag the third baseman was, John was tempted to steal again, but decided against it. Distracted from John's bluffs toward third, the Aviston pitcher flung a poor curveball toward the plate. Wagoner smashed a one-hopper through the hole on the left side, eluding the third baseman and shortstop as the baseball accelerated into left field.

With all eyes upon him, John darted for third base. He lifted his head for a split second to locate Garcia, who was in the third-base coaching box and waving John home.

But in the process of looking at the coach while running at full speed, John also spotted someone else in the background behind Garcia.

Just beyond the third-base dugout was a beautiful young woman, whom John had never seen previously in town. She had a facial expression John would never forget; her eyes were looking right into John's. They were *stunning* eyes, sparkling directly through his soul. She had black, straight, shoulder-length hair and was jumping up and down in a frenzied cheer with a wide smile beaming on her face.

Stunned by her magnificence, John stumbled when he rounded the third base bag. Trying to regain his balance, he ultimately fell to the ground fifteen feet shy of home plate. The third baseman for Aviston turned his head and noticed the mishap. He took his time in making a careful relay throw to the catcher as John was tagged for an easy third out, with the home crowd moaning in disappointment.

John paused afterwards on his knees, his head hanging and his hands resting on his thighs in mild shame until he shook off the dust and forced himself up. As the teams traded places on the field in preparation for the next inning, only one pair of eyes was now upon John.

As he walked over to the Eagles bench to get his cap and glove, the girl, despite the botched play, sent him an approving smile from her radiant face. "That's okay, John!" she called out to him. "Hold 'em right there on defense!"

Jogging back onto the field, John—who remembered his coaches telling him to never look in the stands—peeked back over his shoulder into the crowd. He quickly found her, nodded, smiled, and tipped his cap in her direction.

Buoyed by the support, John homered twice and tripled in his final three at bats on the day, in addition to striking out thirteen batters in a magnificent pitching effort as the Eagles coasted to a 9-2 drubbing of the previously unbeaten Aviston club.

After lingering for a while at the field, the postgame routine invariably took everyone, fans and players alike, to George's. With the onset of Prohibition in 1920, the establishment had been transformed into an alcohol-free diner; its traditional slogan hanging on the sign out front, therefore, had changed only in meaning.

Drop in after the ball game
For a cool and refreshing drink

Garcia remained the proprietor of the establishment. He had a local print shop produce the Eagles baseball schedule on a foldable card, which he made available in a stack for patrons near the cash register. The faithful gradually arrived each Sunday from the ball field later in the afternoon. On this day, John rode over with several other players on the back of a truck, celebrating the big victory along the way.

As he hopped off in front of George's, John was about to walk inside when he stopped abruptly in his tracks.

He spotted Bobby down the block on Louis Street.

Bobby was walking erratically, soberly but nervously, as if beset with some form of paranoia as he glanced quickly from direction to direction. When his eyes turned back toward George's, he saw John. He stumbled away in the opposite direction as John yelled out to him.

"Bob!"

But his catcher kept walking farther away, not even turning around again to acknowledge. In the next instant, Bobby disappeared around the corner, shrouded in the dust of the Southern Illinois drought. John drew a deep breath and shook his head.

At that moment, he noticed a group of three young women approaching George's behind him. One of them was the same, stunning, unforgettable girl he had seen at the field, with the same dazzling smile still on her face as she walked right up to him. For the second time that afternoon, the girl tripped him up.

"Uh, John Laufketter," was all he could muster as he removed his dirty, crumpled ballcap while extending his hand.

"I know who you are," the girl responded confidently. She was still smiling widely. "Everybody knows who *you* are. I'm Rose Huels."

The players who rode in the truck with John began piling inside the front door of George's, looking back at him to see if he would be joining them.

"I don't think I've seen you around here before," John continued in a staggered breath, just trying to keep the conversation going. "So, you like baseball?"

"Oh yes," Rose responded. "My mother, father, and I just moved down here from Vandalia. My father was hired at Farmers and Merchants, trying to help get the loan department back on its feet. I'm done with school, just thinking about what I want to do next. Kind of hard to find stuff to do around here, but the games on Sunday are great. We were at the one last week too."

John nodded while staring into her mesmerizing eyes. Rose continued.

"I asked about you," she said boldly. "I'm told you left school to come back here and take care of your mother. I—I think that's the noblest thing I've ever heard. You must really care about her and this town to give that all up and come back."

With his cap still in his hands, John shrugged his shoulders in appreciation. He then motioned to the door. "Would you like to come inside with us?"

"No, thank you. We're still setting up a place over on Dora Street, so I have to get on home. It was very nice meeting you, though, John Laufketter."

John started to go on into George's when he heard Rose call out to him.

"There really *is* nothing to do around here," she said with a chuckle. "Would you take me for an ice cream sometime?"

"Sounds great," the ballplayer responded with a dust-covered smile.

John and Beckemeyer itself, with new life, sprang forth from the victory over Aviston and would not lose again in the 1930 regular season, finishing with a 12-2 mark. They faced Trenton in the league championship game, where John battled with Trenton pitcher Wes Brooks in a masterful struggle of great hurlers. Unable to get John a run, Beckemeyer lost the crown by a 1–0 score, the lone tally being unearned because of two Eagles errors in the decisive seventh inning.

Despite the disappointing defeat in the league title game, the camaraderie and competition that accompanied the return of baseball to John's life invigorated him. He thrived on the adrenaline that came from preparing for a game or even a practice.

When the season concluded, he found it difficult to wind down during his off-time from the mine—off-time that was gradually increasing for John and the other miners. However, it also left him more time to meet with Rose.

On a Saturday afternoon in September with no work to be had, John went into George's to find the other idled laborers passing the time, sipping iced tea and other virgin drinks. He found a week-old newspaper lying on the bar and skimmed the headlines, many of which lately noted the unrest taking place in Germany. Updates from his father's homeland particularly caught his attention. The featured article announced that the rebellious new National Socialist Party had just picked up 107 seats in the German Reichstag, making it the second-largest political faction in that country.

John flipped the paper aside as he leaned on the bar. It bumped into some napkins, which uncovered a copy of *The Sporting News*. The famed athletics periodical, published out of St. Louis, served as the favored source nationwide for the latest information from the baseball world. The August 28 issue sitting there was nearly two weeks old but was still a valued piece of information, respectfully left near the register for the next person to enjoy. With a tall glass of ginger ale and ice in one hand, John scooped up the paper and leaned against the wall, flipping through the pages with keen interest. He noticed that the Cardinals were scheduled to be in Boston that day. That very afternoon, his favorite player, Jesse Haines, would pitch them to a complete game 8–2 victory over the Braves, which would keep the Redbirds in a first-place tie with Brooklyn, with both teams leading the Chicago Cubs by a mere half game. Less than two weeks later on the twenty-sixth, Haines would wrap up the National League pennant for St. Louis, beating Pittsburgh at Sportsman's Park. With a World Series appearance already in the bag, Branch Rickey decided it was time to summon his prized pitching prospect.

On the final day of the 1930 season on September 28, with the Cards holding an insurmountable two-game lead on the Cubs, Dizzy Dean took the mound for the first time in a major league game. He stymied the Pirates batters in just an hour and twenty-one minutes, a three-hitter in beating the Pittsburgh men by a 3–1 count. He would not pitch in the World Series, however, as the Cardinals fell to the A's in six games, two of which were won by their new ace, Lefty Grove.

Searching for more updates on the Cardinals as he normally did, John noticed a feature article.

Dean Not Only Can Pitch,
But He Has Plenty of Self-Confidence

The St. Louis Cardinals have a rare specimen in Dizzy Dean, the tall, loose-jointed righthander now hurling in style for the Houston Buffs. After he had burned up the Western League at the St. Joseph farm, the St. Louis club promoted him to the Buffs for some necessary finishing touches.

In winning his fourth straight start in the Texas League at Wichita Falls, August 17, Dean fanned 12 of the Spudders and won in a breeze. Since then he has boosted his record to six straight, and has struck out 47 in 49 innings pitched for Houston.

In his debut in the Buffs' uniform, Dizzy struck out 14 of the San Antonio batsmen, allowed six hits, and won twelve to one. Houston scribes, duly impressed with that initial effort, sought out the youngster and requested an interview.

'Shucks, I didn't have my stuff,' drawled the lanky pitcher. 'Can you imagine that bunch of bums making a run off me?'

It was quite evident that if confidence means anything, Mr. Dean should travel far and high.

In fact, as one Texas scribe recently put it, there is nothing that Dean doesn't have. His windup in itself is enough to baffle any batter. It is an arm-flapping windup, and is undoubtedly an asset to him on the mound. But that is only a fore-runner of what is to come. Dizzy has a blazing swift ball with a genuine break on it. He has a sweeping curve, mixes a slow pitch in for a change of pace with rare judgment, and so far, he has displayed perfect control.

While at St. Joseph, he is said to have won two different fistic brawls with players who challenged his greatness, and one of these victories was over a player much bigger than Dizzy.

Branch Rickey, vice-president of the Cardinals who was responsible for the transfer of Dean from one Cardinal farm to another, believes Dean is one of the most promising pitchers in the minors. 'Don't be surprised if Dean is with the Cardinals in 1931,' was a prediction recently made by Rickey.

John's interest in the article began fading. But as he was about to flip the paper back onto the counter, the last couple lines grabbed his attention once again.

The other notable feature of Houston's play has been the hitting of Homer Peel, who has clouted at better than a .420 clip since joining the club two months ago. Many of Peel's blows have been for extra bases.

John thought of Bobby. He remembered his friend making a disgruntled mention of Peel, for some reason, during their drive into the city the previous August. Bobby's whereabouts were unknown since the evening of Beckemeyer's big win over Aviston on July 20.

As daylight faded into the colder months of late 1930, the pain of the Great Depression was intensifying. Fortunately for John, his shifts at the

Breese mine remained mostly steady, due to his work ethic. He never had forgotten the feeling of hunger on many days while at SLU, just a short time ago when times were good, and he never wanted to have that feeling again. Life now consisted of his mine shifts, once-a-week ballgames in CCL during the summer months, playing cards with his mother at the kitchen table, and spending every other available moment with Rose.

He acquiesced that it was enough for him. It was what he was supposed to be doing, he told himself.

Just like his father used to do, John carefully pored over every paycheck and every bill at home. Even with the budget being as tight as a drum, he was usually able to take Rose to a movie in Carlyle once a week (he indulged this activity because she enjoyed it so much, even though he preferred dates where they could talk). Every week, regardless if it had been a good week or bad week in the mine, John made certain that his savings inched forward at the Farmers and Merchants Bank, even if it was only a single dollar. "You're always either getting better or getting worse, and never staying the same," Father Schweighart used to tell John and his St. Anthony's classmates about life.

Their most favorite activity, however, was going to Mass together at St. Anthony's. Each Sunday, John hoped his favorite hymn being sung. It usually was, as it was one of Father Schweighart's favorites as well.

> O Lord my God
> When I in awesome wonder
> Consider all the worlds Thy hands have made
> I see the stars, I hear the rolling thunder
> Thy pow'r throughout the universe displayed.
> Then sings my soul
> My savior, God, to Thee
> How great Thou art,
> How great Thou art.

John knew his hard life had him aging prematurely. Nevertheless, he was determined to marry Rose and ultimately make a better life for *her*. He was her "big guy," she was his "sweetie," and they were always seen side by side in town.

As the spring of 1931 arrived and the Cardinals got ready to defend their National League pennant, fans were hoping that the precocious Dizzy Dean would be brought to St. Louis full-time. Rickey and Breadon, however, resisted the temptation to elevate him from the minors. It proved to be a deft move, as the Cardinals coasted to their fourth National League pennant in six years (and a World Series victory over the A's) without him. Dean instead unleashed his fury on the hitters of the Texas League, posting a remarkable 26-10 record and a 1.57 ERA at Houston, permitting an average of fewer than one base runner per inning.

And just like Dean, John Laufketter also blazed through other teams' bats in an obscure league in 1931. Beckemeyer won its first Clinton County League title in twelve years, losing only once over the entire summer. John's mastery happened with so much ease that he appeared to be toying with Becky's opponents. Even with his sore shoulder that worsened with each passing month in the mine, he was already a man among boys.

It was his success on the mound, however, that ironically led to some tension around town.

One day in late 1931, a lone solitary patron was sitting at a table in George's when John walked in. Looking up at John, the patron returned his eyes back down to his milkshake and smacked his lips after a sip while scanning the *St. Louis Post-Dispatch*. The man was reading an article extolling fact that Dean, the game's newest pitching sensation, was only 21 years old. The pitcher was on the verge of greatness and had the world by the tail.

Hiding behind the paper, the patron's eyes rolled up over the top, gazing once again at John—who, in having just turned twenty, was even younger than Dean.

The man's judgmental stare came upon John from many people whenever a discussion of major league pitchers arose in George's, the barbershop, the lunchroom at the mine, or anyplace else around town. With John's ability, the locals wondered, why was he not getting—or at least *seeking*—a professional tryout? If the Cardinals had no use for him, why not the lowly St. Louis Browns of the American League, which had lost ninety games the past season? Shouldn't *someone* know about him by now?

Since being back home, John had inadvertently overhead the disappointed whispers about Bobby and how *he* had failed. Now, the townspeople were speaking of him in the same manner. No one blamed John for coming home after the death of his father and caring for Leah, and no one blamed him for spending his spare time courting the beautiful, charming Rose. Yet a shadow of disappointment trailed him wherever he went. So much notoriety could be brought to Beckemeyer if he just gave it a shot, the locals figured.

John took one gulp of his Coca-Cola. He slammed his glass onto the counter, stared the man down, and shoved the door open, leaving George's.

While 1932 saw some of the greatest general suffering for the nation during the Great Depression, John, Rose, and Beckemeyer itself enjoyed the most prosperity they had experienced in years. The couple kicked off the summer in grand style by getting married at St. Anthony's on June 18. Much like his father, John had never imagined himself getting married, but he was so in love with Rose that he found himself doting on her perpetually.

Compounding their joy that summer was an addition to their family—a hungry, stray dog that had been wandering around their house and returning more often as Rose gave it bowls of milk. It was a mixed-breed female, its origins unknown, but it appeared to be a cross between a beagle and a pit bull. They named her Little Lady, which stemmed from John asking Rose each day upon returning home, "Where's the little lady?" She soon became a fixture with Rose every Sunday at the Beckemeyer ball field in cheering on John. Little Lady also proved to be a dependable chaser, retrieving the foul balls that rolled along Murray Street.

Then came more good news. The Beckemeyer coal mine, dormant for three years, was to be reopened later in the year. Having earned small semblance of seniority at the East Breese mine, John was one of the first residents able to get himself transferred to the Beckemeyer location, an easy ten-block walk from his house on Lincoln Street.

And topping it all off for the town was the Eagles' unprecedented performance on the diamond in 1932. They did what no team in the Clinton County League had ever accomplished, a perfect 14-0 regular season record. The unblemished slate was followed by a 12–1 trouncing of Bartelso in the championship game, giving Becky back-to-back league titles, with John being the winning pitcher in fourteen of the fifteen contests. Counting the postseason victories, Beckemeyer had won twenty-seven of its last twenty-eight games and had a 41-4 overall mark during the past three seasons (with two of those losses occurring without John on the roster).

Meanwhile, in St. Louis that summer, Dizzy Dean had indeed shown he was ready for the majors in his rookie season. Although the defending champion Redbirds had slipped all the way to sixth place in the eight-team National League with a 72-82 mark, Dean led the league's pitchers in innings (286), shutouts (4), and strikeouts (191).

As Beckemeyer residents spent the cold months of 1932–33 trying to build upon the upturn of their luck, most Americans struggled to survive the fourth winter of the Great Depression. They looked for leadership.

Beginning on March 12, 1933, newly elected President Franklin Delano Roosevelt used the burgeoning medium of radio to take his message directly to the people, reassuring them with his series of fireside chats. As he spoke, the president imagined himself sitting with a few citizens around his living room with warm flames churning. "When you get to the end of your rope," he instructed the populace, "tie a knot and hang on."

A day after the first broadcast, the Dow Jones Industrial Average posted its biggest percentage gain in history—15.34 percent—on March 13. Positive momentum appeared to be on its way.

Ten days later, the Cullen-Harrison Act would be signed into law by Roosevelt, making the sale of beer with an alcohol composition of 3.2 percent legal, as well as some wines with comparable content.

Folks around St. Louis were quick to launch their celebrations. Shortly after midnight on April 7, the day on which the law would be in effect, newly elected Mayor Bernard Dickmann toasted with the Elks Club on Lindell Avenue near the SLU campus, while nearly 30,000 people were in the streets outside the Anheuser-Busch brewery waiting for twelve o'clock to strike. Around the corner from where Dickmann and the Elks were reveling, more than 10,000 others were cheering at the Falstaff plant on Forest Park Avenue, where the trucks were lined up and pumped full of beer, ready for delivery.

But once again, fortunes had shifted in Beckemeyer. There was little to celebrate.

In March 1933, just after it was reported in the newspapers that Adolf Hitler had become dictator of Germany, a fire at the revived Beckemeyer coal mine destroyed the screening plant for the facility.

Less than three weeks later, the supports of an air shaft gave way, and while no one was inside at the time, it was destroyed as well. The mine was immediately shut down, as Beckemeyer once again instantly plummeted into economic darkness.

John and the other workers began trudging back to Breese, hoping for any hours they could get. But upon getting there, they discovered there were now even more workers flooding the Clinton County labor pool. On the morning of Christmas Eve 1932, a methane gas explosion at the coal mine in the town of Moweaqua, seventy miles to the north, had killed fifty-four workers. Most of those remaining had now drifted down to Breese, looking for a job.

A mounting anxiety began overwhelming John. The closure of the Beckemeyer mine was a disheartening retreat, a shattering surrender of ground he thought to be permanently recaptured. He and Rose were expecting their first child—a prospect that, while still a blessing, had been much brighter when it appeared the mine was permanently back in operation.

Like his father had done in his own solitary days, John had never minded enduring hardships by himself; he could always "tough things out" on his own, whether it meant going hungry for a day or doing without extra items of comfort. But, now, the specter of entrenched poverty peered over his family. As he lay exhausted yet sleepless in his bed, it stared down upon him.

To make matters even more challenging, Rose's parents had recently moved in with them, joining Leah. When the economy tanked again, Jim Huels was told that his services were no longer needed in the loan department at the Farmers and Merchants Bank, as there was nothing left for people to borrow. On most days, John came home from the mine to find his father-in-law sitting in a wrought iron chair in the backyard, staring out into the cornfields in a catatonic state.

In early May 1933, just a couple of weeks before the baby's arrival, it occurred to John during one of those sleepless nights that, had he stayed in school, he would now have been graduating from SLU. He could not help but wonder. . . how would life have been different? Certainly, his mother would have been able to take care of herself or, at the very least, there were plenty of people who could have looked in on her. Had he made the right choice long ago in coming back home?

With the bank account evaporating and the baby almost due, John begrudgingly decided to sell the big house on Lincoln Street, his boyhood home that his father had purchased almost thirty years earlier. He moved his mother, Rose, Little Lady, and Rose's parents to a smaller and more affordable house, six blocks east in Beckemeyer on Randolph Street and just five blocks from the mine. For the time being, the air was clean in that part of town with the mine having been idled, but with cleaner air came no work.

A son was born to John and Rose on May 24, whom they named Joseph. Little Lady soon became an overprotective older sister, regularly sitting in the baby's room and keeping an eye on things as she curled up on a pillow in the corner near the crib. She would also howl if John, Rose, or Leah did not attend to Joseph's crying in an expeditious manner.

Also giving extensive care to Joseph was John's mother, who demanded to be a regular contributor to the household so long as she lived with them. Leah had been doing clothing repair to bring in extra income, as people from all over Beckemeyer dropped off their tattered shirts and pants to her at the new residence on Randolph Street. They knew her ten dancing fingers could stretch the clothing's use a bit longer, which was perhaps an important work shirt for the family's breadwinner or some hand-me-downs for a younger sibling in a family with no means for new outfits.

When she first launched her service, Leah accepted and promptly finished all the work she could get. She placed all the clothes in a pile with carefully marked tags that identified each one's owner. With a hot cup of tea, she sat down by the front window, nabbed a shirt or pair of slacks off the top of the pile, and happily started her work. She began by meticulously studying the damaged item through her glasses before reaching into her sewing kit to locate the necessary tools. Throughout a job, she occasionally peeked out the window to see if her son was coming home from the mine.

Over time, as John came through the front door each day, he noticed that the pile of clothes mounted. He also noticed his mother was beginning to quiver as she sewed, working frantically to keep up, despite John and Rose imploring her to not take on so much.

Her desire to help the family—or perhaps her longing for Alphie—finally overcame her.

While on her way to Diekamper's for some extra cloth and thread, Leah suffered a massive stroke and collapsed along Louis Street, passing away on June 19, 1933, just three weeks after the birth of her grandson.

Leah was buried at St. Anthony's Cemetery next to Alphie. John had an inscription placed on her stone like that of Alphie's.

Leah Erlhaus Laufketter
1880–1933
The Most Unselfish Woman We Ever Knew

After the funeral, John lost interest in most things, including baseball, and barely could get himself out of the house to go to work. He decided that he would not play in the CCL for the rest of the summer, as his heart was not in it. The 1933 edition of the Beckemeyer Eagles would not recover from his absence, as it sank to a 6-8 final record after a 4-1 start.

With little work and plenty of time to think, John mostly sat at home, wondering if the Breese coal mine, where he was now spending only a few hours each week, would be where his once-promising life would end.

Conversely, the luck and legend of another young pitcher forty miles away continued to ascend. On July 30, 1933, with second baseman Frankie Frisch taking over as the Cardinals manager a week earlier, Dizzy Dean stood on the mound at Sportsman's Park in the ninth inning of the first game of a doubleheader against the Chicago Cubs. With one out to go, he peered toward his catcher's signs amidst a frenzied, hollering crowd. With his long-sleeved undershirt soaked with sweat seeping all the way onto his white flannel jersey, Dean's labor over the sunbaked afternoon had victory imminent, with the Cardinals ahead by a comfortable 8–2 score.

In the previous moment, he had struck out Chicago shortstop Bill Jurges for the second time of the day. It was the sixteenth strikeout of the game for Dizzy, which left him one shy of the record for a single game. Dean stood ready to go for the new mark as the final Cubs hitter, Jim Mosolf, approached the batter's circle. Mosolf, a 27-year-old reserve outfielder, had only joined the Cubs at the end of June and was now summoned by Chicago manager Charlie Grimm as a pinch hitter.

Diz released a trio of electric fastballs, each of which Mosolf barely saw, becoming Dean's seventeenth strikeout victim. It was the most ever in a nine-inning game, surpassing a record which had stood for almost twenty-five years. Over the course of the contest, Dizzy himself had added three hits to the Cards offensive attack, including two doubles. "Mosolf never took the bat off his shoulder," Dean said later. "I just put three of 'em through there, Dean Specials with smoke curlin' off 'em."

As Dizzy disappeared down the dugout steps while accepting congratulations from his teammates, the St. Louisans in the first few rows of the seats at Sportsman's Park reached out to touch him as if mystical powers wafted from his garments.

With time in between games of the doubleheader, Dean was anxious to greet some of those admirers. "He dressed quickly and went into the grandstand to mix with the crowd," one report noted. "Diz was laughing, flexing his right arm, and signing everything from the cuffs on white shirts to beer labels."

The Cardinals would eventually fade in the standings, but brighter days were undoubtedly ahead. On September 13, Dean would become the first Cardinals pitcher in five years to win twenty games in a season. The team then designated the 17th as Dizzy Dean Day at Sportsman's Park as the laurels continued to pour in. "His gifts included a new Buick, a crate of baby chicks, and five pigs," a writer noted about the occasion. He was the toast of the town, and everywhere he went, people fawned over his every move and hung on his every word. People were making pilgrimages to St. Louis from across the country to watch him pitch. "Farmers come out of the distant Ozarks," Jimmy Powers of the *New York Daily News* would write of him, "and Midwest traveling salesmen arrange their itineraries to catch him."

In living at the plush Forest Park Hotel with his wife Pat, the former cotton-picking country boy never imagined that life could be so grand.

By December 1933, the kegs began flowing once again at George's, as the Eighteenth Amendment had fully ended Prohibition. Despite bordering the east side of Beckemeyer as closely as it did the west, George's was almost always clean, due to the miners following an unwritten local "law" about drinking only at Ed Roach's tavern near the shaft. John was an exception to the rule.

But despite the alcohol now pouring once again, John had little to celebrate and never had found drinking to be a lasting solution, anyway. As men with empty pockets toasted and cheered the restored right to toast and cheer, the soup lines were simultaneously growing down the street, a forlorn image of the Great Depression once seen in the vicinity only in Breese but now having come to Beckemeyer as well. A ration of soup, available just three times per week, was being handed out across from Diekamper's store, just two blocks from George's. Despite his murmuring stomach, John pridefully never stood in the line as he did not wish for the townspeople to see him there.

His family had a growing credit bill at the general store; and while the note was not yet called due, John sensed that the benevolent Mr. Diekamper could not bail him and the other Beckemeyer residents out much longer. The only thing standing between the Laufketter household and ruin was John's scant time afforded him each week at the Breese mine. He had lost his mother, his father, and most of his work; would he ultimately lose Rose and Joseph as well if he could not support them?

And, on top of everything else, he had no idea what had become of his best friend. Throughout it all, during three years of John being back in Beckemeyer, there was still no sign of Bobby since John had seen him on Louis Street in July 1930. Had he left town for good? Was he angry at John for some reason? Was he still angry at Beckemeyer for some reason? At something else?

On Christmas Eve, John and Rose baked a small ham at home, the first meat on their table in nearly two months. The following day in St. Louis, Bernard Dickmann oversaw the first Mayor's Christmas Dinner for the needy. Over 26,000 residents were served.

As 1933 passed into 1934, life for John had become a daily battle to hang on. It was an entire lifetime away from the carefree days of his recent youth.

CHAPTER SEVEN

The Cardinals' spring training practices for the 1934 season got underway in Bradenton on March 3. As Dean drove from his sparkling new house in Palma Sola to the team's training facility in the center of town, he glanced up at the palm trees, which were flapping in the coastal breeze. Feeling strong, with his weight up to 195 pounds, Dean arrived in the best shape of his three-year career. He was nearly thirty pounds heavier than he was at the end of the 1933 season when he had wilted as the Cardinals' most used pitcher. "As he shapes up as a 200-pounder," Joe Vila of the *New York Sun* assessed of how Dean looked, "Branch Rickey says that Dizzy's smoke will surpass that of Walter Johnson and all other speed merchants."

Pulling into the parking lot at Ninth Street Park, Dizzy's famous grin darted in all directions. He emerged from his new Buick to exchange handshakes and backslaps with his teammates at their yearly late-winter reunion.

Greeting him first was his closest comrade on the team, a man with whom he shared a raw background from rural America. Oklahoma native Johnny "Pepper" Martin was straight off the prairie—a sinewy, speedy base runner and full-blooded roughneck. Pepper, in his inimitable style, rolled into Bradenton wearing only overalls in his barrel-nosed Ford pickup truck. He had been accompanied on his 1,300-mile trip to Bradenton by his two beloved bird dogs, sitting happily alongside Martin in the passenger seat.

Dizzy's 20-year-old brother Paul was also in camp, seeking to claim a roster spot with St. Louis for 1934 as a rookie. A year earlier, Paul—also a pitcher—had logged twenty-two victories in hurling for one of the Cardinals' top minor league teams at Columbus in the American Association, a performance that also included 222 strikeouts and two no-hitters. Like Dizzy, Paul's pitching motion included his arm dropping way down, slinging the ball from nearly a side-armed delivery. The action of his arm whipped the horsehide toward the plate with a tailing movement, pushing it away from left-handed batters.

Dizzy wasted no time in advocating his sibling's stock as much as possible. Despite having yet to take the hill in big-league action, Paul was advised by Diz upon arriving in Bradenton to hold out for an extra $1,500 before signing a contract. The press fawned all over the junior Dean, wondering if he would reach the same heights as his elder family member. "He's a great pitcher," Dizzy assured everyone. "He's even greater than I am, if that's possible. He told Mr. Rickey he'd pitch for nothing until he won a certain number of games, say fifteen, and then let the Cardinals pay him $500 for each victory. And he turned that offer down! You can't tell what a club's going to do nowadays."

After only three days had passed in Paul's first big-league camp, Dizzy then declared that the Dean brothers would together win at least forty-five ball games that year, leaving only forty-five or fifty or so, Diz figured, for the rest of the staff to win for the Cards to take the pennant.

Some of the other pitchers resented the implication that Dizzy had already anointed them as also-rans. One of them was James "Tex" Carleton, who had been in the big leagues as long as Dizzy and who himself had won seventeen games for St. Louis in 1933. Carleton did not think that the untested rookie Paul deserved all the extra attention he was getting. "He doesn't have a curve," Carleton said of Paul Dean when watching him throw off the mound for the first time in spring training. Another pitcher spoke to the press under the condition that his name not be printed, suggesting that the poorly lit fields of pitcher-friendly night baseball in the minor leagues had padded Paul's numbers. "He's just a thrower who struck out a lot of guys under the lights at Columbus," one opined. "If he weren't Diz's brother, he'd be long gone. That's the only reason they're keeping him up here."

On March 14, the Cards opened their exhibition schedule in Bradenton against the defending champion New York Giants, greeted by an overflow crowd that bulged down from the seats onto the actual playing surface. The spectators, yearning for a look at the Deans, were restrained by ropes along the left and right field lines. They were treated to an evenly matched contest, as Diz polished off the final three New York batters in the ninth to secure the win, 7–6.

Six days later, Paul entered his first game and promptly held the Philadelphia Phillies scoreless for three innings, suggesting that the dynamic Dean duo would indeed be the leading act in St. Louis in the approaching summer, just as Dizzy had been predicting.

Among ninety-seven sportswriters asked to give their opinion, forty believed the Giants would reclaim the National League title in 1934.

Thirty-four thought it would be the Cubs turn, while thirteen picked the Cardinals, nine selected the Pirates, and one forecasted the Boston Braves as the circuit champ.

Opening Day for both the National and American Leagues would finally arrive on April 17, as over 180,000 spectators poured through the turnstiles, according to a count given by the *Pittsburgh Post-Gazette*. However, owners were upholding a ban on the broadcasting of games on the radio; thus, when Beans Garcia turned on the radio at the now free-flowing George's Tavern on Louis Street in Beckemeyer, Illinois, the familiar voice of France Laux delivering the play-by-play of the Cardinals game was not heard.

Thinking quickly, Garcia then decided to revert to a practice conducted in many taverns before the days of radio—that of keeping the patrons up to date on the game via telegraph reports he received in his office. Once receiving each update, Garcia instructed the bartender to climb a ladder and write the inning-by-inning score on a large chalkboard above the mirror behind the bar.

Despite the attraction of Dizzy Dean, only 7,500 spectators showed up for the opener in St. Louis, as the Cardinals and the Pittsburgh Pirates took the field at Sportsman's Park under partly cloudy skies and a most pleasant 66 degrees for mid-April. The Redbirds coasted to a 7–1 beating of the Pirates.

Dizzy was his usual loquacious self in assessment of the enemy. "You can depend on the Deans winning two games of each series we play with the Pirates," he added as another forecast for 1934 for himself and his brother. "Why, those palookas are lucky whenever they get a run off me and Paul."

The Cards had their first battle of the year with the defending champion Giants in St. Louis on May 9. Diz disposed of the New Yorkers with an easy 4–0 shutout, permitting only two New York men to get as far as second base and sending everyone home in just over an hour and a half. Had he worked any more slowly, however, the teams would have encountered unplayable weather conditions at Sportsman's Park later that afternoon.

Near the end of the game at 4:40 p.m., fans sitting in the seats along the right field line began snapping their heads to the right, as if they were being pelted by tiny bullets. Those sitting on the opposite side of the stadium could see it happening in the first row of seats, then up to second row, and then up to another, the attack quickly ascending toward the upper deck.

Those being assaulted held up their forearms in self-defense, covering their eyes and mouths with their hands. Peeking out, they winced skyward. They were stunned to see that the afternoon sun had been eclipsed by a dark, grainy mass. Approaching through the grandstand from the west on the third-base side of the ballpark, the cloud covered the entire horizon and turned blacker as it drew closer. It was a blanket of dirt, slung by nature onto a wall of wind.

Three hundred million tons of granulated earth had charged across the American heartland from west to east, having been uprooted and carried from the Great Plains. At its ceiling, it stretched to the heavens over two miles high and was nearly 2,000 miles wide from north to south across the continent. A smaller dirt storm had hit St. Louis two weeks earlier on April 24 but was nowhere near the magnitude of the current blast.

As it tore through the press box, the sportswriters had been watching the closing moments of a baseball game taking place *somewhere* down on a field, which was now unseen below them. "Dimly lit through the dust cloud," Tom Meany wrote of the scene that day from his vantage point for the *New York World-Telegram*, "A cloud which has swept southeastward from Nebraska and the Dakotas to envelop this town in a murky haze." Full blackness soon overtook the sun, causing some observers in Sportsman's Park to nervously recall the biblical story of Golgotha.

In states west of Missouri that day, conditions were even more extreme. "Children were dying of dust pneumonia," one writer warned in reporting of the situation in Kansas. "Adults were getting lost in their backyards while fleeing to storm cellars, and many nights entire families were sleeping with their faces covered in wet towels or sheets." In Dupree, South Dakota, that same afternoon, a woman was reported killed as her vision was obscured while driving as she overturned her car in a ditch.

The Dust Bowl had returned, and there was no escape in any direction.

Three hundred miles to the north of St. Louis, Chicago hit a record temperature for the date at 94 degrees, with dust flying through the air "without precedent in intensity" in the city, the Associated Press reported. "Chicago's skyscrapers, which ordinarily loom before the eye at great distances, were virtually blotted from sight . . . dairymen said a milk shortage may develop in July. They declared feed costs were mounting and that pastures were entirely inadequate." It was estimated that twelve million pounds of earth had settled upon Chicago in the past twenty-four hours.

The dust storm would charge eastward, assaulting Boston as well as the nation's largest city. "To thousands of curious New Yorkers, who licked dry lips and felt the grit of fine dust particles in their mouths," wrote one observer, "it was a new experience."

After having passed through New York City, the soil-laden zephyr would ultimately travel over 1,500 miles before plunging to its final demise in the Atlantic Ocean.

The weather had once again added to the misery of the ongoing Great Depression. But as people across the United States and the world scratched through garbage cans for scraps of rotten food, the World Wheat Advisory Commission proclaimed on May 9 from their conference in Rome that the "world stocks of wheat on August 1 this year would be the largest on record, about 1.14 billion bushels."

At Sportsman's Park, fans and players alike scrambled for the streetcars after the game, holding onto the rails against the ravenous wind. Before the dinner hour struck in the city, the atmospheric conditions worsened even further.

Taking a shower was almost futile with the dirt incessantly hovering in the air, but Dean did so, anyway. He walked out of the ballpark and smiled as he obliged autograph seekers while grabbing a taxi back to his suite at the Forest Park Hotel. By then the dust had already jumped the river into Illinois, its sights set on invading Clinton County once again, just as it had the previous November. The storm rumbled into Summerfield and then swept over Trenton, Aviston, Breese, and Beckemeyer, engulfing the communities in rapid succession as man and beast scurried under shelter.

Among those peeking out from their windows were the people at 739 Randolph Street. Inside was a beaten-down John Laufketter, his wife, their son, their dog, and his wife's parents. They wondered if anything good could ever come from the weather again.

After the dust storm had cleared the Midwest, a throng of 6,500 fans—sizable for a weekday Depression-era crowd—returned to the ballpark to watch their Cardinals once again on May 11. "The air was not dust-filled as yesterday," reported Dent McSkimming for the *Post-Dispatch*, "but there was still a brisk wind blowing." Almost half of them were women who were admitted free of charge for a Ladies' Day promotion. "Aiding and abetting the Cardinals," noticed Will Wedge, "was a quota of soprano-shrill female customers, who yipped and yammered at everything, making a fearful din which helped the Cardinals." The women, grateful for their special day at the park, brought a homemade selection of "kitchen-baked pies, cakes, and cinnamon rolls to the handsome Deans."

With the breezes clear but still wreaking havoc with fly balls, Paul beat the immortal Meal Ticket of the Giants. "The famous 'Dean Act' is beginning to pay dividends," affirmed Ray Smith of the *St. Louis Globe-Democrat*. "Matching ball for ball with the great Carl Hubbell, Paul Dean came through like a thoroughbred. He had to travel ten innings before victory was his."

In doing so, the Cards had thus swept all three games from the Giants, as Frisch's men now had taken twelve of their last thirteen overall. Brash and cocky, they were having as much fun as an underpaid team could have. "They possess playing qualities that catch the eye," Gary Schumacher of the *New York Evening Journal* had conceded. "Flash and dash, speed, and an ostentatious aggressiveness." The Cards' fighting spirit had them atop the 1934 National League standings as May ended. But by the end of June, they had relinquished the lead back to the formidable Giants, suggesting that a back-and-forth struggle would ensue for the rest of the summer.

During the battle, a troubling reality was settling in on the St. Louis manager. In reviewing his notes and statistics, Frisch noticed that Dizzy and Paul Dean had pitched in two-thirds of his team's games to that point, leaving him to wonder if any other reliable throwers would surface on his staff for the remainder of the pennant race.

CHAPTER EIGHT

His job keeping him on the road every day from March to September, Jerry Tretiak never went anywhere without hot coffee in his vacuum-sealed metal cup. The cup sat in a makeshift holder he had rigged next to the front seat of his car, a disintegrating, creaking 1928 Plymouth Model Q that had seen every part of Michigan, Wisconsin, Illinois, Kentucky, and Indiana with him.

Beside the coffee cup sat a large binder, filled with various notes and several pencils, all of which, just like his Plymouth, had been ground dull. Occasionally, Tretiak traveled by train with his coffee cup and notes. But due to the spontaneous requirements of his occupation, he preferred to drive. He enjoyed being able to switch destinations at a moment's notice, a flexibility that the automobile afforded. The newly devised metal cup, which some people were calling a thermos, was another contemporary comfort, joining him in his ventures from Appleton to Paducah to Fort Wayne and all points in between. Tretiak knew all the best stops at which to have the cup filled, and he even knew many of the waitresses by their first names. His most preferred oases were in Central and Southern Illinois, including the Mill Restaurant in Lincoln, the Ariston Cafe in Litchfield, and the Tourist Haven Diner in Hamel. He was once married, but his inactivity around the house from September to March proved as much of a strain on his wife as his absence for work in the other half of the year, and the couple was divorced after only seventeen months.

His lonesome calling barely afforded him the luxury of a few close friends. Besides some familiar faces in the restaurants and gas stations he frequented, Jerry's only true companions were the other solitary men in his line of work whom he often crossed on the road—baseball scouts.

At 7:30 p.m. on Saturday June 30, 1934, Tretiak was in the midst of one of those seemingly endless scouting trips for his employer, the St. Louis Cardinals, heading south out of Chicago on US Route 66. Pulling into the Royal Grill in Lockport, another favorite greasy spoon, he limped through the front door with heavy, stiff legs. Jerry had already driven over

300 miles that day; he had attended a noon game in southwestern Michigan before going through Northern Indiana and Chicago up to Janesville, Wisconsin, where he met with the family of a player in whom the parent club had an interest. Afterwards, he headed back to the southwest side of Chicago for the same purpose with another.

Slumping down in fatigue at the counter while mumbling to the server, he requested a ham and egg sandwich with a side of fried potatoes. He gulped down two full cups of black coffee before his plate arrived.

The man on the stool next to him was reading the day's copy of the *St. Louis Star-Times*, making Tretiak wonder how the late edition of the paper had arrived so far north. The man eventually shuffled to the sports section where Tretiak noticed the brief, menacing headline.

Hallahan in Tailspin

Jerry slid his head sideways for a closer look. He saw a quote from Frankie Frisch.

"I've tried everything," Frisch told the newspaper writer. "I've rested him. I've worked him oftener than his regular schedule. When a pitcher gets in a rut, he has to pitch himself out of it. A manager can't help him."

In the next instant, Jerry felt a friendly slap on the back. It was Dave Alexander, a Giants scout.

"What you know, Jerr?" Alexander leaned in to say without sitting down, as the smoke from the nearby sizzling skillets wafted through them.

"Not much. Just making my way back home. But it would be nice to find a pitcher, as always. What are you doing in these parts?"

"Need a fourth outfielder, and we're looking everywhere. Peel's just not cutting it anymore. Terry had to yank him out of the middle of a game last week in St. Louis. It might be his last. He's down to .195 and just not doing us any good. Wasn't he one of yours?"

Jerry shook his head in the middle of another swig of coffee.

"I didn't sign him, but yeah, he's was a Cardinal guy. From Texas, I think."

Alexander continued in his perfunctory tone. "Well, anyway, you know how it is. Out with the old, in with the new. We'll find someone. Maybe Leiber. He's had a helluva spring at Nashville."

"Yeah, I guess that's what we do. Dig up someone else," Jerry affirmed.

The conversation then turned to the Deans, as it always did in baseball talk these days.

"Are they back?" Alexander asked, without even having to say their names.

"Yeah, the strike didn't last long. Dizzy stormed into Breadon's office and threatened not to pitch anymore until he and Paul got more money. But I knew they'd come back. Diz just likes to make a story of himself. Hallahan just isn't what he was, and Carleton's ERA is now up near five. He was horseshit again today. And Dean thinks—"

Tretiak stopped himself, realizing he had said too much. Despite maintaining a friendly fraternity, scouts were nonetheless careful to play their cards close to the vest.

The two men exchanged a small smile of understanding, and the conversation fell silent.

Alexander slid away and took his own seat in a booth as Jerry gobbled up the rest of his meal, eating as if he had not had anything in days. He paid the bill, ordered a refill of strong black coffee for his thermos, and hollered a goodbye to Alexander. Any scout with experienced efficiency was ready to be on the road again in no time. Alexander nodded without looking up from the menu.

As a younger scout a decade ago, Jerry had mastered the vicissitudes of his profession—such as getting by on minimal sleep and food. He took pride in knowing that he could be anywhere Mr. Rickey wanted him at any time, as long as his car or a train could get him there. But now, in his eleventh year on the job for the Cardinals, he noticed that the physical strain was taking its toll. Ulcerous pains ripped at his midsection, as the unrelenting discomfort was compounded with a slow, monotonous throbbing in his head that never seemed to cease.

Adding to Tretiak's physical malaise was the Dust Bowl itself and its intense heat. The merciless weather had added to his exhaustion, while also necessitating that a closer eye be kept on the condition of his beaten-up car as it gagged along in a struggling state like its owner. The temperatures had been particularly brutal in the past week, the spearhead of what would be a devastating furnace-like summer. Jerry had been at the Cardinals game in St. Louis the previous Sunday on June 24, when the thermometer at Sportsman's Park had read 99 degrees as the first pitch was thrown by Tex Carleton at three o'clock. One hour later in the fourth inning, it reached triple digits, one of thirty days that year when St. Louis would be 100 degrees or hotter. "On the field, umpires Bill Klem, George Barr, and Bill Stewart had removed their coats and, supposedly for the first time ever in the majors, called a game in their shirtsleeves," one witness in the press box observed about the playing surface that day. Dean, always the entertainer, drew laughs from some of the 15,000 scorched fans as he gathered debris on the field and started a small blaze in front of the Cardinals dugout. "He fanned his little fire," wrote Powers in the *Daily News*, "rubbing his knuckles, encouraging and soberly inspecting it from every angle to make sure the little wigwam of sticks drew a good draft." After it had burned out, Diz began did a rain dance; in mere moments, it produced imaginary drops of water, in which he lavishly bathed himself to the further amusement of the fans.

Laughing was perhaps all one could do at the weather, which was as bad as anyone could remember. "The current heat wave is steaming at its peak and sizzling at 115 degrees," reported John Drebinger for his readers back east in the *New York Times* as he brushed away drops of sweat before they fell upon his typewriter.

"Bill Terry declared he never played ball in hotter weather, and Bill is a veteran of the Southern and Texas Leagues," added his colleague Meany about the Giants player-manager. "Terry has been coming to St. Louis for a dozen seasons, and he never found it this hot before."

Tretiak had bolted out of the ballpark early that day to ensure he would not be stalled in traffic, hoping to keep cooler air circulating through the car. Thus, he was not on hand to see the Cardinals relinquish an early 5–3 lead and drop a 9–7 decision to Terry's Giants, the loss pinned on pitcher Jim Lindsey after he and Carleton permitted a six-run fifth inning by New York. Hallahan, the former fellow Texas League star of Lindsey's and a fading hero from the 1931 World Series three years prior, was called upon later in the game and permitted a run in less than an inning of work.

The lackluster performance by the other Cardinal pitchers prompted Stockton to sum up the value of the Deans after the game in his *Post-Dispatch* column. "Followers of the Cardinals are wondering how long Dizzy and his brother Paul can keep the team in the pennant race. . . . Frisch's team has battled valiantly under the handicap of having only two consistently good pitchers. Dizzy and Paul have worked in turn and out of turn. . . . If the Cardinals are going to win, Carleton and Hallahan will have to bear some of the burden." By this juncture, the Dean brothers had won a combined twenty games for the season and had lost only four; meanwhile, the remainder of the St. Louis pitching staff, having received a vote of no confidence from Frisch, Cardinal followers, and the front office, had a record of 17-21. "My gang should be pitching hay instead of baseballs. At least they'd be earning their pay," the disgruntled manager muttered the following day to the writers. "We're not going any place unless Carleton and Hallahan win some games, and they might as well start now."

In desperation, Branch Rickey phoned the Reds executives in Cincinnati the next day and purchased veteran hurler Charles "Dazzy" Vance for immediate hire. At the time of the transaction, the forty-three-year-old Vance had a horrific 7.50 earned run average. But Rickey was willing to take a chance on the former star, who once had led the National League in strikeouts seven years running from 1922 to 1928. Privately, Rickey and Breadon shared their dismay with the exigency that was developing on the pitching mound.

"The Deans are all the St. Louis fans talk about," noticed the writer Schumacher. "When anybody else starts on the mound, the fans chant in unison, 'We want Dean.'"

Dizzy could not agree more. "This country may have needed a good five-cent cigar," he said, quoting former United States Vice President Thomas Marshall. "But what the Cardinals need is more Deans."

The high temperatures traveled with the Cardinals as they left town during the final week of June, returning with Vance to Cincinnati to play the Reds. As the train chugged out of Union Station and headed east, the team gazed out upon the withering Southern Illinois farmland. Acre after acre of formerly rich soil now resembled abandoned city lots, with dying cornstalks floundering in the wind. The oppressive sun lurked over the team's locomotive and descended upon the banks of the Ohio River, ominously hovering over Crosley Field like an alien spacecraft ready to emit death rays.

Among the sun's latest victims was major league umpire Beans Reardon. While working home plate of the Cardinals-Reds game on June 29, Reardon would have to resign his position in the fourth inning as he wilted from heat exhaustion.

Leaving the diner in Lockport on the night of June 30, Tretiak heard the bell to start the final round of his drowsy fight, hoping to make it another 200 miles down Route 66 to Litchfield. There, he could finally surrender and sleep for a few hours, refill his coffee in the morning at the Ariston, and then finish the last sixty miles to St. Louis before reporting to Rickey's assistant. Rickey typically demanded that Tretiak update him in person as soon as he arrived back in town, but Jerry knew the general manager would not be in the office on a Sunday, as Rickey had promised his mother long ago that he would never conduct any baseball business on the Sabbath. Rickey would expect Jerry to file his report with a staffer who would be watching the office on Sunday, but at least the scout would not have to run into the big man himself.

Jerry accelerated faster through Coal City and Wilmington, finally hitting a comfortable cruising speed in reaching the open, rural countryside. The stars in the sky were starting to appear, and businesses along 66 became less frequent as he left the brightness of the urban Chicago vicinity behind, plunging into the darkness of the desolate stretches of Central Illinois. His arrival in St. Louis early the next morning to report to the front office was thus paramount—even on a Sunday, and even if not to Rickey himself. There was a cloak-and-dagger process in sneaking a prospect past the other organizations, and new devices and methods for doing so were appearing all the time. The past summer, Jerry and some other scouts had tried using the new *Baseball Telegraphic Code Book*, a secret language through which scouts could cable their reports back to their superiors without other teams intercepting the message, as such thievery had been commonplace since scouts had started using the telegraph to report on players a few years earlier.

But beyond his automobile and thermos, Jerry did not trust most modern technology. A veteran at his craft, he relied upon his instincts to get the job done. In his head, he began organizing his report for Rickey while speeding down 66; he would then put it to paper first thing in the morning, as was his routine on the last leg of each scouting trip he made.

While constructing of the myriad of details in his mind, he dozed off—and was jolted to consciousness when veering toward a steep ditch. He awakened and quickly jerked the car back onto the pavement, the vehicle wobbling to recover from the sudden swerve. If he had strayed only a few feet farther off the road, he would have rolled the car over.

It was the second time that day Jerry had nearly run the car into a ditch, although the first event was not of his own doing. Earlier that afternoon in heading west out of South Bend, Indiana, he narrowly escaped collision with a passing convoy of eleven police cars on US Route 20, flying by Jerry so rapidly that he barely had enough time to elude them. The squadron of cops had been scrambled in search of the men who had robbed nearly $29,000 from the Merchants National Bank at 11:30 that morning and who also had murdered South Bend officer Howard Wagner in the process. The getaway car for which the police were searching was finally recovered later that day, long after Jerry had reached southern Wisconsin. It had been abandoned over a hundred miles to the southwest of

South Bend in Goodland, Indiana, riddled with bullet holes and stained with blood. Goodland was near the home area of one of the passengers of the car, John Dillinger, while the blood in the car belonged to Homer Van Meter, one of Dillinger's associates who had survived a bullet in the head from return fire after Van Meter had killed Wagoner. Dillinger, meanwhile, decided to lay low for a while with friends near Indianapolis while waiting for the chaos to settle.

The South Bend robbery would be the final heist on Dillinger's lengthy rap sheet. A week earlier, the US Attorney General's Office had offered a $10,000 reward for his capture. Another $5,000 was offered for the apprehension of his accomplice, Lester M. Gillis, who also went by the name of George "Baby Face" Nelson.

The few flickering lights of the approaching small town of Odell had revived Jerry. It was now 9:20 p.m. Although he did not want to stop, he knew that a five-minute break would pay off down the road—and perhaps save his life, he told himself.

Jerry's mental map told him there was a Standard gas station and general store off the highway in Odell. Just like his collection of preferred diners, it was one of his favorite stopping places to fuel up. The station had a single pump and a small garage for repairs, with a lovely adjacent park across the road, where Jerry liked to sit and relax for a few moments when he had time.

The attendant was topping off Jerry's tank when the proprietor, Patrick O'Donnell, came out of the store and greeted the scout.

"You hear about Clancy?"

"Yep, just today," Jerry responded, his eyes gazing off into the darkness.

"Hope it works out for him somewhere else," O'Donnell returned.

Passing through one small town after another in the Midwest, Jerry usually tried to recall if a big leaguer had come from a particular community. Odell indeed had its own. It was Bud Clancy, a first baseman with the Chicago White Sox for seven years who, for the past few seasons, was trying to hang on with other teams and had been released by the Philadelphia Phillies just the past Thursday. Clancy had singled off Paul Dean in a pinch-hitting appearance two weeks earlier for the Phillies in St. Louis, in what would be the one of the final hits of his career.

Odell was eternally proud of him; for the past decade, Clancy's success helped further Odell's identity and "put it on the map," and they were grateful to him for it. When strangers would pull into O'Donnell's station, he would usually greet them with, "Bud Clancy's from here, you know."

Jerry paid the bill, told O'Donnell to keep the change, and got in the car quickly to drive off.

His next objective was Litchfield. The Ariston was his aiming point, situated squarely at the intersection of 66 and Illinois Route 16 and next door to the only available hotel in Litchfield, the Schwab Inn.

The place was run by a middle-aged couple named Gary and Linda Schwab, and although Jerry would be arriving late, he was not concerned about getting a room. Hotels across the country were half as occupied as they had been in 1928, as economic troubles from the Depression had severely cut leisure travel for Americans. Tretiak invariably stopped in to see the Schwabs whenever returning from a scouting trip to the north. And like his other favorite places, he looked forward to the warm greeting he would receive.

Like in Odell, the approaching glow of Litchfield revived Jerry once again. As he drew closer to the junction with Route 16, he could see the parking lot lights of the Ariston.

But he also noticed the light was unusually east of the restaurant, in the direction toward town. The typically illuminated outline of the community's buildings on the edge of Litchfield was, for some reason, more difficult to discern than usual.

Figuring it was simply a product of fatigue, Jerry gradually slowed his car after turning left at the Ariston. Yet, as he quietly rolled closer to the hotel, he knew something was wrong. All the lights were off at the Schwab Inn, something he fearfully suspected after turning off 66.

There were no cars in the parking lot. As he inched closer to the entrance, the only sign of life was a note affixed to the front door of the office, which was legible only by Jerry nudging the vehicle up against the front walk and shining his lights upon it.

Must close; cannot operate under current conditions.
Not sure what to do next.
Please send all correspondence for us to the
Whitaker residence on south State Street.
Thanks to all and God bless.
—*Linda and Gary*

Retreating toward his car in disbelief, the stillness of the night covered Jerry with as lonely a feeling as he ever experienced. Until now, he had not personally known anyone close to him who had been forced to surrender his livelihood to the Depression. But this touched him. Like most everyone in the Cardinals organization, Jerry had had to endure salary cuts in recent years because of the conditions; he was now even paying for some of his own meals and lodging while on the road. But at least he still had his income. The Schwabs no longer had theirs.

Submerged back into the paralyzing darkness, Jerry sank into his vehicle and took off.

Forgetting his crucial morning deadline with Rickey, he did not turn back onto Route 66 to continue toward St. Louis.

Instead, he chose to drift in the opposite direction into the downtown portion of Litchfield, hoping to get some glimpse of the Schwabs, even at this late hour. He did not know who the Whitakers were, but he nonetheless drove up and down State Street several times, looking for the Schwab's vehicle. There was no sign of them.

On the last pass, he just kept driving.

The momentary venture out into the fresh air at the abandoned motel briefly reinvigorated him. But soon, Jerry started weaving once again, aimlessly rolling southbound out of Litchfield in a sleepy daze. He turned onto an unnamed backroad of Montgomery County, then another, driving with a blank stare for nearly another hour. How would the Schwabs survive now?

He unknowingly passed south into Bond County and drove straight through a stop sign at an intersection with US Route 40, narrowly missing a crossing car. The scream of the near miss snapped him fully awake once more, the third time he had avoided a major calamity while driving that day.

That is enough for today.

Several more miles down, he saw another sizable group of lights, evidence of another town along the lines of an Odell or a Litchfield.

Whatever that place is, I'll sleep there for the night.

If there were no rooms, he would park somewhere and sleep in the car. *Enough is enough.*

As he entered the town in the dead of night, Jerry could not make out its name on the large sign that greeted visitors. He could only read the subtitle in larger printing below the name, which claimed that the place was "Famous for Friendliness."

Noticing the silhouette of a baseball field backstop on his right, a few blocks later he finally hit US Route 50. Seeing Route 50 made him laugh out loud, as it informed him just how far he had drifted south from Litchfield.

At least he was in Illinois and on Route 50, he figured, coordinates he knew would give him a straight shot back to St. Louis, regardless of his east-west location. He turned west, needing to head in that direction, anyway. Like most scouts, Jerry drove his car more from memory than maps.

A few blocks down on 50, a bright electric neon sign beckoned him.

Knotty Pine Inn and Motel

Beneath the electrified portion, a manual billboard added a hearty welcome.

Brand New – Come on In

CHAPTER NINE

Jerry circled around and stopped under the sign, the front of his car facing the edge of the dark, deserted highway. Getting out of his car, the unknown town was as quiet as any in which he had ever stopped. He looked over to see that the guest rooms were detached from the main building, which housed the restaurant. Jerry was grateful to discover a light was still on in the office.

Jerry walked in and gave a gentle tap to the bell at the front desk. The hotel and restaurant manager, having heard him pull into the lot, appeared before the bell even stopped reverberating.

"Thought we weren't having anyone tonight," the man said with a warm smile. "I'm Frank Colston, and this is my place."

"Glad you're here," Jerry responded. "I take it you've got a spot for me?"

"Oh yeah—any room you want—but they're all pretty much the same. How about Number 1?"

"Sure. Is there any place I could send a cable at this time of night?"

"No, but we can take care of that right here for you in the morning," Colston said while scribbling a few notes. He handed Jerry a rectangular piece of orange plastic, decorated only with a large numeral one connected to a key.

Colston wagged his thumb over his shoulder a couple times. "If you need anything, I'll be over at my place on the corner of Plum and Sixth."

While signing his name on the register, Jerry looked up, confused.

"You mean, no office people stay here overnight?"

Colston chuckled. "No, but don't worry. We never have any problems. In fact, we've been open almost a year now, and no guest has ever needed to come get me, not for a towel or matchbook or anything. But if you do, feel free to."

The men departed the way they had entered, Colston out the back door and Jerry out the front. As Jerry dragged his belongings across the parking lot, the Southern Illinois heat continued to beat on him, even in the complete absence of the sun at one o'clock in the morning. He popped open the door to Room 1, which, like his car on the other side of the lot, sat right along Route 50, only steps from the highway's asphalt.

Immediately dropping his items inside the doorway, Jerry sprawled out on the bed and, in sheer exhaustion, absorbed its softness while not bothering to close the curtain.

A few minutes after laying down, he noticed across the parking lot that the single light from the office had gone dark. Next, he saw Colston leaving the building and vanishing up the street. Jerry was now the lone person on the premises of the Knotty Pine Inn and Motel.

Jerry struggled out of the bed to close the curtain and then collapsed upon the mattress once again, wrapping himself in the blanket without even disturbing the sheets. He slept as soundly as he had in the past three months.

A peaceful, cloudless sky greeted Jerry when he awoke later that Sunday morning, July 1. He took a long bath and put on some fresh clothes. Stepping out the door of his room, the omnipresent heat now did not bother him; instead, Jerry imbibed a strange, soothing calm that overtook his being.

On his way across the parking lot to the restaurant, he stopped and grabbed a newspaper. He read about the *Nacht der langen Messer*, or Night of the Long Knives, which had occurred overnight in Germany. "Ruthless to all opposition," began the Associated Press article, "Adolf Hitler today crushed a revolt that threatened the Third Reich, in a day of summary punishment for those who challenged his authority." Another part of the paper reported on the continued mass starvation occurring in the Soviet Union from the collectivization farming policy established by Josef Stalin at the beginning of the decade. Flipping to page two, Jerry also got an explanation of what had caused his driving calamity near South Bend.

Inside the restaurant, he found Colston again, but this time, instead of carrying a guest registry, he was wearing an apron that was splattered with grease. He was in the process of pouring coffee for two people who had just come in off the street for breakfast. Colston, along with a young, industrious helper named Diane Poettker—who had eyes on buying the place from Colston—did it all at the Knotty Pine, which included the cooking of all meals.

"Good morning, Mr. Tretiak," Colston greeted him promptly. "Care for some coffee?" he then asked, raising the coffeepot he was holding.

"You bet," Jerry responded. "And how about that cable?"

"Already on it," Colston assured. He set the pot down and wiped his hands while hurrying to the desk. "I'm all set to send it. You just tell me what to say."

Setting his thermos down on an empty table, Jerry began his dictation.

"To: Jeffrey Ney
St. Louis National League Baseball Club
North Grand Boulevard
St. Louis, Missouri

Colston took interest in the significant address. He looked up for a moment as Jerry continued.

Will not report until Sunday afternoon.
Thoroughly tired. Accommodations unexpectedly closed.
Tretiak. STOP"

"You a baseball man?" Colston asked.

"Yessss," Jerry sighed after a brief hesitation, even rolling his eyes a bit while still facing away from Colston.

Jerry quickly grew tired of out-of-the-way men who were always asking him about scouting and, then, what invariably followed—trying to steer him toward that town's newest, greatest player in whichever Podunk place Jerry happened to be. But Colston had been very kind to him, and the availability of his inn during Jerry's time of need was indeed serendipitous. So, he indulged him.

"Yeah, I work for the Cardinals," Jerry said a bit more engagingly. "I'm an amateur scout."

Colston was confused. "How can you work in pro baseball if you're an amateur?"

"No," Jerry responded a bit tersely, already tiring of the response he had given people a thousand times but trying not to show it. "That means *I scout amateur players* for the team."

"Oh, I got it," Colston responded. "That must mean you're here for the All-Star Game."

"All-Star Game?" Jerry asked with a spark of sarcasm that he did not intend. He once again tried to hide his disdain for what he knew would follow in the sequence of such conversations—the inevitable reference to the local men's league.

"The CCL All-Star Game," Colston responded with a hint of surprise in his own voice.

"What is the CCL?"

"The Clinton County League. There are games every Sunday. I used to play in the league myself. I was a catcher. I played in the minors until I bought this place.

"Today is the All-Star Game. The All-Stars usually play a team from St. Louis. But with the money troubles this year, no team would come out here. So, the league is playing its own All-Star Game this season, with the towns divided in half."

Jerry had a revelation. "So, *that's* where I am!" he whispered to himself.

Bypassing Clinton County on many trips north during his years with the Cardinals, Jerry had never actually stopped there. He believed, like a growing number of scouts, that better players were now coming from the larger cities and not the countryside, as had been the case in the past. Therefore, he usually dismissed the never-ending tales of alleged star players thrust upon him by people just like Colston and in places just like this.

"Okay, Clinton County. So, which *town* is this?" Jerry asked, feigning interest as a matter of courtesy. "I didn't catch what you said last night."

"Breese."

"*Breese.* I see. And is Breese hosting this *All-Star Game* today?"

"Sure is," Colston replied, now with a little disdain of his own. "There's also the annual church picnic afterwards in the next town over, just four miles away if you'd be nice enough to stay."

Jerry, having enough of the conversation, did not respond. He helped himself to the coffeepot sitting between the hotel desk and the entrance to the restaurant. He filled up his thermos, threw a ten-dollar bill on the counter to pay for his room and meal, gave a quick nod, and walked out the door as Colston watched him.

Though it was only 9:30 a.m., the sun was already melting the parking lot as Jerry strolled back across to Room No. 1. Relaxed from his long sleep and presuming the cable had bought him time with Rickey, he was in no hurry to do much of anything, basking in a lazy Sunday. He would file his report with the staffer at the Cardinals offices later that night.

Jerry stopped short of his room door. Instead of going inside, he decided to take a few steps out to the shoulder of US 50. He gazed east and then west. At first glance to him, there seemed to be nothing unique about this place; it resembled the many other Midwestern small towns he had visited over the years. The same businesses dotted the main drag as they did elsewhere, and the very same poverty-beaten, worrisome countenances painted the faces of the people.

Yet there *was* something about Breese, now illuminated in the daylight, that intrigued him. Maybe it reminded him of Litchfield and the Schwabs—hard-working, kind people who were just trying to make it. People like Colston, whose subsistence during the Great Depression teetered on the fickle finger of fate. *Real* people.

Jerry *wanted* to see a baseball game in this place. It was away from the world of deadlines, reports, Rickey, trying to outflank Alexander and the Giants . . . all of it. He decided to stay for the Clinton County League All-Star Game, which would begin at one o'clock.

When he emerged again from his room an hour later, Jerry noticed more activity on the sidewalk along Route 50, despite it being a Sunday and the increasing heat. The first individual he approached was able to direct him to the baseball field. It was the same field he had passed in the darkness the night before, just a few blocks to the north of the Knotty Pine.

Jerry made the walk to the ball field slowly and with a spontaneous joy, his hands in his pockets while humming his favorite tune "The Wabash Cannonball" all the way. Having already packed the car, he brought nothing with him. No scouting notes, no pencils, and not even his thermos of coffee.

By the time he reached the field, there was over an hour to go before the first pitch. Though the park was modest, he was impressed to find that it had a covered seating area that had obviously been overseen with care. With the lower half of the grandstand already filled, he climbed to the top of the stairs and took a chair in the very last row on the aisle. While most scouts preferred sitting directly behind home plate, Jerry typically avoided this tendency. He was always careful not to convey any characteristic that implied he was a scout; rather, he preferred to remain as inconspicuous as possible. Jerry also typically took very few notes on players while at any game, instead choosing to write them up from memory upon returning to his car.

With nothing on his person, Jerry, while getting an occasional stare for being an obvious outsider, looked to be an ordinary fellow, just as he desired.

One thing he did require at *every* game, however, was a roster of the players. He was disappointed to learn that, despite the special occasion, there was none for this game. When he asked someone sitting nearby how he might obtain one, he was given a look of bewilderment in return. Among all the early arrivals to the grandstand, Jerry was the only one who did not know who all the players were—let alone *any* of them, as more inquisitive looks were now thrown up in his direction.

As the players began filtering into the bench areas along each baseline, they were the most unkempt lot Jerry had ever laid his eyes on. Dirt was caked on nearly every uniform, and most had holes in the pants or jerseys. While the Cardinals themselves were known for keeping their uniforms dirty to respect a winning streak, these players appeared just plain slovenly. Their appearance gave Jerry the courage to ask a different person sitting nearby another question.

"Why are their uniforms so filthy?" Jerry said with a wry smile, now relishing his role as an anonymous outsider. "I heard they only play once a week."

"Yeah," someone responded while turning halfway to face him. "But any extra wash water gets saved for the mine clothes, and that don't even get done 'nough. If they're lucky, they might get to clean their baseball uniforms two or three times all summer."

The crowd swelled quickly. Twenty minutes after Jerry had sat down, every seat in the grandstand was taken. Later arrivals began to gradually assemble along the foul lines in the outfield, jostling each other aside as if seeking the best vantage point for a parade.

Suddenly, a sweet-smelling smoke drifted over the field from behind the grandstand, enveloping the premises in the aroma of sausages and peppers cooking. As game time approached, bottles of three-two beer were clutched in thirsty hands everywhere; for even with the repeal of the Eighteenth Amendment, the lower-alcohol variety was still popular because of its more favorable price.

At four minutes before one o'clock, Jerry and the other spectators looked on as the teams walked out to the first and third base lines. On the first base side, selected players from the towns of Trenton, Aviston, Carlyle, Beckemeyer, and Breese comprised the home team, or the "North." Across from them were those chosen from New Baden, Albers, Germantown, Bartelso, and Hoffman, the visitors from the "South." The South had the youngest All-Star in 14-year-old Julius Schoendienst from Germantown, who had his little brothers in attendance cheering him on. The local buzz was that one of them—11-year-old Albert—might wind up being the best of the bunch someday.

As he did at the start of every game he scouted, Jerry carefully scanned everyone from both groups. Though not working this day, he did so merely out of habit, looking for someone who might physically stand out from the others. Except for a couple of men with above-average height, none did. Rather, most of them appeared exceptionally gaunt and even malnourished, their flannel jerseys dangling off their thin bodies like drapes.

One by one, the players were "introduced" to the crowd. Each man, already known to the entire crowd, took his turn to step forward and tip his cap.

When the bells from the Breese church struck at one, a man stood up in the front row of the grandstand and addressed the crowd in all directions. In lieu of the singing of the national anthem (with no lead singer available), he requested in a bellowing voice that everyone pause for a moment of prayer, asking God for the redemption of the economy, the mines, and the farmland.

After a moment, the man thanked those in attendance as the spectators took their seats once again while the players replaced the caps onto their heads and returned to their benches.

The temperature in Breese was now 96 degrees. There was nothing to assuage the burning wrath of the defiant sun, sitting high on its powerful throne in the July sky as it watched events unfold below. During infield practice, every scrape of a cleat and every bounce of a ball emitted bursts of wafting dirt. There was no watering system to properly care for the bone-dry field, and certainly no recent water from above.

But in their own defiance of the heat, the spectators rose to their feet once again, cheering wildly as the Breese players and their North teammates took the field. On any other Sunday during the summer, the four other teams comprising the North roster were adversaries of the Breese Merchants; but today they were allies against the other five towns.

Jerry watched as the last of the nine players came out. The final one to emerge was the pitcher, as the others dispersed rapidly to their positions.

The pitcher was one of the taller players whom Jerry had noticed earlier, a tired, lurching figure who walked to the mound at a most minimal pace. He, like most of the others, appeared to be emaciated, with a man's body that looked almost too weak to play a boy's game.

Even so, his slow stride also connoted a semblance of purpose. It suggested that, despite his fatigue, he knew he still had a duty to fulfill.

Jerry recognized him from somewhere.

The pitcher picked the baseball up off the mound. He took a few more steps toward second base, staring out toward center field. He shrugged his shoulders a couple of times, took one deep breath, turned on the hill, and faced the grandstand, now ready to begin his warm-up tosses.

The countenance was slightly older, worn, and sullener, but it was *him*, Jerry strained to remember . . . *someone . . . who?*

Jerry began pawing through his endless cabinet of mental notes. Rubbing his brow, he squinted down at the concrete of the grandstand near his feet and then up again at the player . . . *he was someone . . . from where . . . when?*

A few seconds later, and just before the man's first pitch of the game, he heard someone in front of him mumble the name.

"Laufketter."

Instantly, Jerry recalled the day at Forest Park in St. Louis five years ago, when he had seen this young man throw only four pitches—but they were four pitches he had never forgotten.

With the first live pitch came the grunt from the field. It jolted Jerry's recollection of how this player—*John*, he now remembered—had audibly released more power with each of his pitches.

In John Laufketter's case, the groan was from the pain of his long-ailing shoulder.

Coming into the 1934 Clinton County League All-Star Game, John had uncharacteristically already lost two contests during the season, including a 1–0 pitcher's duel to Bartelso on opening day in which the game's lone tally was a long home run to center field. But in watching John intently, Jerry was convinced that he was throwing just as hard today, if not harder, than when John was a freshman in college five years ago.

The first batter for the South team, a speedy center fielder from Albers named Peter Von Hatten, stepped to the plate and tapped an easy grounder back to John for the first out. Three pitches later, the second batter was retired on a routine bouncer as well, this time to shortstop.

Despite being the best which the League had to offer, Jerry noticed that the hitters from the South squad seemed to have a reverent fear of John when they approached the plate. As each batter settled into his stance, he had an expression of imminent defeat, a look of futility in knowing that this pitcher was always one step ahead.

With two out, Bartelso third baseman Jason Rakers—perhaps the league's toughest hitter, and who had homered off John to beat him on opening day—now stepped in, batting third in the order. Rakers was the only former professional player in the CCL, and the only other player besides John whom Jerry had recognized on sight. After a successful collegiate career at Quincy University, Rakers had gone on to play in the Three-I League with farm clubs scattered across Illinois, Indiana, and Iowa.

John got ahead in the count with two quick strikes at 0-2 but then threw a pitch that caught a good portion of Rakers's wheelhouse. The batter jumped on it and drove a sharp double to the gap in right center field.

John was incensed at himself for the mistake and proceeded to fire two pickoff throws toward Rakers at second just to release his anger, the second of which seemed to be directed at Rakers himself instead of the glove of the North's second baseman.

The fourth batter for the South, also from Bartelso, promptly struck out on three pitches, all unhittable curveballs thrown for strikes. When issuing his curve, John released a grunt that had a slightly different sound from his fastball grunt, but even with the momentary advance warning, opponents still could not seem to touch it. The final strike came without a swing, as the top of the first inning ended.

During the break, Jerry did something he never did at any game. He started engaging some of the spectators seated in front of him in a conversation.

"I'm just passing through," he offered, continuing to fake ignorance while fishing for information. "Is this Laufketter guy any good?"

Several immediately whirled around, each ready to volunteer the same answer. "The best I've ever seen around here," asserted the first one to speak up, after laughing briefly at what was considered a silly question. "In fact, you could say he's the Dean of Clinton County."

Jerry stared at John, who was now seated on the home bench. The scout could not believe the weathered figure was not yet 23 years old, completely worn down from the hardness of the world.

In the next hour, John retired twelve of the first fourteen men he faced, eight of them on strikeouts. The home plate umpire, called "Caveman" by the players but whose real name was unknown, flung up his right arm all day long, proclaiming strike after strike.

The game remained close until the bottom of the fifth when Wagoner, the Beckemeyer power source, came to the plate. Booed during his first at bat, Wagoner was the only player from either team who had also been derided during the pregame introductions. But the derision quickly turned to cheers as he slammed a long home run to the trees beyond left field, a three-run shot that gave the North a 4-0 lead, seemingly an insurmountable advantage with John on the hill.

While the pitchers for the South team quickly grew tired in the extreme heat and had to often be replaced, there appeared to be no limit to the personal arsenal from which John could draw as he continued to mow down the opponent in regularity. In recent weeks during league play, he had begun dropping his arm down to a three-quarters delivery in his pitching motion around the seventh inning of games, deviating from his normal overhand action to relieve pressure on his aching shoulder. By the eighth inning John would drop down even farther, throwing almost completely side-armed with his elbow never rising above his chest at any point. With the gradual change of his arm slot over the course of a game, the movement on John's pitches was now of a completely different unhittable variety in later innings from the over-the-top ones with which he had started.

But remarkably, even with variations in his follow-through, John still maintained his pinpoint control, walking no batters on the afternoon. This did not escape Jerry's attention. In the sixth inning, he moved down to a seat closer to home plate.

Initially, Jerry's scouting habits prompted him to consider leaving the game around the third inning as he normally did, but other instincts suggested he had better stay put. He was watching something special, giving witness to a man who seemed to have nothing left to lose. This man was pitching this game as if it would be his last.

The 4-0 North lead held up into the ninth, when John had to face the second, third, and fourth spots in the South lineup to finish the job. He retired the leadoff man on five pitches, the last a "cut" fastball that ran in on the left-handed hitter's fists. It was so devastating that it buzz-sawed the bat handle in two, sending shards of it spraying across the infield as the second baseman from Trenton dodged the last of it and caught the easy pop-up.

Jerry laughed to himself and got up out of his seat to walk back to his car, now having seen enough. Leaving the worn grass of the concession stand area and entering the gravel parking lot, he heard silence for next few moments. Suddenly there was another momentary roar from the crowd. The great Rakers was retired for the third time in a row, this time on a long fly ball to center field, making him one for four on the day.

As Jerry reached for the door handle of his vehicle, he heard one more grunt coming through the silence . . . one more pop of the catcher's mitt . . . and one more holler of a "strike" call from the umpire. A longer eruption then came from the crowd, signifying the end of the game.

Jerry stopped before opening the car door. He whispered to himself as he kicked some gravel underneath the car, torn in thought.

What would Rickey say? . . . His arm is probably shot, anyway.

He smiled and jumped in.

Too bad.

Turning westbound on US 50, he slowed for a moment in front of the Knotty Pine before launching his final forty miles to St. Louis. Like a thousand other days in his line of work, it has been an interesting but fruitless afternoon of baseball for Jerry, another day of finding no one useful.

Twenty minutes later, John was able to catch a lift back to Beckemeyer on the flatbed truck of an Eagles fan. Once inside his home, he greeted Rose with a kiss.

"How'd you do, Big Guy?" she asked about the team's success on the day, as she always did first.

"Four–zip," he said.

"How did *you* do?" she then asked, as she always did for her second question. John always had good news in that portion.

He washed up as best he could, changed his clothes, and, with Joseph on his shoulders, walked with his sweetie over to the St. Anthony's picnic. There, they built up their plates with the wonderful food. At least for one day, there was plenty to eat for all in town.

Later spreading a small blanket in the corner of the churchyard, they got ready for the fireworks. It was John's most favorite few hours of the year, just as it had been for his father.

Tomorrow, a Monday, would soon come. It was a scheduled workday for him in the mine, and more of the grinding labor to which he did not look forward. But it was labor for which he was grateful, and which he was honored to have.

CHAPTER TEN

As John was finishing off the ninth inning at the CCL All-Star Game in Breese on July 1, Dizzy Dean was working in his eleventh inning in Cincinnati despite 100-degree temperatures that continued to engulf the Ohio River valley, reddening faces as "the countenances of the athletes glistened under the violent rays of Old Sol," according to Jack Ryder, covering the scene for the *Cincinnati Enquirer*.

The Cardinals had tied the game in the ninth, and it looked as if neither team would be able to plate another run the rest of the day. The struggle reached the seventeenth inning, when a homer by Medwick put the Cardinals ahead temporarily. The Reds answered in the bottom half with a run of their own, as Cincinnati pitcher Tony Freitas—who just six weeks earlier was a Cardinal minor leaguer—matched Diz, inning for inning, with neither starter willing to give way. The decision by Frisch to let Diz go indefinitely was an easy one, for he had virtually no options. A second game for the day's doubleheader still followed, and Tex Carleton, Jim Mooney, and Paul Dean were unavailable, having been roughed up by the Reds for an 11–4 beating the prior afternoon.

But the manager nonetheless rolled the dice in the top of the eighteenth, as Diz was finally lifted for pinch hitter Pat Crawford, who reached base with a single and came around to score the eventual winning run. In the bottom half, Dean was replaced on the mound by the struggling Lindsey. Lindsey was in his second stint with the team, having been traded by the Reds for Freitas himself back in May.

With Lindsey serving up hittable pitches, it would be Medwick who would have to save the day on defense. Jim Bottomley jumped on a fastball and slammed one that seemed destined for York Street beyond left field. But Ducky turned 180 degrees, sprinted north, and made a superb, running one-handed catch along Crosley Field's famous incline at the wall, as the Reds had stranded their twentieth and twenty-first runners on base for the game. "Medwick cut back toward the scoreboard like a startled hare," described Ryder, "leaped high, and came down with the ball tightly encased in his glove."

As for Lindsey, Branch Rickey had now seen enough. It would be the final week with the team for the former Texas League star, as he and his 7.71 ERA were sent packing.

After a brief rest, Frisch's men got ready for the second game of the twin bill. With no one else to whom he could turn, he handed the ball to the venerable Vance, himself a Red just a few days earlier. The salty veteran lasted three frames in what would end as a 2–2 tie after five innings due to darkness. The Cardinals runs came on another homer by the surging Medwick, a first-inning blast that boosted his average up to .355, as baseball's newest big hitter had not dipped below that mark since May 24.

After a brief two-day break around the major league's version of the All-Star Game, the Cardinals went back to work, trying to catch Hubbell and the Giants in the National League standings.

Diz went the distance for the win in Boston against the Braves on July 19, his first triumph ever in that city, as a brawl broke out between the two teams. At various points during the game, Dean had been harassed by a brash rookie pitcher for the Braves named Tony Stoecklin. The left-handed reliever had not permitted a base runner in his first five major league appearances after being recalled from the minors two weeks earlier. Stoecklin was a St. Louis-area native from across the river at East Alton, Illinois, and considered one of the top young pitchers to enter the game— and he wanted Dean to know it.

At first, his cockiness made Dizzy smile, as the sounds of self-assuredness were all too familiar. But by the fifth inning it had grown tiresome. After the Braves' third out, Dean marched not in the direction of the St. Louis dugout but that of Boston's. He addressed everyone in it. "Whoever's the tough guy in here," he blared while scanning the bench, "step on out and let's settle this. This is coming from the horse's mouth."

Stoecklin, arms folded, calmly stayed in his seat. He spit off to the side and looked Diz in the eye. "I say it's from a hillbilly horse's ass," Stoecklin responded.

The other Cardinals on the field, now realizing what was happening, reversed themselves and jogged over the to the Braves bench, on guard for anything that might boil over. Stoecklin then started in on Spud Davis and the girth he possessed underneath his chest protector.

"Hey fatty," he addressed the catcher, "why don't you lift up that jersey, and let that other guy play for a little while?"

Dean then intercepted Davis as the catcher charged at the rookie, but only because he wanted the first crack at him.

"Just come on up," Dizzy said.

Stoecklin obliged. He grabbed one of the bats laid out in front of the dugout, holding it with one arm as he pointed the barrel at Dean's face as a warning. Tossing it aside, Stoecklin then unleashed a strong left fist to Dizzy's face. Dean returned the blow with a weaker one of his own, at which point cooler heads were able to get them separated as the game resumed.

Being on the East Coast at least had provided the Cardinals some semblance of relief from the devastating Midwestern heat, but cooler heads were indeed hard to find. While the team was in Boston, they had been in the middle of a massive twenty-three-game, three-week road trip. A day after the Dean-Stoecklin fight on July 20, Keokuk would set the Iowa record with 114-degree temperatures. St. Louis would have record highs the same week, reaching 110 and beyond. Over the preceding and succeeding weeks, the city would post its hottest June, July, and August since 1871.

But the rough, tumbling Cardinals fought through the heat, with themselves, with opponents, and fought on. By the time Diz had beaten the Giants in his next start on July 23 at the Polo Grounds for his eighteenth win (and tenth straight), St. Louis had bagged eight victories in their last nine games on their odyssey, closing to within two-and-a-half games of New York for first place in the National League. "I had 'em swinging like a ham on a hook," Dizzy would say of Bill Terry's men. "Give ol' Diz a lead of a run or two after five or six innings, and the other fellows might as well fold up."

After watching the St. Louis boys rampage through town in pursuit of their Giants, New York writers such as Jimmy Powers sensed the Deans' success was related to their country roots and that the razzing from Stoecklin and others only served to motivate them. "Does anyone appreciate resentment small-town people hold for residents of big cities?" Powers offered, thinking specifically of the Dean brothers. "When you hand Paul or Jay a baseball and tell them to pitch against the New York Giants their eyes glow fanatically, they snatch the horsehide and stride to the mound, nostrils breathing fire."

The Cardinals' fighting indeed included scraps with themselves as often as with other teams. Many of the flare-ups had been instigated by Carleton, who one day refused to let Medwick take his turn in batting practice as the two exchanged punches. But Carleton's main target for his rage was Dean, as he was fed up with Dizzy's denouncement of the rest of the pitching staff.

But despite the wear and tear on the team which the weather, the road trips, the competition in the National League, and the players themselves caused, Breadon and Rickey refused to go for outside help. The front office continued to show their lack of confidence in any prospects from the minor league system, instead permitting the active roster to fall short of what was allowed by the league. "The Cardinals are trying to compete for the pennant with less manpower than the other teams have," J. Roy Stockton pointed out in his *Post-Dispatch* article on August 3. "The Cubs and Giants have 23 men, but the Cardinals struggle along with 21, and in bitterly contested games that is not enough."

The number was whittled down even further in the following week, from twenty-one to nineteen.

After a doubleheader loss to the Cubs in St. Louis on Sunday, August 12, Dizzy and Paul refused to accompany the team to an exhibition game in Detroit on Monday and were both suspended and fined by Frisch. It was the second time during the summer in which Dizzy refused to pitch and the second time Paul had been an accomplice, willing or not. "I pulled something loose in my right elbow in the fourth inning," Diz tried to explain. "I didn't have my stuff after that." Dizzy then suggested to Martin Haley of the *Globe-Democrat* that he might not be able to throw for several weeks because of the injury. "I'm not going to pitch again until the arm is healed," Dean went on to declare. "Other pitchers don't work if they have sore arms, and I'm not going to, either. If I went out there, I might ruin my career." Paul had expected Dizzy to pick him up for a ride to the train station for the trip to Detroit, but the older brother never showed up.

The second miniature "strike" of the season by the Dean boys only served to bond the rest of the team together, as well as their loyalty to the manager.

"Out of the mess a new team spirit has been born," reported Stockton. "The team morale and allegiance to Manager Frisch reached a new high. 'There are only 19 of us left, including Frank,' the boys in the dugout announced, 'but the 18 of us will fight with everything we have to show Frank we're for him.'"

Diz, meanwhile, remained defiant, using the incident of the missed Detroit exhibition to renew his call for more money for him and Paul. He also pointed to individuals among the remaining eighteen to illustrate the brothers' worth to the ball club. "It might interest the public to know," Dizzy told Bill McCullough of the *Brooklyn Times-Union*, "that we know of one pitcher who gets more than both of us combined who can't hold Paul's glove, let alone mine."

Many in the press supported his sentiment, agreeing that the Dean brothers had no help. "The St. Louis Cardinals are a two-pitcher outfit," wrote Cy Peterman in the *Philadelphia Evening Bulletin*, "needlessly exciting the National League in a phony bid for the flag . . . they are not to be taken seriously for the pennant."

Things came to a head on August 14 when, in a fit of rage, Dizzy destroyed two of his Cardinal uniforms in the locker room after being ordered to take the field by an angered Frisch. After being fined by Breadon for each day he chose to sit out, a contrite Diz returned to the team a week later with Paul in tow once again. Recommitted to their work, the Deans were forgiven by the team as the pennant race reached its final stretch.

On Sunday, September 16, in New York, both brothers pitched before the largest crowd in the history of the National League to date. A total of 62,573 baseball fanatics came out to see a critical doubleheader between the Cardinals and Giants. "The Giants never before had played to more than 55,000 at the Polo Grounds," informed Dan Daniel. "As the Harlem plant has less than 52,000 seats, one may imagine how the 10,500 extras disposed themselves. They jammed the aisles, crowded two in a seat, and clung precariously to rafters. They stood at points from which only home plate was visible.

"At 2:30 [a half hour before the first pitch], the Fire Department ordered all gates locked. At that time more than 15,000 were trying to fight their way into the park . . . a hard shower drenched the park just before game time, but thousands kept crowding through all entrances."

The afternoon became yet another showcase for the siblings. Dizzy won the first game 5–3 and Paul the nightcap 3–1, with the latter having to go eleven innings toe-to-toe with Hubbell to secure the triumph. The Cards had now topped the Giants' great lefty in four of five tries on the year, with the Deans having beaten Terry's club twelve times by themselves.

Next for the St. Louis assault was Brooklyn on September 21, as they faced off against the Dodgers and their first-year manager Casey Stengel in another doubleheader. With the tight pennant race, every game was critical, and despite the compacted games, Frisch continued to trust no one on the mound except the Dean brothers.

The Dodgers had won their last six in a row but still sat in last place with a 65-77 record. They, like their crosstown cousins the Giants, struggled against the Deans, as the Dodgers were a combined 0-7 against the Deans so far in 1934. Dizzy started the opener in Flatbush and won a laugher, 13–0, not permitting a Dodger hit until one out in the eighth inning when speedy Brooklyn outfielder Buzz Boyle beat out a slow chopper to Leo Durocher at short. It was Dean's twenty-seventh win, the most ever in one season by a Cardinal in breaking the thirty-five-year-old record of Cy Young.

But the little brother outdid him in the nightcap. "The Stengel athletes marched to the plate and back again with monotonous regularity," wrote Roscoe McGowen of Paul in the *New York Times*.

The younger Dean surpassed Dizzy, approaching lofty heights Diz himself had never seen. He kept every opposing player from hitting safely over the course of the day.

With two out in the ninth inning, Paul was threatening to become the first Cardinal to throw a no-hitter since Haines had accomplished the feat ten years earlier.

The last batter with a chance against him was Boyle. Just as he had done in spoiling Dizzy's effort earlier that day, Boyle would test Durocher again, this time on a hot shot to the shortstop's right. Leo knocked the ball down, snatched it quickly off the dirt with his bare hand, and let fly on a throw with everything he had. Watching the bag and first baseman Rip Collins's glove intently was Ziggy Sears, a rookie umpire from the Texas League who had been calling games in the majors for only the past seven weeks. Sears's right arm shot up into the air, declaring that Durocher's throw nipped Boyle by the slimmest of margins.

In addition to being the first no-hit game by a Cardinal in a decade, it was also the first no-hitter in the National League since Hubbell had achieved the feat against the Pirates five years earlier.

When visited by Stockton at his locker after the game, Paul was asked how he would have felt if Boyle had reached safely.

"It wouldn't have bothered me none," Paul answered nonchalantly. "Of course, I was thinking it would be kinda nice to have the no-hitter, but if Boyle had been man enough to sock one, I'd have taken it without crying."

The Deans had now won a combined forty-five games on the year, just as Dizzy predicted they would back in spring training. Later it was revealed that, earlier that day, Diz had issued another of his amazing predictions. "The dizziest prophecy of all," McGowen continued in his account, "was voiced in the Cardinals' hotel yesterday morning when Dizzy said, '[Brooklyn pitchers] Zachary and Benge will be pitching against one-hit Dean and no-hit Dean today.'"

The two losses pushed Stengel's record to 0-9 against Dizzy and Paul for the season. "How would you feel?" the dejected Brooklyn skipper would say to the writers at the conclusion of the long day. "You get three itsy-bitsy hits off the big brother in the first game, and then you look around and there's the little brother with biscuits from the same table to throw at you."

Dizzy felt it was now an opportune moment to raise the issue of his and Paul's salaries yet again. As their performance became more dominant, their case continued to resonate in the newspapers of other cities, particularly in New York.

"Instead of being encouraged to outdo themselves as they probably would if shown the least bit of consideration," claimed Dan Parker of the *Daily Mirror*, "they are underpaid and treated like striking mill hands whenever the flagrant injustice of their case leads them to register a protest. Any other club would recognize the value of this colorful brother act and pay them at least twice as much as the Cards. But the nickel-nursing Cardinal owners look at it from the angle of how much they can save by underpaying the brothers."

Tommy Holmes of the *Brooklyn Eagle*, who had just watched Dizzy and Paul overwhelm his hometown team, put it in sheer numbers. "Eighteen thousand saw the Deans pitch a weekday doubleheader. And more than 62,000, a league record, saw the Deans win a doubleheader at the Polo Grounds Sunday. And the combined salary of the Deans is still $10,500."

But Paul, humbly thankful just to be in the major leagues, remained more reticent than Diz. "We've had our misunderstanding," he said of himself and the St. Louis front office. "But, after all, Mr. Breadon is a businessman, and he is grateful when you deliver."

That same afternoon, Giants owner Horace Stoneham and his secretary, Jim Tierney, announced they were accepting applications from the public for World Series tickets, while his field manager Terry revealed that Hubbell was his choice to start the first game in the championship round. "Although the Cardinals are the best team in the National League right now," Stanley Frank of the *New York Post* admitted, "the Giants will play Detroit [the American League pennant winner] because they cannot possibly blow the pennant no matter how hard they try."

The Cardinals moved on to Cincinnati on their way back home, as Dizzy pitched in relief in both games of a doubleheader against the Reds on the September 23. His next start would come at home in Sportsman's Park two days later.

After another long road trip that had spanned six cities, seven teams, and nearly four weeks (including two stops in Chicago and three in New York, counting Brooklyn), the Cardinals were back in St. Louis to finally play their first September home game on the twenty-fifth. As the players left their hotel rooms and apartments that morning to head to Sportsman's Park, they were pleased to find that cooler temperatures greeted them. Over the course of the many train rides they had endured in recent weeks, the team now saw the lethal summer heat of the Dust Bowl at last giving way to the gentle, refreshing breezes of the fall. The folks of Missouri, Illinois, and the rest of the Midwest hoped good things were finally coming with the drop in the mercury.

The surging Cards themselves, however, had not been quenched, as they brought a hot streak back to the city with them. Victorious in nine of their last ten games, no one on the club dared to mess with the momentum by changing—or even washing—his uniform. Crackling with caked mud and emitting an almost intolerable stench, the Cardinals road grays were removed from their travel bags and heaved into the laundry bin in the washroom at Sportsman's Park.

Clubhouse man Butch Yatkeman had already dutifully hung the white home uniforms into each locker by the time the players arrived back home. If not for the league rules that required the host team to wear white, however, the Cardinals would have insisted upon further use of the grays. The latest expedition into enemy territory had brought them back to the corner of Grand and Dodier with a 90-57 record, closing in on the first-place Giants, now standing just two games back.

Back in spring training, New York manager Bill Terry had joked to reporters by asking if the struggling Brooklyn Dodgers were even still in the National League. But, now, as fate would have it, his Giants had to face Stengel and his charges in the season's final days with the pennant on the line.

The former Giants second baseman Frisch, meanwhile, feeling that luck was now on his club's side, had his old team squarely in his sights. The St. Louis manager made it clear that every game was of dire consequence and no potential victory could afford to be wasted. "What we're trying to do is win every game possible. There won't be a letdown so long as we have the slightest chance to win. Anything can happen in baseball, and if the wind should miraculously blow our way, we'll have our sails set."

The confidence of his team shone the most brightly from Dizzy Dean, who had become indomitable as the league schedule now stood in its final week. The former sharecropper, unbeaten in almost a month, got into his uniform as his spikes clicked on the concrete tunnel that led to the field. In town to face him today were the Pittsburgh Pirates, certain to be his next victim as the Cards continued their sprint upward in the standings.

Diz warmed up in the bullpen along the left field foul line as the first-pitch hour of three o'clock approached. The early autumn sun was dipping low in the west, settling into the hills of Dean's roots out in Arkansas and Oklahoma as he was ready to pitch the Cardinals to within a game of first place by the end of the day.

By now, Breadon had backed away from his banishment of radio broad-casts, allowing approved stations to air Cardinals games mostly without stoppage. At George's in Beckemeyer over the past few weeks, gatherings of various sizes had thus encircled the Philco radio as the Cards accelerated their charge toward the pennant since Labor Day.

As Dean took the mound on this Tuesday, September 25, it was a day of the week when most adults were still occupied with work, or at least the pursuit of it, even during the Depression.

But John Laufketter was not among those working this day. He was among those sitting idly at George's, pondering his future.

John had been on the job the past Friday when a representative from the Beckemeyer Coal and Mining Company had pulled him aside and told John he was being considered for a promotion to a foreman's position. The role would include moderately better pay, slightly less filth, and an improved degree of job security than the typical laborer's spot. He was permitted to have one week to think about the offer. If he did not give the company an answer by the following Friday, the twenty-eighth, the opportunity would go to someone else.

John was certain he wanted the promotion. Even so, he did not respond to the company immediately, as he did not wish to appear too anxious. He told no one of it, not even Rose.

On the morning of Tuesday, the twenty-fifth, John eagerly made his way to the company's office trailer at the Beckemeyer mine to give his agreement to the offer. But as he reached out for the door handle, his optimism was suddenly dashed.

Two men in business suits came charging out, impervious to John standing in the doorway and not bothering to excuse themselves when bumping past him. John overheard their brief discussion, and as the two men jumped into car a few feet away, he caught their last few words.

"Yep, soon, there won't be no need for one more rock of coal from around here. All these folks will be gone."

John did not go inside the trailer. He fell back against its outer wall, his hand covering his mouth.

The mine must be closing.

For the first time in as long as he could remember, John did not want to go home to Rose. He slipped away like a ghost down First Street to George's, trying to withstand yet another raising and dashing of his hopes.

CHAPTER ELEVEN

After St. Louis had burned soft coal for nearly a century—the cheap and plentiful type mined in Clinton County and other parts of Southern Illinois—a suffocating black pall permanently floated over the city, a dirty film darker than anything even the vaunted Dust Bowl could muster. One section of the city, stretching from the river to Kingshighway and north to south over the same distance, seemed to be perpetually smothered in coal residue. Mornings and afternoons often looked like dusk, as the smoke soiled daily life. By 1934, the culmination of various research studies concluded that St. Louis had developed the worst air pollution of any city in America.

City residents complained to local officials and demanded that action be taken. Among those who fielded the grievances was Mayor Dickmann, who had been on the job for just over a year. To find solutions to the problem, Dickmann formed the Citizens' Smoke Abatement League, with his secretary, Raymond Tucker, directing the work.

After several rounds of investigative work, Tucker's group recommended the installation of more efficient and cleaner-running furnaces and machinery in homes, businesses, and vehicles. Handing out leaflets downtown, the League informed people of a recent report of a researcher at Washington University, who had been examining the impact of coal smoke on mice. The researcher had discovered that, over an eighteen-month period, twice as many mice had died when exposed to city's average smoke level as those that had been quarantined from it.

In lobbying its case to local and state lawmakers, the League finally decided that St. Louis should no longer utilize the softer coal found across the river; instead, it would get its supply going forward from the harder anthracite found in Arkansas.

Almost overnight, the lifeblood of Southern Illinois had sustained a lethal hit, taking with it the livelihoods of thousands of people who depended upon the mines.

When residents of Clinton County read about the activities of the Smoke Abatement League in the newspapers, they paid little heed. It would be too expensive and cumbersome, they figured, for all of St. Louis to completely overhaul its chief source of energy.

Yet, as the months had passed in 1934, reality began setting in upon the residents of Beckemeyer and the surrounding communities. Gradually, fewer and fewer shifts were required of workers at the mine, and by late September, little evidence was seen of the shaft operating at all. The idle miners, growing in numbers each day, started roaming the streets in the center of town in front of George's with ghastly and bleak expressions. Ignoring the traditional social stratification, the miners no longer followed local expectations for them to stay in "their own section" of Beckemeyer on the east side and to limit their drinking in "their own place" at Roach's Tavern. They now went and drank wherever they pleased.

As a local hero, John was always exempt from this prejudice, even though he now lived on the east side and toiled at the mine like the rest of the laborers. He was one of the very few residents who had ever attended college, and among the even fewer still who had done so and came back to town. But, now, both the educated and the uneducated would be battling side by side for work, sustenance, and survival.

Forgetting about his supposed promotion at the mine, John plopped down sullenly at George's. He looked over and saw a group of his follow workers huddling in the middle of the place. With only a couple of coins in each one's pocket, they were trying to pass the hours slowly by savoring one precious beer. Some with a little more money opted for a highball, a mixture of Coca-Cola and hard liquor for those who could afford the extra ten cents.

John did not share with anyone what he had overheard at the trailer. He watched as the men flung glassy stares in no particular direction. They were making their drinks, and the peaceable moment, last as long as possible.

It was nearing three o'clock, and the Cardinals game was about to begin. John moved to a spot close to the radio, as Laux informed his listeners that Dean was heading to the mound. The others in George's seemed to display no interest in the ballgame.

As refreshing as a beer would have tasted to him and perhaps tamed his growling stomach a little bit, John chose water. With the imminent collapse of the mine, even one draft was an unfathomable indulgence at this point. The family was struggling just to eat regularly, and even harder days were surely to come.

With the Cardinals having relented on its ban of broadcasting, following the team on the radio had recently become John's lone leisure activity.

Through Laux's descriptions, John had always loved how he could paint his own picture of the ballgame in his mind, how he could drift away to his own make-believe world in Sportsman's Park. In his imagination, the grass at the stadium was as green as he wished it to be, or perhaps worn brown; sometimes, the stands were full, or they were nearly empty; sometimes there was excited chatter coming from the players in the dugout and loud cheers from the crowd, or sometimes the stadium sat in silence, anticipating a crucial moment in the game.

It was all up to him. He closed his eyes, picturing what it was like inside the gates at Grand and Dodier. John still had never been to a Cardinals game in person and figured it would be a long time before it was even remotely possible, if ever. The idea of taking himself, let alone Rose as well, to a game in St. Louis was completely out of the question due to the cost. Newspapermen agreed that such barriers existed, even for those people who lived in the city. "Young men and women are unable to pay the [ticket] prices," John Wray had written in the *Post-Dispatch* earlier that year. "When a youth escorts a girl to a baseball game, it costs him upwards of $2.50, including carfare. For this sum he could take his companion to the neighborhood picture show five times. His choice is inevitable."

Listening to the Cardinals games at George's also brought John out in public, as he had chosen to stay out of sight since Beckemeyer's final game of the 1934 Clinton County League season a few weeks earlier.

It was *that* game, and not the one resonating through the radio from St. Louis, that now drifted into John's mind as he sipped his water. He tuned out the Cardinals broadcast from his attention and glanced through the window, recalling what had happened a couple Sundays ago.

For the second straight year, Beckemeyer had not been at the top of the league standings at season's end. After the team had collapsed in the middle of 1933 when John abruptly quit upon the death of his mother, he and the Eagles had appeared to have rebounded in 1934, caroming off John's magnificent performance in the All-Star Game to clinch an early spot in the championship contest. But when Becky met Germantown in the regular season finale on August 26, John had uncharacteristically permitted three ninth inning runs as a stunned Beckemeyer outfit lost, 7–6.

Their momentum depleted, the Eagles had collapsed in the title game on September 2. Having pitched every inning that summer, fatigue had finally caught up with John as he was overpowered by the Centralia Buds in an 11–3 drubbing. Centralia had scored five times in the first inning, chasing John from the hill by the third as a relief pitcher entered a game for the Eagles for the first time all year.

John had remained in the game to play right field, as local whispers resumed about John possessing a dead arm. He spent the rest of the afternoon with a blank stare back toward home plate, similar to the one now held by the idle miners at George's. He was disgusted with himself. It seemed that even his recreational baseball career was now in its twilight. To what else could he now look forward? Could he dare even dream of a better life for his son, if not for himself and his wife?

As the crowd at Sportsman's Park roared through the radio with Dean's appearance out of the dugout, John snapped himself from his second-guessing daydreaming of the CCL championship game. The cool, early autumn air brushed into his face through the street-side window of George's. The pleasant drop in temperature, however, only reminded John that another winter was on its way, leaving him to wonder if there would be enough work around Beckemeyer to keep the stove heated in the family home.

He did not want to think about such things right now. He inched closer to the radio near the bar.

It was three o'clock. In St. Louis, Dizzy Dean went to work on *his* shift.

Even with Laux's radio microphone far from the field in the press box, the patrons in George's could hear Dean's fastball smacking like a pistol into the mitt of Spud Davis again and again.

POP!   *POP!*   *POP!*

After Pittsburgh was set down in its initial turn, hits by Frisch, Medwick, and Collins, as well as a fielding error by Pirates shortstop Arky Vaughan, staked Dizzy and the Redbirds to an early 3–0 lead in the first inning.

Through five innings, the only Pirate base runner Dizzy would permit had reached on a bobbled ground ball by Frisch near the second base bag in the first inning. The idle, listless miners in George's now took more interest in the game, as did others who had just come in off Louis Street.

Along with John, there was one man who made sure he sat as close as possible to the radio. He could not hide his admiration. "Dean! Amazing! He is indestructible!" the man declared. He sat squarely in front of the Philco, careful not to let anyone nearer to it than himself.

The man grabbed his glass of Falstaff beer with a grip that a pair of pliers could not break. Taking a long, refreshing slurp, he then turned his head, peering back toward John.

"Never has arm trouble," the man went on to assert, looking John in the eye and then turning his head back to the radio. He downed another long gulp of his beer. "Did y'all know that Dean has pitched more innings than anyone the last two years?"

"I think Hubbell has a few more," offered another man nearby.

"No way," the first man shot back. "No one throws like Diz. He'd pitch every day if Frisch would let 'em."

The Pirates continued to flail erratically at Dean's pitches for the rest of the afternoon, with Dizzy scattering a mere three hits and walking no one. Pittsburgh began its final try in the top of the ninth with the 3–0 score still standing. The Pirates leadoff hitter was Woody Jensen, who was quickly retired as well on a great play in the hole by Durocher.

At just that moment, word arrived at Sportsman's Park that the Giants had lost to the paltry Phillies, as Terry's troops were shut out by Curt Davis at the Polo Grounds 4–0. If Dean could hold on, Laux told the listeners, New York's pennant lead would be down to a single game.

Next up was Paul Waner, the National League leader in hits on the season and, according to Dizzy, the toughest batter he ever had to face. Waner, who had homered off Diz in Pittsburgh back in July, was fooled by a Dean curveball and tapped a light grounder toward Durocher at short. Fearing Waner's powerful bat, Leo had been playing deep at his position, even on the opposite-field side, and was unable to get to the ball in time to prevent an infield hit as Waner reached first safely.

Vaughan was next to the plate, another of the National League's top sluggers. Looking to atone for his fielding miscue earlier in the day, which had contributed to the game's only runs, he grabbed hold of Dizzy's second pitch and sent a long home run far off the premises, sailing high over the pavilion beyond right field. To the surprise of those turning and watching in last row of the bleachers, the ball finally crashed down upon the northbound lanes of Grand Avenue as the Pirates were suddenly within a run at 3–2.

Angry, Diz slammed his fist into his mitt several times as he circled the mound and got a new ball from the umpire, incensed that his sixth shutout of the year was now ruined.

The next hitter was Harold "Pie" Traynor, the Pirates third baseman who, like Frisch, was also in his first year as a player-manager. Dean reached back for his best fastball, a "real fogger" as he liked to call it. The ball sailed up toward the head of Traynor, who eluded it just in time.

The veteran was unfazed by the message, standing his ground in the batter's box in readying for the next offering. He promptly deposited a single into the burnt center field pasture of Sportsman's Park as the potential tying run was now aboard.

The look on Dean's face now visibly changed. His normally playful demeanor took on a presence of rage, his eyes twisting angrily at the next man in the Pittsburgh order, first baseman Gus Suhr. Working the count to 2-2, Dizzy—wanting to finish off the game with a couple more mighty salvos—let loose with everything he had on his fastball. Driving off the mound for extra power, he fired the ball past the flailing Suhr for strike three and the crucial second out.

But in doing so, a twinge hit his right leg when he let go of the ball. Pepper Martin, over at third base, later claimed to hear something pop. Dizzy let out a howl that echoed throughout the ballpark and that was even slightly audible over the radio broadcast. It was Dean's hamstring, which, with the cooler weather, had blown from overexertion.

Diz retrieved the ball from Davis and hobbled back to the rubber, trying not to look at Frisch at his second base position. He was afraid that if he made eye contact with the manager, Frisch would be compelled to take him out of the game. Their eyes did meet, and Frisch did not budge; rather, he nodded back at his pitcher as he kept his hands on his knees. This was Dizzy's game to finish.

Second baseman Tommy Thevenow was next. Dean, gingerly rotating the injured leg on his first offering, lobbed a weak curveball toward the plate. To everyone's surprise, it induced the former Cardinal to pop up softly to Frisch for the culminating third out.

Victory again belonged to the rampaging St. Louis Cardinals in a contest lasting only an hour and twenty-seven minutes. They were now only a game behind the panicking New York Giants, with five left to play. "No team in major league history ever went into September with a seven-game lead and lost it," Gary Schumacher pondered in his column the following day. "The Giants haven't done that yet, but it now appears inevitable. They're tired and worn, their spirit has sagged. They can't hit, and their pitchers have yielded to physical weariness."

The victory for the Cardinals, however, was a pyrrhic one.

Leaving the field, Dizzy forced a smile to the fans as he accepted congratulatory handshakes from his teammates. But once underneath the stands in the tunnel leading to the clubhouse, he released a yelp of pain and collapsed to the floor. Martin and Durocher grabbed him quickly, placed him around their arms, and carried him into the treatment room of Doc Weaver, the team's trainer. Dean had nearly torn his hamstring, and even in its merely pulled condition, the injury placed the Cardinals' entire championship run in doubt.

Unusual for a Tuesday, a beehive of activity was seen in front of the Chase Park Plaza Hotel on Kingshighway in St. Louis later that night. Five well-dressed men, though there was supposed to be six, clandestinely dashed out of taxi cabs at the front door and were ushered quickly inside. The men were escorted one by one to small meeting room in the back of the first floor of the hotel, where Branch Rickey sat waiting. The five guests were his top Midwestern scouts and personnel advisors, two of whom had to immediately drive in from Cape Girardeau and Rolla.

Rickey gave them the details of the disheartening news. It was determined by physicians that it was not possible for Dizzy Dean to make his next scheduled start three days later on September 28 against the Cincinnati Reds.

A two-and-a-half-hour discussion ensued, as the men attempted to decide which pitcher from the Cardinals minor league system should be summoned to take his place, at a minimum for the twenty-eighth and perhaps into the World Series if the Cardinals could overcome the Giants.

At 10:33 p.m., a consensus was reached. While not unanimous, it was agreed that left-hander Bud Teachout would be purchased from the Cardinals farm team at Columbus, Ohio.

The thirty-year-old Teachout, originally from Los Angeles, had previously starred at Occidental College, where he had accumulated a 30-6 record and authored a no-hitter against the University of Southern California. The decisive factor among Rickey and his men was that Teachout, unlike most of the other available pitchers, had previous major league experience. He had posted a fine 12-6 aggregate mark with the Chicago Cubs in 1930 and 1931 before being traded with legendary slugger Hack Wilson to the Cards in exchange for Burleigh Grimes.

Since being traded to the Cardinals, Teachout had pitched only one inning for St. Louis, which occurred during the first week of the 1932 season. In spending most of the past three years in the minors, Teachout had earned his return trip to the big leagues by leading Columbus with seventeen wins during the 1934 summer.

At 12:13 a.m. on the twenty-sixth, a stunned Teachout was awoken by an incessant knock on the door of his room at the Great Southern Hotel. A bellhop handed him an envelope and quickly departed. In a brief telegram from Rickey, Teachout was informed that the general manager of the Columbus team would be waiting for him in front of the hotel on High Street at 7:00 that same morning. The orders from Rickey included that the Columbus GM was to surrender his personal vehicle and give it to Teachout, the latter of whom was then to drive to St. Louis at once. A track operators' strike in Indiana had disrupted train travel throughout the region, and Rickey did not want to take any chances. The pitcher was directed in the final line of the telegram to get himself to St. Louis "as expeditiously as conditions permit."

Notwithstanding the strange request, Teachout dared not question Rickey's command. Nervously, he climbed in and got behind the wheel, driving a car for the first time in over a year. He fumbled with a map as he yanked the vehicle into gear to start his westward trek.

Teachout had studied the map only briefly before departing. He knew that US Route 40 would be a logical road with which to start, as it was the major east-west passageway in and out of Columbus. After a short distance, however, he cut south and headed for Route 50. He knew this was the direct path traveled by teams between Cincinnati and St. Louis, albeit by train. While Rickey gave him no deadline of the time for his arrival, he had to get to St. Louis and report sometime on the night of the twenty-sixth.

He made it through Cincinnati without incident, carefully navigating the perilous curves of the Delhi and Cleves neighborhoods before reaching the rolling hills of Southern Indiana. The earth ultimately flattened with the approach of the Illinois state line, as the green of the Hoosier forests gradually gave way to the stark reminder of the Dust Bowl with the downtrodden prairie lying dead ahead.

Stopping for a bite to eat, Teachout learned over a radio in a coffee shop that the National League had stood firm after the games on the twenty-sixth from its status of the previous day. New York had lost to the Phillies by permitting a run in the ninth, but Paul Dean had also lost to the Pirates 3–0 in Sportsman's Park as the Redbirds were shut out by Waite Hoyt on only two hits. Thus, the Giants had successfully maintained their one-game advantage over the Cardinals.

By 7:30 p.m. Teachout had made it to Salem, only seventy-five miles from St. Louis. The fall sun was setting rapidly and never in his life had he driven such a long distance under the darkening sky. Though fatigued, he pressed on. His guide had been the railroad tracks, sitting faithfully at his left along Route 50. Teachout glanced over at them regularly; they were the same tracks he had traveled in his brief time previously in the majors with the Cubs when the team had left Cincinnati to play the Cardinals in St. Louis. He knew that if he stayed on Route 50, which was always parallel to the rail line, he would find his destination. His confidence growing as he was leaving the west end of Salem, Teachout felt comfortable in accelerating to a faster speed.

As soon as he left the city limits of Salem, Teachout noticed that an overcast sky was now greeting him. Taking his eyes off the road for a moment, he stared in amazement at the clouds. Upon closer scrutiny, they seemed darker to him than any he had ever seen, even darker than those which might precede a violent thunderstorm. Glancing again at the tracks to the south side of the road, he noticed the trees lining the railroad had started swaying, bobbing up and down like evil specters. With the fierce wind now swirling and the trees bending further as the approaching blackness grew closer, Teachout scanned the horizon for a funnel cloud. Relieved to find none, he nevertheless remembered a time in the minor leagues when the team's driver spotted an approaching tornado, as the players piled out of the vehicle and laid in a ditch upwind of the bus.

In the next instant, a small, repeating knock hit the windshield. Teachout figured the rainstorm had finally reached him.

tick-tick . . . tick-tick-tick

But to his surprise, the windshield was dry.
The sound continued.

tick-tick-tick . . . tick-tick

In mere seconds, the knocking increased in volume and force.

pock-POCK . . . pock-POCK

Teachout was now unable see to the hood of the car. The vehicle had been completely and instantly engulfed in dirt. The attack came upon the helpless victim in no time, like a swarm of angry bees.

Without slowing down, Teachout panicked and jerked the automobile to the left. Awaiting the impact of an oncoming car he could neither see nor hear, he prepared for the end of his life.

To his surprise, there was no collision. The car kept veering to the left. As he recovered and attempted to bring the car back to the right side of the road, the front wheel caught the edge of the embankment. The dirt had now engulfed the entire cabin of the car. Teachout could see or hear nothing at all, as the deafening noise of the storm made him believe he was now on the railroad tracks and perhaps heading for an oncoming train.

All he could do was feel himself helplessly fall along with the vehicle. The car rolled down the embankment and over itself twice before coming to a rest, the driver's side flush with the ground.

Teachout, who had been playfully flapping his pitching arm out the window for most of the trip, now realized the left side of his body was immobilized. He drifted into unconsciousness.

He would lay there for the next nine hours, invisible in the ditch to those passing by. The Dust Bowl had claimed its latest victim and crept on past him toward its next.

When the air over Salem cleared as the sun rose on the morning of the twenty-seventh, a farmer traveling down Route 50 spotted Teachout's car while heading into town. The farmer, unaware that anyone was still inside, roused the occupant by rattling the tipped-over vehicle. Teachout mumbled something about St. Louis, and the farmer brought him to the small hospital in Salem. The pitcher had sustained no life-threatening injuries but suffered lacerations on his face, four broken ribs, and a cracked radius in his left arm.

By 10:00 a.m., Branch Rickey was incensed that he had not heard from Teachout, with the left-hander supposed to be pitching a crucial game for the Cardinals the following day. But minutes later, Rickey's secretary handed him the telegram with the news. Teachout would not be coming any closer to St. Louis than his Salem hospital bed.

As his team was getting ready to play the series opener with the Reds down the street, Rickey once again called all the scouts together to the Chase Park Plaza at noon, in the same room in which they had met just over twenty-four hours earlier.

"Gentlemen," Rickey began, "by now you are aware of the great misfortune which has befallen Mr. Teachout. I have been told that, thankfully, he will convalesce. Yet we are faced with the same question: who can pitch for us tomorrow?"

The men looked down at their laps. No one offered an answer.

Aside from the Deans, Rickey held no confidence in any of the other current Cardinal pitchers. As his law training had taught him, Rickey listed the evidence in outlining the crisis. "Since the fifth of September, the Dean brothers have had to pitch in two-thirds of our games in either a starting or relief role. Because no one else is rested, we must throw Walker and Hallahan today and maybe Mooney as well, even though Walker is not fully recovered from his broken arm in May when Medwick hit him in batting practice. Mooney has not thrown for a month, and his earned run average is nearly five-and-a-half. He, Vance, and Haines cannot help us. Someone should replace Haines right now, in fact. Winford and Grimes are long gone.

"And the most recent dust storm causing Teachout's accident has impeded most train and automobile traffic from the eastern states or halted it altogether. This precludes anyone else arriving from Columbus in time.

"Rochester, our other top farm team, is twice as far as Columbus. So is our next-highest one, Houston. The other lower minor league affiliates of Lufkin, Huntington, Greensboro, and Greensburg also report that the distance and weather prevents them from getting anyone here in time."

As he continued, Rickey started shaking visibly in furor.

"And nobody in Springfield is picking up the dadgum phone, so no one is available from there, either."

He closed his eyes for a second. Breathing deeply, he calmed himself and went on.

"There are a couple of nearby high school pitchers I have seen. They could probably go a few innings if we can outhit the Reds, but I refuse to put that much pressure on a young person. And none of the local colleges will let me touch any of their players, as they cannot return to college to play after they throw one professional pitch."

Rickey's utterance of the word "college" caught the attention of one of the men at the table. The man had missed the initial meeting the previous day when Teachout had been the choice of the group. His head perked up.

"We are one day away from the biggest game of the season," Rickey said in conclusion. "And we do not have a single full-strength pitching arm that is available to us. Pepper Martin has at least attempted it previously. He or Mooney may have to be the one."

The man absent from the first meeting hesitated at first but then forced his mouth open.

"Mr. Rickey," he began. "I might have an answer, but it's the *longest* of longshots, at the very best."

Rickey's eyes grew wide in interest. He chewed on his unlit cigar while staring at the speaker

"Nice of you to join us, Mr. Tretiak," he said in sarcastic admonition for the man's absence the previous day. "Go on."

Jerry drew a deep breath and continued.

"Out in Illinois, not too far from here, certainly reachable, is a possible guy. He pitched for SLU four years ago as a freshman in the spring of 1930, so he's only twenty-two – maybe twenty-three, twenty-four at the most."

Tretiak realized a mistake he had made with his revelation. John could not have pitched in a game as a freshman, and Rickey would know that.

"It was an intrasquad game I was watching," Jerry said in righting himself, not breaking stride with his story. "Something strange happened that year, and he left school abruptly after one season. He never told anyone he was leaving—not his coach, his teammates, his professors, no one—and that was the last anyone ever saw of him in St. Louis. He's now throwing in a men's league, and as far as I know, he's not under contract with any club.

"But let me tell you something, Mr. Rickey, and I will stake my reputation on this. He has major league stuff *right now*."

Others around the table wanted to snicker in the way scouts do when one of their brethren endorses an obscure player, but they held their breath, first waiting to see Rickey's reaction.

After a moment of more staring and cigar chewing, it finally came.

"*If* he has major league stuff," Rickey interrogated while bobbing his head flamboyantly, "what on God's green earth is he doing now besides pitching in a semipro league?"

"I don't know, sir. Most of the men in that part of Illinois—Clinton County, I think it is—are either farmers or miners. He must be doing some form of tough manual labor, though, because even though he's skinny, he is as strong as an ox. In that league's all-star game, he toyed with the best players that county had to offer, whatever that is worth. He completely dominated them. It wasn't even close."

"How he hasn't been picked up by some other club, I have no idea. Maybe it's because he's in a remote area, or maybe he's just not interested in leaving his hometown. From what I saw, I will say he is better than anyone we have in our farm system right now, in my opinion. So, you don't need to bring anybody from Houston or Rochester. This guy is right across the river, he has the goods, he's not doing anything, he would be cheap, and he probably has nothing to lose."

"But *we* certainly do," Rickey retorted quickly. "I will tell Frisch to start Haines before some nobody pitcher ascends to *my* mound. When is the last time you saw him throw?"

Jerry could barely spit it out. "The first of July."

Now, some of the other scouts finally did snicker nervously.

Rickey resumed chewing on his cigar for several seconds, seconds that felt like hours to everyone in the room. All the while, he was staring directly at Jerry.

"All right," he finally blurted out. "Get in your car right now, find him, and have him throw a few to someone, anyone. Even you, if necessary, so bring a mitt. If he's in shape and you think he still has what you say, tell him we'll give him a one-day contract. Once he signs it, bring him to me. I want to ask him a few questions."

With that, Rickey abruptly stopped talking. The cigar still clenched between his teeth, he looked down and shuffled papers, signaling to the men that the meeting was over.

One by one, the scouts pushed themselves up from their chairs and departed, looking at each other incredulously. They could not believe that the Cardinals' season had come to this, their chances resting on an absolute nobody. Yet, none of them could offer up an alternative.

As Jerry and the others headed out the door, Rickey interrupted the exodus without looking up from shuffling his papers. "Mr. Tretiak, a word?"

Jerry reversed himself and slowly waded through the others to return to the table, as Rickey resumed speaking in his urbane murmur.

"I know I don't have to remind you, Jerry, that our season hangs in the balance. This can't be some organizational guy we're talking about. This man must win a major league baseball game for us, nothing less. If you are not 100 percent certain he is the one, I'm directing Frisch to give Haines the ball."

Rickey grunted before concluding. "And let me be frank. It has been a while since you have forwarded someone who has helped this organization. If this fails, the mantle of responsibility is going to fall completely on you. And if that occurs, I think you'll need to make other arrangements for your employment."

As directed, Jerry picked up the contract from Rickey's secretary. The boilerplate document was typically used by Rickey for a one-day recall of a player from the minor leagues. Jerry stuffed the contract into his satchel, tossed it into the front seat of his car, and sped toward Downtown. Shortly after leaving, he noticed he had forgotten to grab a catcher's mitt as Rickey also directed, figuring he could find one once he got there. But got *where?* Was Beckemeyer small enough to find a man named John Laufketter quickly enough? Cruising through the St. Louis streets, he tried to mentally map the route he had taken from Clinton County a couple months prior.

After a quick stop to pick up a sandwich and coffee at the Eat-Rite Diner at Seventh and Chouteau, Jerry made his way along the makeshift tenements, which still lined the river near the train tracks. Pulling up onto the Municipal Bridge, he exchanged glances with the glum expressions of the destitute people down below.

His scout's instincts took him to Route 50. Within forty-five minutes, the town names of Trenton and Aviston, came into view, familiar to Jerry as two of the teams comprising the Clinton County League.

Next was Breese, still claiming to be "Famous for Friendliness" with a sign at its western boundary, a copy of the greeting Jerry had seen in approaching the town from the north back in July. He smiled when speeding past the Knotty Pine, making him wonder how Colston and Poettker were doing—and if they had fared any better than the Schwabs in surviving the Depression. Jerry wanted to stop and say hello, but there was not a minute to lose.

Next was Beckemeyer. He had made good time, arriving ahead of schedule at 2:30 p.m. Jerry had not gotten this far east in Clinton County back in July, but the town was just as he imagined it. It was quite like all the others nearby, though not as big as Breese.

Beckemeyer's lone major avenue off Route 50 was very apparent to the visitor, as Jerry turned where a sign reading Louis Street was affixed to a lamp post.

With the only sizable buildings visible, it must be the town's main street, Jerry figured. He still had no idea where to begin looking for the player; if he could just find a barbershop, a bank, or a tavern, that would be a start.

Going a few blocks, he slowed to a stop alongside the curb. Getting out of his car, Jerry gazed up the street. He noticed only one place where people were coming and going, with a sign reading George's on the outside.

As Jerry entered, he slung his suit coat over his shoulder informally and loosened his tie, trying to convey a friendly approach. Even so, the few men in the place turned and gazed upon him with suspicious curiosity. To them, he was an outsider; not necessarily a troublemaker but an outsider all the same . . . perhaps a motorist stranded or lost somewhere along 50.

While staring at Jerry, the men were arranged in exact same seats they had occupied for the past three days. The place was silent, except for the voice of France Laux coming through the radio at the bar in reporting the Cardinals game. The familiar sound of Laux made Jerry more comfortable and gave him the courage to speak up. He could not delay his purpose any longer.

"I'm looking for John Laufketter."

Heads darted away from Jerry and toward the opposite end of the room.

There, another man sat by himself on a barstool. He was bent over, his elbows resting on his knees and his hands folded. The man peered back at Jerry through the top of his eyes.

"Who wants to know?" answered the man defensively, thinking the stranger was a representative from the bank who had come to call the note on his mortgage, which was now three months in arrears.

"My name is Tretiak," Jerry answered, delighted to see the man again and flashing a quick smile. Jerry began moving cautiously across the room. He stopped halfway. "Can we talk outside for a minute?"

John rolled his eyes and got up slowly, as if to comply but not really caring one way or the other.

Jerry did not say another word until the door closed behind them and they were out on the sidewalk along Louis Street. The other men inside the bar had left their tables and crammed the windows. John's countenance changed dramatically in the next moment.

CHAPTER TWELVE

Ten minutes later, Jerry had retraced his steps of the past two-and-a-half months.

"So, that's the deal," he told John. "You give the Cardinals the best you've got for one day, and you'll make seventy-five dollars plus a free train ride back here. And if it goes well . . . well, we'll see what happens from there."

"I haven't picked up a baseball in almost four weeks," John said. "Don't you even want to see me throw?"

"Don't have to. How does your shoulder feel?"

"It's fine."

"Well, fine then. I already know what you've got."

John laughed aloud, trying to comprehend what was happening.

"So, I'm to pitch for the St. Louis Cardinals tomorrow? Do I have any time to think about it?"

"Not much—hardly any. You probably shouldn't think too much about it, anyway. What do you need to do?"

"I just need an hour," John said.

"You can have an hour."

John left Jerry and pondered the decision where he did his best thinking—roaming the Beckemeyer streets. The first stop he needed to make was home.

When he turned the corner onto Randolph Street, Rose was in the kitchen, drying her hands with a dish towel. She saw John approaching the house and lovingly watched him come up the walk. With the erratic schedule of the mine in recent months, she had grown accustomed to him coming and going at any time during the afternoon. But his expression today suggested something was different.

The screen door rattled as he made his way inside, its deteriorating hinges having loosened like the ones on the back door. Rose tossed the towel aside as she looked at John quizzically. He gazed silently back at her.

"What's wrong?" she finally asked. "Did somebody get hurt at the mine?"

"No," he replied. "Let's just talk for a minute."

He invited her outside, and they sat down on the front porch swing. Alphie had built it for Leah at the house over on Lincoln Street, and it was one of the few things John was certain to bring with them when they moved.

"Sweetie," John began, "I love you more than anything this world has ever given me or ever will give."

Rose cocked her head slightly, smiling wryly back at him. She was both appreciative and suspicious.

"That is why," he continued, "anything I ever do, or ever would do, has you in mind, first and foremost. I would never do anything that would hurt you and would only do things that are good for you. You're on my mind, all day long, every day—"

"Okay," she finally interrupted. "What's this all about?"

He took a deep breath. "This will be the most ridiculous, unbelievable thing you've ever heard." John turned away and looked out into the street at nothing. "I'm pitching for the Cardinals tomorrow."

He turned back to face Rose and see her reaction. She barely showed a hint of surprise. She was excited but otherwise unfazed.

"Doesn't sound so crazy to me," she said with a shrug. "I know what you can do. But—how the heck—"

"I was just told fifteen minutes ago. A guy from the Cards saw me pitch in Breese at the All-Star Game. He happened to be passing through. He asked me why I wasn't pitching for someone else, and I told him about the shoulder, about the trouble finding and keeping regular work, all that stuff.

"The mine is dying. St. Louis doesn't want our coal anymore. Pretty soon, there won't be any work around here at all. But, by the grace of God, if I can do well in this one game . . . I might get something more."

"You mean, a permanent spot with the Cardinals?"

"Yeah, maybe, according to the scout."

That ended the upside of the deal, as John laid out the other possibilities roaring through his mind. The tone of his voice went from one of excitement to angst.

"And then again, the scout might be just leading me on. Even if I do well and they want to keep me, they might say that I must go off to one of their minor league teams instead of staying in St. Louis. It would be decent, steady pay, but I'd be away from you and Joseph for who-knows-how-long to who-knows-where, and with no guarantee that I'd even get to return to the Cardinals ever again.

"And if I get hurt tomorrow or next week or next month in the minors somewhere—you know how my shoulder has been—it won't matter to them. They'll just put me on the train back here like an old hog's carcass, back in Beckemeyer and out of a job, just like B——. Anyway, a guy with a destroyed shoulder can't work in the mine.

"The scout asked me how my arm is, and I lied through my teeth. It hurts so bad most days that I want to chop it off. What if I pitch this game and injure myself to the point where I can't even work anymore? What will we do then?"

"It would be tough," Rose acknowledged—yet still smiling. "But I would be the proudest wife in the county."

Her confidence made *him* smile. "You and Joseph could not come to the game. I know that."

She nodded.

"Hell, am I really good enough to toe the slab in Sportsman's Park? I've never even *been* to a big-league game."

"Big Guy, that scout wasn't in the right place at the right time—*you* were. This is what you were *meant* to do. I know you love me, but you also love baseball. It's okay. *It's what you're supposed to do.* This is your destiny, John. It's not right for anybody to keep that from you. Not even me. Besides, I wouldn't want to do that, anyway."

John cracked a smile. "Do you mind me being gone for the night?" He had never spent a night away from Rose since they were married. Again, Rose smiled. He held her as tightly as he could and laid out the rest of the details, the few of which he knew.

"If I'm going, I have to leave with the scout in the next half hour. I had to tell you first, but I also need to go to church. Look all the way down Second Street thirty minutes from now. If I'm waving, I'm going. If I'm walking back home, I'm not."

She smiled again, recalling the time he had stumbled when their eyes first met.

"Just watch out for those things that can trip you up when you're heading home."

John went inside and put on his Sunday church clothes. After jamming a few personal items into the same duffel bag he had carried off to SLU five years earlier, he hustled back downstairs and gave Rose the longest kiss he could before hurrying back through town toward the west side.

Stopping for a moment when he reached Louis Street, John looked north and could see Jerry a few blocks up, his back towards him. The man who had been sent to save the St. Louis Cardinals' season by Branch Rickey was still standing out in front of George's Tavern in Beckemeyer, his hands stuffed in his pockets, patiently waiting.

John continued four more blocks, sprinting past his old house before arriving at the steps of St. Anthony's. The door to the church was always open; despite golden chalices and other valuables perched on the altar, no one ever considered taking any of them, even if one's family was starving.

John walked inside, dropped his bag in the third row of the nave, and fell into a seat. He cast his eyes downward as he mumbled an impromptu prayer.

What does this mean, Lord? Why was I chosen for this role? This has *to mean something.*

In the quiet stillness, John Laufketter prayed in solitude for the peace, health, and happiness of Rose. He prayed the same for Joseph. He prayed for his departed parents. And he prayed for Bud Teachout.

When finished, he also prayed for the restoration of his fortitude. "St. Anthony, patron saint of lost items, please help me regain my confidence."

A familiar voice then softly emerged.

"He will."

John turned, grinning before he even faced the person. He knew it was Father Schweighart.

"Hey, Father. I need some help."

John explained what had transpired in the last hour. Father Schweighart, always stoic, sat and listened intently as he always did, with one arm resting on the back of the pew.

"You have more support than you realize, John," the priest reminded him. "Your dad, your mom, they're up there. They are your greatest cheerleaders."

"I know," John responded, shaking his head while still staring at the church floor. "But I think there's just too much at stake here."

"What do you mean? What can happen from which you can't recover?"

John looked away, having surmised many possible things that could go wrong, other possibilities that he did not have the heart to share with Rose on the front porch.

"What if I fail? What if it's a disaster, if I embarrass myself, and then even *more* people around here keep looking at me as the guy who should have made it but didn't? I was supposed to be the guy who would *get out* of Beckemeyer and the mines—for *good*. You remember Bobby Durstmiller from here? Same with him. He was the *best*, the best I ever played with or ever saw. He was better than me. And the game chewed him up and spit him out.

"And then there's the Cardinals. This is the last week of season, and they're trying to catch the Giants for the National League pennant. Sure, I can get guys out in the CCL. But do the *St. Louis Cardinals* really need a *coal miner* pitching for them? I could ruin everything for them.

"The game will end at some point. I then come back here, and I can't even work because someone took my place at the mine while I was gone—however long the mine is going to be open. Or in the game, I permanently hurt my arm and *can't* work. What if I can't support my wife and son? What will I be then, if I can't even be any sort of meal ticket for my family?"

As he was rambling, John remembered the hordes of starving people he had seen along the riverfront in St. Louis long ago when he had returned home from college, blighted figures who were no more than scarecrows, crowded together in the Hooverville.

"You know . . . all things considered, I'm actually *lucky* to have my spot at the mine, lucky just to have some work," he resigned. "I'm fine with that. Isn't that who I'm supposed to be?"

Father Schweighart was still stoic and calm. He smiled, got up from the pew, and patted John on the shoulder.

"This is *your* life, John. All you have to remember is that you are a beloved son of a gracious God. You don't have to *be* anything. You just have to *be*.

"Just one piece of advice if you decide to do it: Leave nothing behind."

John managed a little smile as Father Schweighart left. He knew what he meant. The last two axioms were two of Father's famous phrases, having shared them with John and his classmates since they had first walked through the school doors long ago.

The pastor departed, and suddenly John was once again alone in the church. When he closed his eyes, a new peace came upon him; God enveloped him with all the goodness of Beckemeyer—the same goodness his father had always cherished. Regardless of where he found himself tomorrow, and in whatever tough situation, John knew he would be carrying that goodness with him.

He drifted off to sleep for a moment.

When through the woods and forest glades I wander,
And hear the birds sing sweetly in the trees
When I look down from lofty mountain grandeur
And see the brook and feel the gentle breeze.

He awoke, drew a long breath, raised himself up, and exited the church.

How great Thou art.

Exactly thirty minutes after he had left Rose, John returned to the intersection of Louis and Second Street. He looked east and saw her standing four blocks away in the middle of Randolph and Second. He waved both hands above his head, a gesture she returned and followed with a whisper.

"I love you, Big Guy. Don't get tripped up heading for home."

John turned up Louis Street and spotted Jerry. The scout's hands were now on his hips as he kicked at the loose gravel on the sidewalk, pacing a few steps in every direction. The hour John requested had turned into nearly two. It was now almost five o'clock.

John Laufketter, about to become the newest member of the St. Louis Cardinals, called out while running up the dusty main drag of Beckemeyer. "Mr. Tretiak, I'm ready. I've got my glove and cleats in here," he said, pointing to the duffel bag. "What else do I need to bring with me?"

"Nothing at all, if you don't mind wearing those same clothes for the trip back here," the scout summarized in a businesslike tone as they jumped in the car. "The ball club will provide your accommodations for tonight and will have everything you need for the game tomorrow."

Jerry quickly spun the vehicle around in a U-turn on Louis Street. Instead of slowing down to look for traffic before pulling onto Route 50, he accelerated onto the highway without hesitating, leaving John little time to take a last look at Beckemeyer as they sped off. "Everything I need," John mumbled to himself, thinking of his wife, his catcher, and his parents.

The drive to St. Louis transpired much faster to John than when Bobby had driven him five years earlier. His mind was swirling as they passed Breese and then Aviston. Soon Trenton appeared, and the towns were going by much too quickly; the comfortable familiarity of Beckemeyer was fading as the imposing big city and its many pitfalls lay ahead. The bluffs above the Mississippi River soon came into view.

His defining hour was at hand. It was a chance he was supposed to have long ago, under more agreeable circumstances. Trying to put self-pity aside, John looked at the railroad tracks along 50 and could hear his father nudging him from beyond. *"Mach Heu, solange die Sonne scheint!"*—"You have to make hay while the sun shines!"

They soon made their way past the St. Louis riverfront, where the lost, destitute souls seemed to grow in number with each passing. When Jerry turned onto Grand Boulevard and headed north, John did not even care to notice his old classroom buildings of SLU.

A few minutes later, they arrived at Sportsman's Park, a twenty-block trip from the campus but one that John had never made during his brief time at the university. Jerry swung the car left onto Dodier Street, parking directly in front of the ballpark with a two-story structure sitting between the street and the actual stadium. Signs on the building denoted Browns Offices and Cardinals Offices, located approximately a hundred feet apart, with the Browns office closer to the corner at Grand. As John emerged from Tretiak's car, he slowed to a stop in imbibing the magnitude of the complex. Jerry had to shoo him toward the Cardinals office entrance, where the door was already open. "We gotta go," the scout said, taking his arm.

They wove through a maze of hallways, winding up in a large meeting room with an imposing table. As they entered, a man with his back to them suddenly spun around in his chair. John did not recognize him but suspected who it was.

Branch Rickey had yet another cigar clenched tightly in his mouth. He nodded to the men, pleased to see that everything was on schedule.

"Ah. Mr. Laufketter, I presume," he blurted while grabbing the cigar out his mouth with all five left fingers on his left hand, offering John his right.

"Yes, sir," John answered.

"Welcome."

Rickey replaced the cigar between his lips and waved an open hand above the meeting table, an invitation for John and Jerry to be seated.

"Mr. Laufketter, I apologize for your expedited delivery, but we are in quite a predicament here," the general manager began. "I am certain the past several hours have been quite frenzied for you. I am glad you have decided to join us. Mr. Tretiak speaks highly of you."

"Thank you, sir."

Rickey sank back into his plush chair. "Before we go any further, I wish to know. What brought you here today?"

John squirmed a bit in his own seat, not knowing the answer that was sought. He suddenly heard himself speaking frankly, and once he started, he could not stop.

"Well, sir, I love baseball, and I love the Cardinals. More than anything, to be honest, I need the money. I'm a coal miner. And I just got offered a small promotion, but I think the mine is closing, anyway, and I don't know what's going to happen from one day to the next. . . ."

Rickey was intrigued and tilted his head in captivation. "Go on," he said, raising the cigar between two pinched fingers.

"I don't know what . . . what I mean to say is, why . . . why was I the one chosen, sir?" John wondered aloud.

Rickey nodded, closed his eyes for second, and took another long draw of his smoke.

"According to Mr. Tretiak, and he is one of my longest-tenured scouts, you are as good as anyone in our system. Yet, to be frank, we have nobody else. We need you, and you were close by. It was a good fit for us."

Rickey paused for a moment, tapping the cigar on an ash tray, and continued.

"You know by now that you're taking the spot of Dizzy Dean. He is being paid $7,500 for this season. Therefore, we are willing to give you one one-hundredth of that figure for your day's work tomorrow. If you do well, there might be more work for you. If you do not—well, I will do us both the courtesy of not describing such a contingency."

"It would be an honor to work for you, sir," John replied.

As John spoke, Rickey was already nodding and looking down at the table with a finger pointed at the bottom of a piece of paper.

"Please sign here."

The document, less than a page long, was adorned with the club's letterhead at the top and had Rickey's signature already present at the bottom, as well as Jerry's as a witness. It stipulated that the Cardinals would give John train fare back to Beckemeyer and seventy-five dollars for being the starting pitcher in their next game on September 28, payable upon the game's official completion and with no performance bonuses included. The contract also made clear that no implication of further employment with the team would be guaranteed beyond the twenty-eighth, nor would the Cardinals be responsible for anything that happened to John from the moment he signed his name.

The last line of the document, just above the place for John's signature, included one final clause.

"The St. Louis National Baseball Club is, and will be, held harmless from any injury resulting from the baseball actions of the party undersigned."

John wrote his name.

"And here again," Rickey said, uncovering the player's copy. Rickey returned attention to his cigar, wheeled back around to the desk that faced the wall, and shuffled some papers. "Mr. Tretiak will show you to your quarters."

The meeting was over. The scout and his new signee emerged from the building, back out onto Dodier Street.

"Hungry?" Jerry asked.

"Sure," John responded, not certain if he had enough money to pay for any sort of dinner. Hunger was a constant menace, gnawing at him regularly. He often sacrificed meals to ensure that Rose and Joseph had plenty to eat.

Jerry went back down Grand and took John to one of his favorite restaurants in the southwest part of town—Amighetti's on Wilson Avenue, where Jerry had gotten hearty Italian sandwiches since the place had opened in 1921.

Few words were exchanged as Jerry stared down to devour his salami hoagie, looking up only to request a refill of coffee from the server. John finished his plate of pasta quickly then looked around the room nervously, sipping his glass of water. He finally asked Jerry about his chances to remain with the Cardinals organization beyond tomorrow.

"What do I need to do to stick with the club?"

Jerry blurted out an abrupt laugh before another chomp of his sandwich. "Win."

John was becoming paralyzed with the tension. He felt the walls of all the big buildings in St. Louis, on every block, peering down upon him.

Riding north on Kingshighway, John leaned around Jerry to look at Forest Park, the place where the pitcher and scout had encountered each other long ago for the first time. Jerry paid no notice.

After a right turn, the pair arrived at the Forest Park Hotel a few blocks down, the place where John would stay for the night. Jerry still had said nothing. He stopped the car along the curb, handed John his bag, and finally spoke up.

"Let me be honest. I've always liked you from the first time I saw you pitch, and you seem like a good man. But this is probably a one-time deal.

Don't expect too much from this. I'll pick you up outside the locker room after the game tomorrow."

It was the same advice he had received from Bobby five years earlier, when his friend had dropped him off in the city for John's other life-changing opportunity.

With that, Jerry sped off without a wave.

Entering the hotel, John had never been in such a fine building. The lobby itself was so ornate that he had trouble finding the front desk. When the bellhop offered to carry his bag for him, John politely refused. He did not want his few possessions out of his sight.

Once inside of his room, the opulence continued to overwhelm him. To his left and right were expensive furniture, classic artwares, and gold-plated utensils. Though it was only eight o'clock, John turned out the lights and covered himself under the fine linens, not wanting to look at the extravagance surrounding him. He could not escape the thought of his crumbling house in Beckemeyer that meagerly sheltered his wife, child, and in-laws tonight, as he lay far from them.

After twenty minutes of staring at the ceiling, John knew of only one solution. He decided to take a walk and turn over the issues in his mind, just as he and his father did in Beckemeyer.

Roaming the dark, he reached the corner of Euclid and Lindell. To the west stood Forest Park; to the east, a bit farther down, was SLU at the intersection of Grand Avenue. He decided to turn left and wandered past the large, lovely houses on Lindell, the biggest he had ever seen. While not envious, he could not comprehend that people lived in such places.

After an hour, John felt he was sufficiently tired for sleep. Returning to the corner of Lindell and Euclid, he gazed eastward back toward SLU and beyond, toward the riverfront workplace of his father and great uncle and farther beyond toward Clinton County. "Good night, Sweetie," he was sure to say, as he always did.

Upon entering the hotel for the second time, John noticed a beer joint off one end of the lobby. He gave it a passing glance as he continued to the elevators. But out of the corner of his eye, a man and woman emerging from the bar caught his attention.

Both were well-dressed and flashed broad smiles as they waved to other people in the lobby who were calling out to them. The woman was wearing a flaming red dress that drew extra attention, while the man—John's equal in height, or perhaps an inch taller—wore a tailored suit with his long, sloping shoulders and arms running through it. The man was thin yet muscular, with large hands that dangled too far beyond the length of his dress shirt. He was showing a slight limp as he walked.

John smiled for a brief second when he finally recognized the person. In the next instant, however, he frowned, partially hiding himself behind a pillar near the corner of the lobby while hearing several people call out to the man.

"Diz!" they exclaimed.

John peeked out past the pillar. It was, indeed, Dizzy Dean.

Still laughing and shaking several hands, Dizzy had his arm around Patricia as the two sat down on a sofa. Others in the lobby, in respecting the couple's privacy, now drifted away back into the bar or out onto the street. Soon, the only people in the lobby at this late hour were the Deans, the clerks behind the front desk, and John, still peeking out from behind the pillar.

Gathering himself and tucking in his shirt, John walked over to them.

"Mr. Dean?"

Diz had just planted a big kiss on Pat's cheek. The greatest pitcher in baseball turned and looked at John, another wide grin shining through his face.

"Yep, I am."

"Not sure if you know me. I'm John Laufketter—you—I—when you—"

Dean's smile disappeared. He studied John up and down, with a cross look on his face.

John stared right back at him, unflinching, though his nerves now racing. He was readying himself for a fight. If the roles had been reversed and somebody appeared at the mine trying to take *his* job and possibly take food out of his child's mouth, John would have battled such a person.

But Dean's joviality spontaneously returned.

"Well, hellfire!" Dizzy exclaimed with a laugh. "You're *him!*"

John smiled back and nodded.

"Have a seat, John," Diz offered as he slid to the edge of the sofa, making a space in the middle between himself and his wife. Dean looked back at his bride. "Pat, would you excuse us for a bit?" Mrs. Dean nodded and disappeared, heading into the elevator and up to the couple's suite.

There sat the two of them, John Laufketter and Dizzy Dean, two pitchers for the St. Louis Cardinals. For the next twenty-four hours, however, the team's chances were in the hands of the former, not the latter.

John tried to be friendly. "You want a beer?" he offered Dean, not knowing what else to say.

"Naw, I don't drink. Never sat well with me. I think we should talk a bit, though. But not here. Let's go somewhere where folks won't see us. Word is already out on you. Someone might know who *you* are."

Dean got up, motioning for John to follow him. They walked out of the lobby and past the elevators, winding through the hallways and doors, which led them to the rear of the building and out onto the loading dock. They descended the steps and ambled down the back alley behind the hotel. Dean threw on his overcoat and fedora hat. John had none.

"How much time you got?" John asked him. "I can't believe I'm talking to you. There's so much I'd like to ask you about pitching—"

"Not much," Diz jumped in. "I need to get back to Pat, as she keeps pretty close tabs on me. I've got about ten minutes."

"That would be great," John said appreciatively. "I'm sorry about your injury. I'm just going to do the best I can tomorrow." With time short, he went right to the top of his list of questions. "What do you think pitching is all about?"

"Power and more power," Dean replied without hesitation. "Smart pitching, this so-called pitching to the weaknesses of hitters, is bunk. It's okay to know about a guy but do too much of that and you finally get to where you're outsmarting yourself. If you can get the ball over the plate with something on it, there's no call to be smart. That plate's only a few inches wide and that ballpark is as big as all get-out."

The authority, yet simplicity, with which Dean spoke about pitching amazed the newcomer.

"Watch batting practice and see how many balls are hit into the stands," Diz added, his finger pointing up in the air. "Not many. And in batting practice, the hitter knows what's coming, and there's nothing on the ball. So, how's he going to do it when you're wheeling 'em in there with smoke on 'em?"

John just smiled, bouncing his head in agreement.

"And another thing. I think pitchers are a better judge of what to throw than catchers. The pitcher's throwing it, ain't he?"

John was unable to disagree with that logic. They proceeded to discuss fastballs, curveballs, changeups, Hubbell, the Giants, and things for John to look for in the Cincinnati Reds batters tomorrow.

While talking, they had made three trips down the length of alley behind the hotel and back. They snuck back covertly in through the rear door after the fastest twelve minutes of John's life.

Another minute later, they entered the elevators. John's room was on the next floor up from the ground level, while Dean's suite was at the top of the building.

"I just want you to know, Mr. De—"

"Call me Jay."

"I want you to know, Jay, that I'm not trying to take your place, or anyone else's. I'm just a hayseed from nearby, a nobody from nowhere. But I'll do my best for Mr. Frisch and the others."

Dean shook his head. "It's okay, John. Baseball is made for country boys like us. Heck, I was just eighteen when Rickey found me in the pasture. When you go out there tomorrow, you show 'em what you got. You'll make your people proud no matter what, so don't worry about it. When me 'n Paul take the mound, we can feel our kin right there with us."

As the elevator door opened and John got off on the second floor, they shook hands. Before the door closed behind him, John turned toward Dean one more time, looking for any last morsel of advice he could acquire.

Dizzy sensed it and spoke up. "Just go out there tomorrow and pitch for *yourself*. Don't accept any guff from nobody. You're in charge on the mound. Take the white meat."

John retired to his bed, a mattress with clean sheets and the most comfortable on which he had ever rested. Tomorrow, he would make his major league debut four years to the day that Dean made his.

Still unable to comprehend the past six hours, at least he was now more at ease. He drifted off to sleep with the smiles of Rose and Joseph dancing through his head.

CHAPTER THIRTEEN

Despite sleeping soundly for several hours, John awoke in a startled state at five o'clock in the morning, thinking he had to get over to the mine. Not immediately recognizing his surroundings, he panicked as his wife and son were nowhere to be found in the dark room. After calming himself down, he had to force himself to get back to sleep.

At eight, John awoke again. Rubbing his eyes, he stumbled over to the sink to wash his face. He put on the same clothes he had taken off before going to bed, grabbed his duffel bag, and was out the door.

Jerry had written out directions for John to get to the ballpark. He was told to take the city bus eastward along Lindell all the way to SLU, at which point the 70 Grand streetcar would take him north from there the ballpark.

Rickey required that John be at the ballpark by noon, so that there was time to go over the Reds batting order with Frisch and the Cardinals starting catcher before the three o'clock game. However, since it was only 8:35 by the time he got to SLU, John was compelled to interrupt his itinerary and walk around the campus one more time, knowing he would likely never return.

He saw his old apartment, the West Pine Gym, and the academic buildings in which he had his classes. A larger sense of confidence took hold of him as he reflected upon the few months he had spent there, acknowledging the experience as some semblance of achievement.

Not wishing to tempt fate, John delayed no further. He beckoned the next passing of the 70 Grand streetcar and jumped on board. During his year at SLU, John could not afford to take the trolley anywhere, so it was a new adventure for him, like everything else in the past day. After a short distance, he could see the corner of the right field grandstand of Sportsman's Park up on the west side of the street. It was now only 10:30.

Exiting the streetcar, John fished through his pocket for the crumpled piece of paper containing Jerry's directions, for it also had instructions for finding the players' entrance at the ballpark. Walking halfway around the stadium, he finally found the entry with a guard on duty, who had risen from his chair well in advance in seeing the stranger approaching. He stepped in front of the entrance as John approached the gate.

"Sorry, players only," the guard said, with hand held up.

John said nothing in return but instead pulled Rickey's business card out his pocket to serve as his credential. Although the guard let him pass, John did not feel like he belonged.

Once through the gate, he stepped carefully straight ahead and saw the nondescript door with no signage through which he was directed to enter. Upon opening the door and before he saw anything, John was immediately engulfed by the unmistakable smell of perspiration, dirty flannel clothes, shower mold, and liniment oil.

At this early hour, there were only two players in the Cardinals locker room. One was right fielder Jack Rothrock, who was thumbing through the morning edition of the *Post-Dispatch*, and Buster Mills, a rookie backup outfielder who was working on a crossword puzzle that he had torn out of Rothrock's paper. Neither looked up when John walked in.

John scanned the room from right to left. He saw the famous names above the lockers—*Medwick . . . Martin . . . Carleton . . . Durocher . . . Walker . . .* but no Laufketter. He looked back and forth another time, and then again, but could not find the space assigned to him. John took a few more steps inside for a closer look at the room, which still revealed nothing. Rothrock now looked up for a moment from his newspaper and back down again.

Finally, another man appeared. He was one of the smallest adults, male or female, John had ever seen. The man had silently entered by way of the equipment cage, which stood adjacent to the locker room. Further down from the equipment cage was the manager's office, from which John heard voices behind the closed door.

Like Dizzy Dean the previous evening, the equipment man was the first person to smile at John so far that day. Twenty-six-year-old Butch Yatkeman had toiled in Sportsman's Park for ten years, first serving as the visitor's clubhouse boy before working his way up to overseeing the Cardinals' area.

"Hello," Yatkeman offered simply and amiably. Pointing his finger over John's back, he added, "Got you set up right over there."

"Over there" was a four-foot-wide space in the corner of the locker room, partly obscured behind a couple of bat bags on the floor. The space possessed one hook on the wall, which suggested to John that this was where temporary players were housed.

Sitting on the floor beneath the hook was a large piece of white cloth. Upon seeing it, Yatkeman sprang into action.

"Ooops," he blurted out on his way over to the corner.

Grabbing the cloth, he attempted to un-wrinkle it by snapping it in his hands a couple of times. Casually dusting it off, he replaced it on the hook.

It was the Cardinals home jersey number twenty-three, the one that had been issued to John.

The jersey had been worn a year earlier by former pitcher Allyn Stout, who also had donned number twenty-one before being traded to the Reds in a deal that had brought Durocher to the Cardinals. Although not being used recently by any player, it remained unwashed out of respect for the team's hot streak, just like the regulars' uniforms.

After departing for a moment, Yatkeman returned after a second trip back to the equipment cage.

"See if this fits," he said, handing a Cardinals cap to John. Unlike his jersey, it was brand new, gleaming white on top with red pinstripes and a red bill.

Yatkeman then bent down behind the bat bags that sat in front of John's space and began digging like a terrier after a bone. Underneath, he uncovered a three-quarters undershirt, a pair of white uniform pants (dirty like the jersey), a pair of sanitary socks (the only other new item provided to John), and red-striped stirrup socks. From his knees, Yatkeman carefully folded all the items and placed them on a shelf under the hook. Going over a checklist in his mind, he nodded while pointing a finger at what John was holding—his glove and his worn-out cleats, as the Cardinals would not provide these items. John excitedly put on the jersey right away, although the moment was less climactic than how it had been played out in his boyhood dreams.

By 11:15, he was already fully dressed for the game. While some players would change shirts after batting practice, this was the sole uniform being loaned to him for the day.

John was scheduled to meet with Frisch in forty-five minutes. He knew that the manager was in his office but debated on whether he should go and introduce himself. How much did Rickey or Tretiak tell Frisch about him, if anything at all?

Not knowing what else to do and not being greeted by anyone, John sat idly on a stool in front of his space in the corner. He looked across the room and saw the open space in locker number 13, the one Dizzy Dean always requested at home or on the road, thumbing his nose at superstition.

John spent the next half hour gently thumping his fist into his glove a couple hundred times, hardly looking up.

At three minutes before noon, Frisch emerged from his office. He placed his hands on his hips as he scanned the room, wearing his baseball undershirt but still in civilian trousers. Combing the room with his eyes, he found John in the corner. He summoned him with a flap of his hand.

Simultaneously, a large man with tobacco drooling out of his mouth also rose and made his way to Frisch's office. Bill Delancey smiled at John with a closed mouthful of Beech-Nut while extending his hand. After the handshake, the smile quickly disappeared.

"Have a seat," Frisch said to John after extending his own hand, not wasting time in introducing himself. He nodded to his assistants. "This here is Coach Wares. Over there is Coach Gonzalez. We need to go over a few things."

John, thinking he was perhaps supposed to take notes, searched for a pencil and paper. Frisch spoke up again while John was still looking around.

"We need this game, John," the thirty-seven-year-old manager said while leaning back in his chair, running his fingers through his thinning, graying hair. "I've heard good things about you. The best thing we can do now is to get you as prepared as possible. Let's talk about Cincinnati."

One by one, Frisch went down the Reds projected batting order for that afternoon, as well as those in reserve. John leaned over the notes that the coaches had compiled, taking in as much as he could process. As Frisch was reciting the litany of names—well known to John with his religious reading of *The Sporting News*—the task before him finally settled in, and a tremendous fear began to stir in his belly. John cringed when Frisch reached some of the names, such as Lombardi and Pool, but visibly recoiled when he spoke of Hafey and Bottomley.

Chick Hafey, suffering from an injury, had not been in the lineup for the past week. But the fearsome Jim Bottomley—like Hafey, another former Cardinal hero of the 1920s and the boyhood idol of John's best friend—would be batting cleanup in the Reds order.

When finished with all the Cincinnati hitters, Frisch tossed the lineup card aside on his desk. "One other thing," he concluded. "I don't want you to try and strike anybody out. I mean *nobody*. You've got good players behind you on defense. Make the Reds put the ball in play, and let your men help you out."

My men, John thought to himself. Sure, they would be behind him *physically* on the field. But would they be truly *behind* him?

When John opened the door and exited Frisch's office, he discovered that the locker room was now full of players, preparing for the Cardinals' round of batting practice to begin at one o'clock.

The room quieted slightly as John made his way back to his space while eyes shifted and followed him. He hoped that some signs of encouragement would be offered, such as a couple of pats on the back or a "Go get 'em." Nothing came.

After eyeballing the newcomer, the players returned to their conversations. After a win by Bill Walker the previous day, the Cardinals stood a mere half-game behind the Giants (who were idle that day) with three to play. Fully aware of the implications of the afternoon's outcome, the St. Louis players did not want to add to John's anxiety. But why was this guy being brought in? Pitchers Lindsey and Vance, in fact, seemed to be glaring angrily at the new hurler.

John sighed, continuing to sit in his small space in the corner of the locker room as he resumed the slamming of his fist into his mitt. Pepper Martin sensed the tension that John was feeling. "Don't worry 'bout the boys," Martin said while walking by, patting John on the shoulder. "They just don't trust outsiders. We've been a tight-knit group all year, and they'd be the same way if someone were sent here from Columbus. Pay no mind. Once the game starts, they'll all have your back."

John nodded, appreciating the sentiment.

"With the way things are these days, they just need that extra World Series money," Martin went on. "So do I, to be honest. We all have other jobs in the off-season just to pay the bills, so we really could use that little bonus."

John snapped his head in Martin's direction, concerned. "How *little* is it?" he wanted to know.

"I think it's about five or six grand for the winner," Martin said.

John hunched in his seat in angst. The responsibility being heaped upon him was almost unbearable. In addition to the pressure of winning the game for the Cardinals in their quest for the pennant, potentially losing his job in the mine, and then having to vie for a permanent roster spot in the Cardinals' organization to take the place of his mining job, John had been unaware that players got bonuses for appearing in the World Series.

The amount of postseason money that Martin mentioned was more than twice what John made in the mine in an entire year. He went from being anxious to having a sick stomach.

Frisch reappeared in the room. "All right boys, let's go," he commanded in summoning them to the field for batting practice. While the other players joked with each other while walking down the corridor from the clubhouse, John walked alone.

Down ahead of him in the tunnel, John could see the dugout steps that led up to the field. He stopped at the end of the corridor; he could not see the grandstand yet. John took a moment to stare out only upon the playing surface. The grass was not green as he had expected, and instead had been worn to an unsightly brown due to sun, drought, and overuse by two home teams, with mere flecks of green sprouting in random places.

Once inside the dugout, John's eyes raised upward from the playing field.

For the first time in his life, he imbibed the grandeur of the interior of Sportsman's Park in all its glory—the famous unknown cathedral from his youth. He examined it from left to right and then back again. The double-decked ballpark sprawled so far and wide that, to John, it looked twice as big as from the outside. The seats seemed to go on forever in all directions.

The ushers were already patrolling their assigned sections, unfolding and wiping down the wooden chairs and picking up leftover trash from yesterday's game. The gates had just opened, with a few fans starting to sprinkle their way inside the park. John soon noticed some children peeking over the roof of the Cardinals dugout, trying to get a glimpse of their heroes. None were looking at him, instead trying to get the attention of Martin and Durocher, who were sitting on the bench with their arms folded while having a leisurely chat.

Stepping out of the dugout, John turned in a complete circle and further absorbed the immensity of the place. He gazed at random places and things . . . at the buildings beyond the ballpark along Sullivan Avenue down the left field line, at the towering pillars holding the upper deck in place, at the faded green paint on the outfield wall, and at the flagpole that sat in play in far center field.

Wanting him to get a few swings in batting practice, Frisch placed John in a hitting group with Ernie Orsatti, Pat Crawford, and the slugger Medwick. As the first group got ready, John jogged toward the outfield, thinking he was required to shag some flies, but Frisch directed him back to the dugout bench, ordering him to take it easy.

Balls started whistling off the bats with the first group. "Bucket!" yelled Coach Buzzy Wares, laboring on the mound as the day's batting practice pitcher, requesting a fresh supply of baseballs. On cue, Jim Mooney ran in from his post behind a screen in shallow center field to refill Wares's basket on the mound.

When it was time for John's group at the plate, Crawford grabbed a bat first and was followed by Orsatti, Medwick, and finally the rookie pitcher. Each one received six throws from Wares in the first round.

On Medwick's sixth and final swing, he tapped a weak foul that trickled to the edge of the dead grass near the stands on the first-base side of the park. After watching the ball roll to a stop, John twirled his bat to display fake confidence and walked inside the cage to take his turn.

"What the hell you doin'?" Medwick barked at him, not moving from the batter's box.

John said nothing in return. But having grown tired of the cold reception he had been getting all day, he stared back. Thinking it was a challenge, Medwick got louder.

"You lookin' at somethin'? I'm done when I *say* I'm done. You got it, boy?"

John turned and walked away, still mute. He heard others laughing.

"Let's have another, Buzzy!" Medwick yelled to the mound. John heard an authoritative crack of the bat as Medwick shot a liner through the outfield to the delight of the team, but most of all himself.

John attempted to enter the cage for a second time. After taking his stance, Wares directed him to bunt the first pitch. John got the ball down but pushed it foul. "Okay, okay," Wares said, dismissing it quickly.

"Hit this one behind the runner," the coach next commanded, wanting John to drive the ball to the right side of the field. John did so expertly, sending a brisk two-hopper in the hole between first and second as Medwick, now on first base rehearsing baserunning situations, galloped to second.

Wares then informed John he could swing freely at the final four pitches. Gripping the bat tightly and overstriding anxiously, John fouled off the first two into the netting behind him. But he caught hold of the next one, driving it far down the left field line as the ball caromed off the wall.

"Comin' out!" Wares yelled, warning the fungo hitters that it was the final pitch and that John would be emerging from the cage.

Unlike the previous swings, John waited back on the last one, trusting his hands to be quick enough. Jumping on the ball at the last moment, he caught it on the fat part of the bat and could feel the horsehide give way to the wood. By the time he had taken three strides out of the batter's box, John, Medwick and everyone else watched as the ball sailed long and high toward left center field, carrying and carrying. Its voyage did not stop until it was over 450 feet from home plate, ending with a thunderous *BOOM* echoing off the Gem Razor Blades advertisement next to the scoreboard.

Curious heads turned back toward the batter, who was running out the play as if it were a potential double in digging around first in a maddened hustle.

Frisch gave John an approving nod from behind the batting cage and instructed him to retreat to the clubhouse until 2:30, at which time he would return to the field for his pregame warm-up regimen. Once back inside the locker room, John spent most of the time in a restroom stall praying to St. Anthony, still seeking the full restoration of his confidence.

Frisch and Rickey had done their best to conceal John's signing to the newspaper writers, to avoid the pitcher having to deal with any pregame interviews. Once the batting orders were released in the press box, however, the feeding frenzy began, as the scribes worked to uncover and disclose the identity of the stranger.

At 2:30, John left the clubhouse and walked back down the corridor toward the field, hearing the hum of the crowd as he got closer. Once he reached the dugout, he looked up and was surprised that many of the seats were still unoccupied, with the stadium perhaps only a quarter full. Walking down to the left field bullpen relatively unnoticed by the fans in the first few rows, he dropped his glove on the ground near the foul line and began nervously circling his arms to loosen up, followed by a slow jog out to the flagpole at the base of the center field wall.

Turning around at the pole, his scanned the entire park once again. As he did so, his eyes stopped at the pitcher's mound in the center of the scene, off in the distance. It was the place which, in a few hours, would determine John's fate—his own, as well as that of his family, the Cardinals season, the hopes of their fans—and, likely, whatever love or hatred the locals in Beckemeyer would have for him tomorrow.

When John jogged back to the left field foul line across the rock-hard grass of the outfield, he noticed Wares and Spud Davis were standing there waiting for him. Wares was wiping his sweat from batting practice with one towel and had another slung over his shoulder for the pitcher. In recent weeks, the hot-hitting rookie Delancey had taken over much of the work at catcher and was in the lineup today as well. Thus, Davis was charged by Frisch to handle John's warm-up throws.

Out of habit and ignorance, John never stretched before throwing. Taking one more run through the outfield, he finished with some basic calisthenics and arrived at the bullpen five minutes later, where Davis and Wares were still chatting. Wares took a spot behind the mound, while Davis squatted behind the plate. "Not too hard here, rook," Davis advised while spitting tobacco through his mask.

John flicked his glove forward to indicate a fastball was coming. In his smooth, easy delivery, he let one fly. Then another. Then another. And another, all having late movement, which impressed Davis. After about twenty pitches, Wares jumped in. "Hold it there," he said, flinging the towel onto John's shoulder. "That's good. How do you feel?" John, still afraid to say anything to anybody, nodded and shrugged.

Game time at three o'clock was now ten minutes away.

While walking back to the Cardinals dugout, John peeked into the stands a couple of times but was careful not to look beyond the first few rows. He figured it best to keep the game "small" and to limit distractions, imagining he was back at the Beckemeyer field where the bases were ninety feet apart, just as they were here in Sportsman's Park.

But at that moment, he smiled in recalling how the Beckemeyer field had the *ultimate* distraction—the beautiful face of Rose cheering him on that day just over four years ago, when he had tripped in rounding the third base bag. He wondered how she and Joseph were getting along.

As he approached the Cardinals bench, John looked to his left and saw the Reds over on the visitors' side along the first base line. Despite being in last place with a record of 52-96 the Reds, like the Cardinals, showed John what the self-assuredness of major leaguers looked like. Cincinnati outfielders Adam Comorosky and Harlin Pool had been sitting on the top step of their dugout, watching John return from the bullpen. As John was about to descend into the Cardinals' area, Pool grabbed a bat and pointed it right at him in a threatening manner. As John turned his head away, he could hear Pool and some of the other Cincinnati players laughing.

Trying to ignore the derision, John was happy to spot a familiar face on the third base side of the stands. Branch Rickey was seated in the second row, hunched over in what appeared to be a serious discussion with a gentleman in front of him. Like Rickey, the other man was impeccably dressed, donning a pristine white suit and hat that had a wide brim, and like Rickey's, the outfit complete with a neatly arranged bow tie. Fifty-year-old Harry Truman was enjoying a day at the ballpark but also was in the process of trying to grab more votes for his upcoming election for Missouri's United States Senator, the vote to take place just six weeks later on November 6 against Republican incumbent Roscoe Patterson.

The general manager never budged from his conversation with Truman, only offering John a quick but dismissive wave of his hand.

At five minutes to three, the umpires emerged from the screened gate behind home plate, as Frisch sent his captain Durocher out with his lineup card. Cincinnati manager Burt Shotton, another former Cardinal who had played for Rickey long ago when Branch had managed the team, brought out his own.

As the Cardinals got ready to take the field, there was still no one speaking to John. It was almost as if he was not even there.

Then, he received his first kind word since leaving the locker room. It came, ironically, from one of the men whose place he was taking.

"So, where ya' from?" Jim Mooney asked in a friendly tone.

"Not far from here; just over the river, really," John answered. Hearing himself say those words convinced him that his presence was probably mere convenience for the Cardinals.

But regardless of the reason he was at the corner of Grand and Dodier, it was his new workplace, and it was time to go to work. John took a long breath as he grabbed his glove off the steps and followed the rest of the Cardinals onto the field.

To his surprise, his emergence elicited little in the way of an audible response from the small crowd of barely 7,000 that had gathered. John could hear the scorecards shuffle, however, when his number twenty-three jersey became visible to them.

As he jogged out to the field, more kind words came from Pepper Martin, who ran alongside him in taking his spot at third base. "Don't you worry none, John," Martin said. "Throw 'em low and tight, and I'll knock 'em down when they come."

In approaching the pitching mound, John located the tiny object that would determine his life to come. The baseball sat there waiting for him, as it had many times before—but never under any circumstances like this.

John grabbed it and looked out toward center field, where the big, colorful signs bellowed back at him.

Always Buy Chesterfields
Falstaff
Hyde Park Beer
Sayman's Soap
Better Buy Buick!

John tried to keep his warm-up routine the same as he did back in Beckemeyer, even though this surely was no Clinton County League game. Still facing the center field wall, he drew another long breath, shrugged his shoulders, circled his right arm a few times, and wheeled around to face Delancey, who was already squatting in awaiting the first practice throw.

Also staring out at him was Cy Rigler, the home plate umpire for today's game. To John's left stood first base umpire Beans Reardon, while the legendary arbiter Bill Klem was over at third to complete the three-man crew. Rigler held out two fingers to John, indicating the warm-up throws were about to end.

At that very instant, a man in street clothes entered the field of play, sat down on a stool at the backstop, and closed the gate behind him. It was Jim Kelley, the de facto emcee at Sportsman's Park, wiping his brow and just returned from his journey to every corner of the stadium. While most of the big-league stadiums had installed electronic communication systems by 1934, Kelley was continuing his spectacular role he had performed since 1926—that of running around the ballpark with a megaphone to let the crowd know of the lineups and substitutions. Quite often during a game, play would resume before Kelley could inform the faraway bleacher observers of a pinch hitter or relief pitcher entering the contest.

Rigler nudged his chest protector aside and checked his pocket watch. It was now thirty seconds before three o'clock. Delancey caught the last pregame pitch and fired the ball to second base as John's lower lip started quivering. Despite the cooler temperatures, marks of perspiration had already formed on John's flannel jersey. Like with the imposing city buildings John had seen the night before as Tretiak drove him back to the hotel from dinner, it felt as if Sportsman's Park was swallowing John like a vast abyss, the stands inching upon him ever closer.

In getting ready to step on the rubber for his first big-league pitch, John suddenly realized he was facing southwest, which meant his back was mostly to Clinton County. It made him imagine—or at least hope—that all his family, friends, and neighbors were behind him, even those who always thought he had underachieved.

His hopes were true.

At George's, they were standing in the doorway and even out onto the sidewalk, all hoping to hear Laux's call of the game with the Philco turned all the way up. Word had quickly spread all over town of what was happening, and Beckemeyer was electrified with excitement.

Rose was not among them. There was no radio in their home, and needing to care for Joseph, she could not join the crowd at the bar. And besides, she figured, she could not bear to listen and hang on every pitch. So, just as with a day in the coal mine, she decided she would wait for John to get home and tell her about his workday.

John hesitated in taking the hill, causing Rigler to spring up with impatience. The pitcher peeked behind him back toward home once again. In doing so, John saw another advertisement on the scoreboard. It was for Alpen Brau beer, with the tantalizing word *COLD* printed underneath the brand name in big letters. The sign made him smile, recalling his father's beginnings as a beer brewer on the river.

It was now exactly a half century after his father had set foot in this city. He had arrived being able to speak no English; nonetheless, he had made a name for himself through his hard work. John was determined to do the same.

John was ready. At that moment, his favorite passage from literature popped into his mind from his schooling at St. Anthony's. It was a stanza from *Julius Caesar* that, for some reason, he had always memorized.

> *There is a tide in the affairs of men,*
> *Which, taken at the flood, leads on to fortune;*
> *Omitted, all the voyage of their life*
> *Is bound in shallows and in miseries.*
> *On such a full sea are we now afloat,*
> *And we must take the current when it serves,*
> *Or lose our ventures.*

The man unknown to nearly everyone in Sportsman's Park stepped carefully to the top of the mound, put his toe on the pitching rubber, and looked up for his first sign from Delancey. Rigler pointed at him, signaling "play ball."

First up for Cincinnati was Alex Kampouris, a cocksure twenty-two-year-old rookie who, in the past week, had taken over the starting spot at second base for the Reds.

As John rocked back into his windup, the stadium went silent in his mind. He knew all eyes were now upon him, just as they were back in the Clinton County League.

In the middle of his delivery, John closed his eyes. He envisioned it was not Delancey sixty feet away but Bobby.

His catcher.

CHAPTER FOURTEEN

John was tentative in letting the ball go, expecting the familiar pain to shoot up through his right shoulder once again.

But to his surprise, there was no discomfort. The ball was in Delancey's glove before John knew it. He started Kampouris off with a curveball, twisting it over the plate for strike one.

John did not question the pitches for which Delancey called; he threw whatever was requested. The next two offerings were both fastballs on the outside corner. The first Kampouris took for another called strike, and the second he flailed at feebly. Three pitches, three strikes.

The small crowd, which until now had studied John in silent curiosity, erupted in delight. The ball went around the horn on the infield after the strikeout as John made a long circle behind the mound. Taking the baseball back from Martin, his heart was now racing again. The quick success did nothing to calm him.

Next was Gordon Slade, the Reds shortstop. Slade attacked the first pitch, another curveball that, in the sweat of the pitcher's nervous hand, slipped out of John's grip and sailed higher than he wanted. Slade chopped at it, whizzing a sharp one just past John's ear. But the clever Durocher had positioned himself perfectly before the pitch and snagged the line drive in the tip of his glove before it could reach the outfield. Two batters, two out.

The Reds third baseman, Mark Koenig, was third in the lineup. Seven years earlier he was part of the New York Yankees' famed "Murderer's Row" lineup, which included Babe Ruth and Lou Gehrig. Delancey set up inside, and John obliged, running the ball in on Koenig's hands. Koenig swung defensively and was only able to bloop a weak pop-up to Frisch near the second base bag.

John Laufketter, a nobody from nowhere, had been perfect in his first inning at baseball's highest level.

Out of his respect for the game, John broke into a sprint off the field. But when he looked up and saw Frisch in the dugout, the manager had both hands extended out in front of him, wanting John to slow to a walk and conserve his energy. Durocher patted him on the backside on the way in, and Medwick did as well.

The Cardinals threatened to score with a couple of hits by Martin and Medwick in the bottom of the first but were unable to cross the plate.

Meeting John in the top of the second was Bottomley, the St. Louis legend admired by John and his friends since they were kids. The former National League Most Valuable Player could cover the whole plate with his bat and proved it by stroking a double into the left field corner, coming on a fastball that John had sent well off the outside part.

Pool, another left-handed batter, followed Bottomley. He had been a great surprise for the Reds as a rookie, coming into the game batting .326 and taking over a regular outfield spot for Cincinnati since late May. Like Bottomley, Pool had great bat control; he squared around and laid down a perfect sacrifice bunt, which John pounced on quickly to throw him out at first by a mere step as Bottomley headed to third. The strategy by Shotton surprised the Cardinals, suggesting the Reds may have been impressed with John's early showing. "Playin' for a run, huh?" Durocher chirped at his former Cincinnati teammates from his shortstop position. "Probably a good idea. You won't get much more."

The sixth spot in the Reds order saw Ernie Lombardi, the imposing young Cincinnati catcher who was nicknamed "Schnozz" for his notable nose, come to the plate. With his great size and strength, Lombardi reminded John of his Beckemeyer teammate Wagoner, and John, thus, did not want to get anything out over the plate whereby Lombardi could extend his arms.

But, unfortunately, he did so accidentally. Lombardi drove the ball deep out of the ballpark to left center, a rising homer that nearly touched the Griesedieck Beer sign high up on the scoreboard.

John recovered to retire Comorosky and Wes Schulmerich, but like Lombardi, both men hit John's pitches very hard as well—the first being Schulmerich's sinking liner to center field on which Orsatti had to make a diving catch and Comorosky's screaming shot to first that nearly took the glove off the right hand of Rip Collins.

As the Cardinals left the field, only limited damage had been done with the two runs scored on the Lombardi homer. Even so, every man who came to the plate that inning seemed to have his way with John. As he walked toward the St. Louis bench with his head down, John once again heard bits of laughter emanating from the Cincinnati side, which were even more audible with the disappointed silence in the stands, the fans doubting the ability of this unknown pitcher to keep the Cards in the game.

The third inning started roughly for John as well, as he already began to feel a hint of pain in his shoulder—pain that, during Clinton County League games, normally did not surface until the sixth inning or later. Pitcher Benny Frey and Kampouris posted back-to-back doubles on him, extending the Cincinnati lead to 3–0. John was then able to get both Slade and Koenig to fly out. But the presence of Bottomley struck fear in him once again. Sunny Jim belted a triple, this time to the gap in right center where he had hit them so many times as a Cardinal, increasing the score to 4–0 as restless boos were heard. The pejorative term "Busher!" was now being hurled toward the mound from the Cincinnati bench, as well as from some parts of the grandstand.

John looked skyward for a moment, holding some of the same doubt that the spectators held in him. He wondered what he was doing here. Pool came to the plate, again grinning at him.

Before starting his motion, John stepped off the rubber abruptly. For some reason, a horrifying image entered his mind.

He pictured Rose and Joseph on the streets of Beckemeyer, begging for food.

He shook his head to dispel the vision, returned to the rubber, and gripped the ball tightly. Something had to be done. He had to stand his ground.

On the very first pitch to Pool, John hit him squarely in the back with a blazing fastball. As soon as he let it go, John knew it was harder than any he had thrown during the summer in the CCL. Beans Garcia had always taught John to hit the batter in the upper middle of the back when such a statement was necessary. Never at the head to seriously injure nor at the legs to give the batter a chance to avoid it. If the ball was planted in the middle of the back, Garcia reasoned, it is almost inescapable.

There was no doubting John's intent. The laughing ceased on the Cincinnati side, as the Reds angrily lined up on the top step of the dugout. The snickering now came from John's impressed teammates behind him in the field. A small smile was now seen from the corner of John's face as well, his first of the day. He issued Pool a stone-cold stare as the batter struggled his way down to first base.

Five pitches later he got his revenge on Lombardi, striking him out on a devastating curveball. Leaving the mound, John slammed his fist into his glove three times in satisfaction. The boos suddenly turned to cheers in Sportsman's Park; for despite the 4–0 deficit, the crowd felt this unknown man was going to fight for them.

But in heading to the plate for his first major league at bat as he led off the Cardinals' third, John knew what was coming for him.

Frey, a five-foot ten-inch right-hander, had a dislike for the St. Louis organization. Originally with the Reds through 1931, Frey had spent less than a month in a Cardinals uniform in early 1932. At that juncture, Rickey considered him expendable with the development of Dizzy Dean, so the general manager sent Frey back to Cincinnati for a nominal cash payment.

Firing side-armed, Frey sailed his first pitch high and tight on John, nearly grazing his chin as John turned inward to protect himself.

Thinking that he would be hit no matter how many pitches it took, John was surprised to find the next offering from Frey to be out over the plate. Trying to swat it at the last moment, he swung wildly and nervously as the bat nearly sailed out of his hands with his continuing perspiration.

John anxiously swung at the third pitch as well, pulling off a curveball on the outer edge. He tapped a light rounder to the charging Koenig at third but made it a reasonably close play at first with his hustle down the line.

In crossing back across the field, John had noticed that, since his hitting of Pool, the derision coming from the Reds dugout had essentially ended.

In the fourth inning, the Cardinals—rejuvenated by John's effort—finally got on the board. Medwick drove a ball on the outside corner over the wall to the deepest part of center field for a home run. And in the fifth, they inched closer. After Durocher led off with a single that bounced over Frey's head and into center field, John followed with a perfect sacrifice bunt and was congratulated when returning to the dugout. Martin followed with a triple to push across Durocher and scored himself on the same play, as Kampouris's relay throw sailed high and wide of Koenig at third, bounding into the stands and sending Pepper home. The Cards now trailed by a single tally at 4–3.

And their new pitcher was settling in, as the Reds started going down at the plate in quick order. The grunts John issued with his pitches, which had been met with teasing by the Cincinnati players earlier in the day, now grew louder.

With two out in the seventh, he went right after Bottomley, challenging him to hit a fastball on the inner half. The slugger, unable to extend the bat, bounced meekly to Collins at first. It was the first time John had gotten Bottomley out all day, as he had now retired nine batters in a row.

Despite his run of success, John left the mound grimacing as he looked at the sky. His shoulder was burning in pain, and his jersey was soaked with sweat. Even so, he was rejuvenated when hearing the crowd work itself into a frenzy in cheering for him.

A scoreless Cardinals' seventh brought Pool to the plate to start the Reds' eighth inning. John induced him to pop up in foul ground to Delancey for ten men retired in a row.

Lombardi then singled to end the streak, as John—now showing evidence of fatigue—uncorked a wild pitch to the backstop with Schulmerich batting. The Cincinnati right fielder then singled, setting up a potential insurance run for his team on third with one out. But on the next pitch, a sinking fastball was tapped back to John by Comorosky. John leapt on it and launched a throw to second base, even though Durocher had yet to arrive. Like a quarterback leading a receiver perfectly in a football pass, John's toss met Leo in stride, as the shortstop glided across the base while snagging the ball, dragged his foot over the bag, and got himself airborne to avoid Schulmerich while firing to Collins at first to complete the double play. The crowd roared once again, as John and the Cardinals remained within a run of evening the game.

Orsatti was first to start the Cardinal eighth, and he took four straight wide ones from Frey and walked. But then Durocher, normally a skilled bunter, failed to get the ball down and popped up as the potential tying run remained at first base.

John did not follow Durocher out to the on-deck circle, as he expected Leo to successfully complete the sacrifice and move Orsatti to second, thus paving the way for a pinch hitter. But now, with one out and a man on first, Frisch—believing that John was better than anyone else in the bullpen for one more inning—let him bat. The manager had a plan in mind.

John looked down at Frisch in the coach's box. The skipper flashed the sign, and on the first pitch, Orsatti took off for second. John used an inside-out swing, just as he had done earlier in the day in batting practice. He drove a ground ball through the hole on the right side vacated by Kampouris, who was going over to cover second base on the steal attempt. The ball rolled safely into right field, as Orsatti raced to third while John stood at first with a single for his first major league hit, representing the potential winning run if he could make it all the way around the bases.

From his box seat behind the Cardinals dugout, Branch Rickey threw his head back and yelled his admiration. He then tapped Truman on the shoulder, still in the first row in front of him. "Man may penetrate the outer reaches of the universe," Rickey said to the senatorial candidate above the roar of the crowd, "but for me, the ultimate human experience is to witness the flawless execution of the hit-and-run."

The momentum was instantly suffocated, however, when Pepper Martin struck out, leaving it up to Rothrock with the tying run on third with two out.

On a 2-2 count, Frey held onto a curve too long and it bounced far in front of Lombardi, the ball skidding fifteen feet off to his right. Sensing an opportunity, the fleet-footed Orsatti—a stuntman in Hollywood for his off-season employment—dashed home and slid across the plate just out of the reach of the Reds catcher, who dove at him in vain with the ball on the tips of his throwing hand fingers. John scooted on down to second base, where he stood looking back at the roaring fans behind home plate, just like in Beckemeyer, with his hands on his hips.

"That's the Cardinal way to score a run!" Rickey proclaimed to Truman about the sequence of events, having to yell over the stadium noise once again.

Frey got Rothrock to fly out on his next offering, as the pitcher flailed his arms in disgust in being one pitch too late. The game entered the ninth inning tied, 4–4.

Despite being permitted to bat for himself in the bottom of the eighth, John looked down the foul line at the bullpen before emerging from the dugout. To his disbelief, there was no one warming up. This was his game.

He did his best to put things out of his mind. . . .

About the absolute exhaustion that had now set in—

About the unrelenting pain in his shoulder, which throbbed with every movement of his upper body—

About the implications of this game for him, the Cardinals, and the city—

And about Rose and Joseph back in Beckemeyer, whom he had not seen for the past twenty-four hours, nearly twice as long as he had ever gone without being with them—

It was the mental fatigue that gnawed at him the most, a culmination of the surreal events of the past day.

Leave nothing behind.

Shotton inserted pinch hitter Sparky Adams to start the Reds' ninth. Adams was yet another former Cardinal who had been shipped over to Cincinnati, and yet another part of the May 1933 trade that had sent Durocher to St. Louis.

John drew a deep breath, shrugged his shoulders, and went back to work. His first two pitches had virtually nothing on them, balls that drifted high and wide to put Adams ahead in the count. The next one floated on in the inner half of the plate, and Adams sent a line drive to left field for a clean single. On the very first pitch to Kampouris, Adams bolted for second, stealing it safely.

Everyone in the ballpark now expected another bunt as Frisch arranged the defense. When Kampouris turned slightly in the batter's box, Collins and Martin came charging in from their respective positions as Frisch rotated over toward first. But at the last moment, Kampouris pulled his bat back as the Cardinal defenders stopped in their tracks. He took a swing with his hands choked up high on the stick and dumped a soft single to right field. By the time Rothrock had chased it down, Adams was already nearing the plate. When he touched it, the Reds had reclaimed the lead, 5–4.

Frisch called time and made his way to the mound. He held out his hand as he got within a few steps of the pitcher.

"Let's have the ball, John," the manager said. "You fought a good fight today."

But John kept it in his glove. "Let me get you out of this inning," he responded.

Frisch grumbled, looking at the ground. "Okay," he agreed. "I'll give you one more hitter, and we'll see how it goes."

Slade grounded a hard one to Martin at third, which Pepper let bounce off his thick chest. With no chance for the double play, Martin picked it up and unleashed a rocket over to Collins for the first out. Afterwards, Frisch stayed put.

Koenig then swung at the first pitch thrown to him and drifted a long fly ball back toward left, which Medwick caught in front of the Alpen Brau beer sign for two quick outs.

Next was Bottomley. All waited for Frisch to go to the mound again, with the southpaw Mooney available to face the left-handed Reds bomber.

But no change was made. John reached back for everything he had on his first pitch, a fastball, hoping that it would catch the strike zone and that Bottomley would hit it to one of his defenders. John, in immense pain and fatigue, did not think he could muster even a second pitch.

The pitch was a most hittable one, thigh-high to the batter with little movement and over the middle of the plate. Bottomley saw it plainly and jumped on it, nailing a drive that he would later say was among the hardest he had ever hit. It was a screaming liner that exploded off his bat, headed right back at the pitcher. John, in finishing his delivery, was bent over to the left side of the mound. He was defenseless.

But instinctively he raised his left arm, covering his face. The split-second reaction kept the missile from shattering his skull, as the ball rested in his glove in nearly the same instant he heard Bottomley make contact. The batter took two steps out of the box and was stunned with the result. Bottomley tipped his cap to John, as the pitcher and his team departed the field with the third out.

Part of the scattered crowd on the third-base side of Sportsman's Park—now roughly half of the 7,000 figure at the start of the day—went into sudden motion. A hundred people or so scrambled down toward Cardinals dugout and, despite the Cardinals falling behind again, gave John a standing ovation. He tipped his cap in appreciation.

J. Roy Stockton, Sid Keener, and the other St. Louis writers up in the press box had been feverishly pecking at their typewriters all afternoon, but the intensity of their work now accelerated. The identity of the mysterious pitcher had finally been unmasked in the fifth inning, as word arrived on what had transpired in the past day.

Warming up in the Reds bullpen and ready to take Frey's place on the mound in the bottom of the ninth was Stout, who had been yet another promising pitching prospect from Rickey's minor league system. He had won eighteen games for Houston in the Texas League in 1930, just as Dean arrived. Stout would face the heart of the Cardinals order in Frisch, Medwick, and Collins, who came into the game hitting .302, .317, and .331, respectively.

But after two pitched balls that went well wide of the strike zone, Shotton headed to the mound. He wanted the left-hander he had warming up, as the switch-hitter Frisch had batted only .258 against southpaws during the season.

As Frisch stepped out of the batter's box and looked down the right field line, he realized his Cardinals were not alone in having a newly signed mystery pitcher. Jogging in from the bullpen after tearing off his warmup jacket was Tony Stoecklin, recently purchased by Cincinnati from the Braves and who had challenged the entire Cardinals bench to a fight back in July. Stoecklin grabbed the ball off the mound, took only four warm-up pitches, and aggressively went right after the St. Louis hitters with his devastating two-seam fastball.

Anxious to tie the game quickly, Frisch swung wildly at the next three pitches, all of which veered screwball-like out of the strike zone off the outside corner, as he struck out for only the eleventh time all year.

Medwick, as was his custom, swung at the first pitch as well. He drilled a hard grounder to the left of Kampouris that seemed destined for right field. But the second baseman stretched out in a dive, grabbed it, got up, and threw to Bottomley in time for two quick outs.

The Cardinals final hope, Collins, also went down quickly, skying a high fly ball to Comorosky in shallow center field. The Cardinals lost, 5–4, falling a full game behind the Giants in the standings.

John joined the other players in stepping out of the dugout for a moment upon the game's completion. He looked over and saw Rickey, still sitting in his seat in the second row while Truman had since departed. John made his way slowly over to him, afraid of what Rickey would have to say about the loss.

"Thank you, John," the general manager simply said, shaking hands with him.

"I'm sorry I couldn't get you any results, sir," John replied.

Rickey nodded understandingly but then returned to his businesslike speech. "Mr. Breadon and I will meet and decide where we go next. If your services are required further, we will let you know."

John was hoping for a more conclusive statement one way or the other, but he did not press the issue. He went back toward the dugout, anxious to shower and get on the train back out to Beckemeyer. The players who remained on the field also shook John's hand, and again, the fans on the third-base side started cheering him wildly, despite the defeat.

Finally, he was permitted to descend the dugout steps. Just as the box seats left his view, something caught his eye in the stands.

It was a man weaving down the stairs of the grandstand toward the field, a lone figure swimming against the mass of the other spectators who were walking up toward the concourse to exit the ballpark.

John thought nothing further of the person. But then he heard the voice, a tongue shriller than all the music.

"Johnny!" the man cried out.

John stopped on the steps, peddling back up and looking out over the dugout roof. Shading his eyes with the western sun now setting through the stadium, John identified the man and hurried to meet him at the railing.

"Bob!" John cried out.

"How did you—Where—What are you doing here?" the pitcher uttered, exasperated in exhaustion and surprise.

"Do you think I would miss this? Well, I almost did—"

John pointed over the top of the upper deck of the third base side of the stadium. "Meet me out there."

After receiving more appreciation from the Cardinals in the locker room and an ice pack taped around his shoulder, John showered, put his street clothes back on, grabbed his cleats and glove, and made his way back out through the players' gate. Looking in all directions, he finally found Bobby, who was staring in awe at the top of the grandstand, imbibing the size of the stadium—just as John had done before taking the mound that day.

John smiled broadly as he approached him. "Well, well. What brings you here?"

"You know what the hell what."

"So, you saw it?"

"Just the last two innings. With the broadcasts now back on, I was listening at a place over at Newstead and Laclede. It's a spot I like to go, near where I live."

Bobby's eyes trailed off for a moment with his voice. Then he continued. "It was loud in the bar, so I didn't even know it was you until the seventh inning. I knew the Cards had called up somebody to pitch the game. But when I heard Laux talk about some rookie getting his shot, that's when I stopped listening—just another guy getting his chance besides me. But then I heard your name, and I couldn't believe it. I started telling everyone in the place, 'He's my pitcher!' They know I'm from Becky, but they all laughed at me. Didn't believe me, of course. I sprinted out of there and got a cab here. There's no way I would've missed it."

Bobby stopped himself again. He pointed up the block toward a place called Palermo's at the corner of Spring and Sullivan, across from the left field corner of the stadium. "Could we go over and sit a bit?" he asked John.

Palermo's was a popular spot among baseball fans, a mere forty steps away from the left field gate. It had spent its first ten years as a Sicilian restaurant and bakery. But when Prohibition had ended, Paul and Mary Palermo, with help from their sons Jimmy and Joe, had immediately began serving drinks as well. On game days, a sidewalk grill featured flame-broiled meats and onions, while inside, the counter at the cash register held different kinds of tobacco and chewing gum. It was also one of the few places in the neighborhood to have "refrigerated air," although it was not needed on this cool September evening.

The postgame crowd inside Palermo's, as it was in the ballpark, was sparse. John and Bobby were mostly alone as they entered, picking a spot at the bar in the middle of the stools. "Two Griesediecks," Bobby directed the bartender.

They grabbed the bottles and saluted each other, wasting little time in pouring them down. The beer was ice cold, melting inside John's parched throat. Not having indulged the expense at George's, it was the first beer he had tasted in nearly a year. After each of them had a long gulp, something needed to be said. John started.

"What happened to you, Bob?"

His friend began his journey of the past five years.

After being released from the Tigers, Bobby had been ashamed to go back to Clinton County. Hating the idea of working in the mines, he had figured he might as well come to the city for good. He had done so and worked odd jobs but none for any more than a few months at a time.

"There was just no way I could go back to the county," he said. "I mean, I was supposed to be the guy to get out of Beckemeyer and do something. I *can't* go back."

John slammed his bottle on the counter in sudden anger.

"That's bullshit. *Supposed to get out.* What the hell does that mean? You're telling me *that's* why you're so embarrassed to go back to Beckemeyer? Because the Tigers released you, and you don't want to dig coal?"

Bobby kept looking down at his bottle before speaking up. "No, there's more. You remember Sally Verhoeven?"

"Yeah," John responded, calming down. "She was a year or two behind us at St. A's, I think."

"Well, when I first got back to Beckemeyer from Texas, she and I got together. You were already gone, and I had no one else to talk to. Outside of my father, she was the only one who would listen. I convinced her to run off with me, and we eloped to St. Louis. But over time, she could see how bitter I was, that I wasn't doing anything to move forward with my life.

"I found out too late that it's okay to remember the past, but not to *live* there—that's what I was trying to do . . . make believe like I was still playing, like I *could* play again. Then, when another one of my jobs fell through—the same one for the third time, actually—that was it. I couldn't take it anymore, not being able to support her. I just up and left her. I told myself that she was better off without me, and that's how I justified it. I didn't want her standing in the soup line alongside me. Thankfully, we don't have any kids. But I lost all my confidence. That was it. I just quit on her.

"Then, I spiraled further. I couldn't find any work at all. I got involved with loan sharks. Last year, a bunch of goons jumped me in an alley off Washington Avenue. One guy punched me several times, and another had me down on the ground with a knife at my throat, saying that if I didn't square my ledger with the boss within forty-eight hours, he was coming back to kill me.

"I told myself, 'No more.' I paid this guy what I owed. The next day, I walked into the CCC office—they got me my first government job, and I have been saving my pennies ever since."

John pressed his lips in an approving smile. He noticed that Bobby was more decently dressed and groomed than he ever remembered him.

"I've forgiven myself," Bobby continued. "It does me no good to stay angry. It took me way too long to figure out that I get nothing out of it. All my anger all these years has never gotten me one damn thing. 'The game cheated me,' I used to tell myself. Carey Selph, Homer Peel, the injury, the Cardinals, the Tigers, baseball, St. Louis. . . . I could find blame anywhere I could point a finger, except in the mirror.

"An old guy I played with, Joe Cobb, tried to tell me the way it really was. But I wouldn't listen. I was young, stupid, and thought I had all the answers. And I never forgave baseball. Maybe I haven't even totally forgiven it yet.

"But today, baseball and life were *perfect*. It was like a dream when I realized they were talking about *you* on the radio. By the sixth inning, I was out of that bar on Newstead, and by the seventh, I was at the ballpark.

"Then, when I saw you battling Bottomley to stay alive in the ninth, with blood and sweat and dirt all over your jersey—your *Cardinals* jersey—I was never so damned proud of anyone in my life."

John just smiled back at him, not knowing what to say. Bobby said it was a perfect day, and the more John thought about it, it was. He realized that, despite losing the ballgame, he had won a victory for both of them.

"But it's okay," Bobby went on. "Now I've got good, steady work with the WPA. We're building a new school down off Weber. And, you know what? The work is all above ground. That's probably the main reason I stayed out of Becky. I sure as hell wasn't gonna dig coal for the rest of my life."

At that point, the bartender, who was stocking a cooler at the other end of the counter, laughed to himself and shook his head. "You a coal miner?" the bartender asked Bobby.

"No, but my father is. And so is he," Bobby answered, motioning toward John.

John—whom the barkeeper did not recognize from the day's events and who could have easily joined the discussion—said nothing. He just sat, listened, and smiled again. *This was vintage Bobby*, John thought. He would talk to anyone, anytime, about anything.

"Where about you from?" the bartender finally asked.

"Not far," Bobby replied. "In Illinois. Clinton County."

"No kidding. I dug up some of that same rock myself. I'm from Willisville, south of you guys about fifty miles."

"Why'd you leave?" Bobby felt compelled to ask.

"Just wanted something different."

"What about home?"

"What about it?"

"Don't you miss it?"

"What for?"

Bobby shrugged his shoulders as the barkeeper continued.

"Willisville is fine, but home doesn't really matter," the man said as he wiped beer glasses. "Home is where you hang your hat. If you work hard, you can make a success of yourself anywhere. In the city, in the country, wherever you choose. Life is pretty much the same all over."

Work is an honor, John thought to himself, agreeing with the sentiment.

John and Bobby downed the rest of their beers. Dusk was coming over the city as they emerged from the tavern. The imposing size of the stadium across the street startled both men once again.

They walked slowly down Spring Avenue along the third-base side of the ballpark. Tretiak, who had promised John a ride to the train station after the game, was nowhere to be found. John was on his own to get to Union Station for the train back to Beckemeyer.

Turning left on Dodier down the first-base side of Sportsman's Park, Bobby continued to stare up at the roof. "You've never been to a game here before today—have you?" John realized.

"Nope, this was the first one," Bobby admitted. "It was all that bitterness that kept me away. Wanted absolutely no part of it. Even just last week. Even yesterday."

John looked for another comforting word. "Well, it's just a game," he suggested. It was a phrase he often used after a ballgame, but only when his team lost.

He then corrected himself.

"No, it's a *great* game, Bobby. Playing pro ball or not playing pro ball, it doesn't matter. It's not *those* things that make it great. It's sharing it with your family, your friends, and your teammates."

John stopped in the middle of the sidewalk, grabbed Bobby, and turned him to face him.

"Sharing it with your *catcher*!"

Bobby smiled, understanding.

"You make the game great by making it your *own*," John continued, "By making it whatever you want it to mean."

They turned right onto Grand Avenue and walked twenty blocks south, all the way down to SLU. John's shoulder, despite the ice treatment, throbbed each time his right foot hit the ground—but he didn't care. They talked about the old days in town—about St. Anthony's, pickup games against guys from Germantown at the ball field, Father Schweighart, and Beckemeyer life in general. John steered clear of mentioning the Clinton County League and the success the Becky team had enjoyed over the past five years, as he did not want his friend to feel like he had missed out.

They finally reached Olive Street. Although many people who had attended the Cardinals game were on the streetcars and the sidewalks as they passed by, few of them recognized John, even with the melting icepack still slung on his shoulder.

"Well, I need to get back," John said, looking for a cab to Union Station. After a moment, he added, "You wanna come back with me?"

Bobby shook his head. "I still can't, John, I'm sorry. I'm not ready. I just *can't* go back there."

John put his hand gently behind his friend's neck. "You *can*, Bob. It's all right. But that's up to you, and nobody else."

The two shook hands as men do but decided it wasn't enough. They hugged each other tightly, not wanting to let go before Bobby finally started west and waved a final time, walking back to his place in the Central West End neighborhood of the city. Just as he had five years earlier, he was leaving John there on the SLU campus. But this time, both he and John felt better about things. *All* things.

John looked in his pocket and noticed the return ticket to Beckemeyer was for the last train at 8:45 p.m. He therefore postponed his search for a taxi, as there was plenty of time to wander around the university some more.

He grabbed a cup of coffee at the student union, sitting in the same chair where he used to read Stockton's columns in the *Post-Dispatch* about the Cardinals games each day. The late edition, which covered the day's game, was not yet out. He wondered what it would say.

When the cab finally dropped him off at Union Station for his train out to Clinton County, John purposely took a seat as far away from others as possible. Nonetheless, he could still hear people's lament of the Cardinals' loss that day, which threatened their pennant hopes, unaware that the anonymous man sitting by himself was the pitcher charged with that loss.

After crossing the bridge, however, John smiled out the window, no longer bothered by the conversations. With a seat next to the window, he looked down upon the tracks—the very same tracks his father had built and the tracks that would take him home.

He had left nothing behind in St. Louis. Giving it all that he had, John had proven to himself he could compete at baseball's highest level. That was enough for him, regardless of the outcome. He wasn't just another guy from the county.

And he was done with baseball. John Laufketter had lost the last game he ever pitched for Beckemeyer in the Clinton County League, and he had lost the last game he ever pitched for St. Louis in the National League. But he was at peace with it. Coal mining in Beckemeyer was just fine, if that was what he wanted to do and if there was a job still waiting for him. But if not, that was fine as well. The words of his English teacher from high school once again rang in his ears, as John recalled the final lines of Milton's *Lycidas*.

> *At last he rose, and twitch'd his mantle blue:*
> *To-morrow to fresh woods, and pastures new.*

Turning in his seat, John's shoulder burned in pain once again from his day's work—as it often did after a day in the mine. But hearing the train engine quickly soothed him once again, as it always did. *Work is an honor.*

When John departed the train in Beckemeyer, there was no welcoming party for him. Most people in town had assumed he had signed a long-term contract with the Cardinals and was leaving Becky for good.

As he stepped down from the train car into the Clinton County night, John noticed the wind was suddenly swirling, suggesting perhaps another dust storm was on its way. It occurred to him, strangely, that the wind had been quiet all day during the game.

He walked past George's, where more noise was heard inside than usual, even for a Friday night. He was tempted to stop in for a moment but continued toward home.

John's heart raced as he turned onto Randolph Street. The light was on the kitchen. The silhouette of a beautiful, dark-haired girl floated toward the front door. She was smiling at him. Of course, she had heard what happened.

"I'm proud of you, Big Guy!" he could hear through the Beckemeyer darkness as he came up the walk.

As always, his favorite part of the day was when he arrived home from work.

John permitted himself to sleep past five o'clock the next morning. In no hurry, he decided he would make his way over the mine at some point to check on his job status.

When he got out of bed, John went out on the porch and looked out over Beckemeyer. He watched as the first train of the morning was approaching down the tracks, his second-favorite part of every day.

At the train stop in Beckemeyer, the newspapers were thrown off in bundles early each day, on the same spot where John had been dropped off a few hours earlier. Getting there early before most of the town was up, he walked over and picked up the morning edition of the *Post-Dispatch*. Flipping to the sports section first as he always did, John found the box score from yesterday's game:

	1	2	3	4	5	6	7	8	9	R	H	E
CIN	0	2	2	0	0	0	0	0	1	5	12	1
STL	0	0	0	1	2	0	0	1	0	4	8	0

Cincinnati	AB	R	H	RBI
Kampouris 2b	5	1	3	2
Slade ss	5	0	0	0
Koenig 3b	5	0	0	0
Bottomley 1b	5	1	3	1
Pool lf	2	0	0	0
Lombardi c	4	1	2	2
Schulmerich rf	3	0	1	0
Comorosky cf	4	0	1	0
Frey p	3	1	1	0
a-Adams ph	1	1	1	0
Stout p	0	0	0	0
Stoecklin p	0	0	0	0
Totals	**37**	**5**	**12**	**5**

St. Louis	AB	R	H	RBI
Martin 3b	4	1	2	1
Rothrock rf	4	0	0	0
Frisch 2b	4	0	0	0
Medwick lf	4	1	3	1
Collins 1b	5	0	0	0
Delancey c	3	0	0	0
Orsatti cf	3	1	1	0
Durocher ss	4	1	1	0
Laufketter p	3	0	1	0
Totals	**34**	**4**	**8**	**2**

a – batted for Frey in 9th
E: Kampouris (6, throw)
2B: Bottomley (31), Frey (1), Kampouris (2)
3B: Bottomley (12)
HR: Lombardi (10, 2nd inning, one on base)
SB: Adams (3)
SH: Pool
SF: Comorosky
HBP: Pool (by Laufketter)
Team LOB: 9

3B: Martin (12)
HR: Medwick (18, 4th inning, none on base)
SB: Martin (23)
SH: Laufketter
Double Plays Turned: 1
Team LOB: 10

Pitching

Cincinnati	IP	H	R	ER	BB	SO	HR	WP
Frey (W, 12-15)	8	8	4	3	6	5	1	0
Stout	0	0	0	0	0	0	0	0
Stoecklin	1	0	0	0	0	0	0	0

St. Louis	IP	H	R	ER	BB	SO	HR	WP
Laufketter (L, 0-1)	9	12	5	5	1	7	1	1

Pitches-Strikes: Frey, 113–67; Stout, 12–8; Laufketter, 127–76
Umpires: HP—Cy Rigler, 1B—Beans Reardon, 3B—Bill Klem
Attendance: 7,243   Time of Game: 2:16

Two days later, on the very last day of the National League schedule, the Cardinals clinched their spot in the World Series against the Detroit Tigers. Returning from his injury, Dizzy Dean shut out the Reds 9–0 in front of over 35,000 at Sportsman's Park, five times the number of people who had seen John pitch in his place forty-eight hours earlier.

"Dizzy Dean became king of St. Louis yesterday," proclaimed the *Globe-Democrat* about the clincher. "Thousands of people surged onto the field, many seeking autographs from players. Others went to the mound and rubbed their feet on the rubber from which Dizzy pitched. A group of policemen and firemen rushed out and formed a cordon about him and hustled him away to the showers."

Afterwards in the locker room, one Cardinal was solemnly grateful for all the blessings the season had brought, including those from the most unlikely of places. "Manager Frisch was very quiet," James Gould of the *Post-Dispatch* had noticed. "In a few words, he thanked everybody who contributed for their efforts."

CHAPTER FIFTEEN

July 18, 1963, was a tranquil, warm Thursday in Clinton County. Unlike most summer days in the area, the temperatures were mild for the time of year. The corn was getting high, and walleye and channel cat fishing was in full swing on the rolling Kaskaskia River.

Just before six o'clock in the evening, a man was driving his car along North Fourth Street in Breese. He slowed to a stop in front of a motel and turned to his fifteen-year-old son Brad in the passenger seat. "Seen enough for today?" The driver smiled, gesturing toward the building as their place to rest. Brad nodded.

The past few hours had encompassed the first time John, now fifty-two, had been back in Southern Illinois in nearly three decades. Several factors had kept him away; the duties of raising a family 300 miles to north kept him busy, but there was also the slight embarrassment of adding a few pounds, as he was no longer the fit athlete whom all would have remembered.

But it was time. He and Brad had left their home near Chicago early that morning, a trip they had planned and eagerly anticipated for months. They were on their way to the Mickey Owen Baseball School in Southwest Missouri, which had been opened four years earlier by the former major league catcher bearing its name. The school offered young players aged eight to eighteen intensive training in the fundamentals of the game. Brad, heading into his sophomore year of high school, was going to spend a week there. He had just acquired his learner's permit to drive and asked his father if he could handle a portion of the road along the way, to which his father had agreed.

John and Rose had welcomed Brad to the family long after Joseph and a daughter, Marie, had arrived, and their youngest child had long been excited about the trip, the first one that he and his father had taken by themselves. Brad was most interested to see Beckemeyer, about which he had heard so many stories.

In early 1935, just a few months after his lone major league appearance with the Cardinals, John had moved the family out of Beckemeyer. The day after returning from St. Louis, he had discovered that the foreman's job at the Beckemeyer mine, previously offered to him, was still John's for the taking. Yet his fears about the future were proven true.

With the ban on soft Southern Illinois coal being enforced in St. Louis and with new, competing forms of energy in hydroelectric power and natural gas, the Beckemeyer facility downsized its operations in the coming year. A large percentage of the workers would be dismissed in 1935, while others (with more seniority) were offered positions at the Centralia mine. Centralia was a twenty-two mile commute each way, making the trip for an impoverished Beckemeyer resident difficult, even if one was among the lucky handful to be chosen. John was assured by company executives he would have the same foreman's job in Centralia. But as part of the deal, he would also be required to log more hours of regular labor in the mine. John agreed to the terms but also began formulating other plans immediately.

He waited for the winter to thaw. In March 1935, John sold the house on Randolph Street at a significant loss. He bought an old truck from a man in town and loaded as many family belongings onto it as possible, while selling some others. He, Rose, and Joseph, the latter nearing two years of age, climbed in and drove an hour and a half south, settling in the small city of Carbondale.

A few weeks later in April, the worst dust storm the nation had yet seen passed through Clinton County, causing further devastation to those in the area.

Transferring his old credits from SLU, using up most of their savings, and taking the maximum course load possible to expedite completion of his degree, John graduated from Southern Illinois University thirteen months later with a major in Physical and Health Education, which included teaching certification at the junior high school level.

After sending cover letters and résumés that made no mention of his "work" with the Cardinals, John was offered several teaching positions in Northern Illinois. He decided upon one at Larsen Junior High School in Elgin, a northwestern suburb of Chicago. The job included coaching junior high basketball and football—but not baseball.

In addition to a regular, steady paycheck, his teaching and coaching career finally gave him the comfort and stability he had always wanted from the coal mine but could never attain. John also took pleasure in the soothing rhythm of the school year, watching the progress of his students with the advance of the seasons. While Rose always thought John undervalued himself and that he should have been pursuing collegiate coaching jobs, John preferred to stick to the junior high regimen and its abbreviated sports seasons. He did not even want to consider moving up to the high school level and its longer schedule of games, as he cherished his extra time with the family, especially over the summers and the restful stretch at Christmas as well.

Unable to break old habits, he was still waking up at five o'clock every morning and was at Larsen by six every day. And like others who got only a brief stay in the big leagues, John's exploits on September 28, 1934, remained unknown to most of his new colleagues and neighbors.

He encouraged Rose to go back to school as well. She did, earning a degree in elementary education from Northern Illinois University, after which she took a job at a Catholic grade school in a small community north of Elgin. Both of them earned master's degrees in education along the way. Marie was born in 1942 while Brad followed as the final child, arriving in 1948.

In returning to the county over twenty-eight years after leaving, John discovered in 1963 that several things had changed but much remained the same. Before pulling into the motel, he had driven Brad over to Beckemeyer earlier in the day, going slowly past Alphie's and Leah's house on the west side of town.

After looking at his boyhood home, they parked the car for a moment near the house on Randolph Street on the east side, with the gravel shoulders giving way to steep ditches on both sides. Turning the corner eastward, the Beckemeyer baseball field came into view.

The park was silent and empty. Brad jumped out of the car and instinctively went to investigate home plate, taking an imaginary swing. He took off through the dirt, sprinted around the bases, and ended with a standup triple at third. In pulling up at the bag, he looked up to find his dad staring at the rusting bleachers behind the dugout.

"Come on," he beckoned his son. "I want to show you something else."

The two walked down the left field line and away from the ball field. They continued for a couple of blocks as they crossed First Street, where they stood on the railroad tracks.

"Look back that way," John said, pointing west toward St. Louis. He then pointed down at the rails. "Your grandfather put that down."

They walked north from the tracks. "There's something else," John continued.

Within fifty yards, they came upon a small hill. Brad noticed that the hill was evenly tall along its summit, like a levee guarding a river.

Reaching the top, they gazed down upon the other side, the former site of the Beckemeyer Coal and Mining Company. The shaft had finally closed for good in 1946, with nearly all the workers transferred over to Centralia.

Weeds had overtaken every portion of the lot. A few years earlier, the ground had been declared contaminated as the health department deemed it unsuitable for further building. The only evidence of human activity now on the premises was a few municipal vehicles, as the county government used it as a parking area. As they walked back to the car, Brad had many questions about the mine. His father could not answer some of them.

Heading back to Breese and the motel, John suddenly screeched the car to a halt in the middle of quiet First Street and paused for a moment. "Brad, there's one more thing I need to show you." Wheeling the car around, they headed east on Route 50 instead. A half hour later, they arrived at a small park just south of Centralia, which sat on the former site of the Wamac Number Five coal mine.

John pulled the car to a stop and began to tell Brad the story of what had happened here—and what could have happened to him if he had stayed in the area.

On March 25, 1947—eight months after the Beckemeyer mine had closed—an explosion in the Number Five mine killed 111 out of the 142 men in the shaft at the time. The horrific carnage was caused by rock dust from the coal that had not been properly cleaned, leaving it highly flammable.

Only a week prior to the explosion, state inspector Driscoll Scanlan had issued a foreboding report on the imminent dangers of the Wamac site. Before leaving Centralia, Scanlan had affixed his findings to the walls of the mine shaft—which were discovered by recovery workers who descended into the aftermath to retrieve the bodies. Among Scanlan's warnings were the following:

"Ventilation inadequate. . . ."

"A loose roof on the haulage roads in a number of places. . . . "

"The wall supporting the hoist in the underground machine shop is broken and bulged and presenting a hazard to repair men using the hoist. . . ."

"The mine is not adequately rock dusted."

Under Scanlan's recommendations for the immediate repair of the above items, he added the following comment:

"Recommendations of previous inspections, that have not been complied with, should be complied with."

Several victims of the blast were John's friends. Among them was Gus, with whom John had walked to work when they labored at the Becky and Breese mines.

And Virgil Mazeka, whose wife would permit young John and his friends to pick apples from her trees while running around town.

And Anton Skrobul, the manager of the Beckemeyer team in the Clinton County League.

Other Beckemeyer natives who perished in the disaster included Alfred Stevens, Rodrigo Alvarez, Joseph Koch, Andrew Farley, John Placek, Joseph Peiler, and Luther Frazier.

And Bobby Durstmiller.

Bobby had ultimately found the courage to return to the county and embrace the same honorable work as his father. Nine months after the blast that took Bobby's life, Joe Cobb died on Christmas Eve, 1947.

In 1951, four years after the Wamac tragedy, 119 men were killed at another coal mine explosion in West Frankfort, Illinois, an hour south of Centralia. The two incidents remain the worst coal mining disasters in United States history since 1917.

Once back in Breese, John turned off Fourth Street and into the parking lot of their motel. The Knotty Pine was a place where John had passed many times as child and young man but had never entered.

They checked in and opened the door to room Number 1. John kicked off his shoes and stretched out on the bed to watch television, while Brad took command of the small desk near the door. He immediately went to work, removing some dice, cards, and charts from his backpack. The cards, one for every player in Major League Baseball, had printed numbers all over them. They were the tools of Strat-O-Matic® Baseball, a table game in which results from the dice rolls for each player accurately mirrored his actual performance in real life. The game had been recently invented by a mathematics student at Bucknell University named Hal Richman, and Joseph had seen it advertised while flipping through a sports magazine and ordered it for his younger brother as a gift.

Brad grabbed a handful of the cards and shuffled through them all, taking a moment to study each one carefully. "You ready?" he asked, smiling as he turned to his father.

"I'm gonna win this time," the father declared, accepting the challenge. Pushing himself up from the bed, John felt the familiar pain in his right side. He patted Brad on the back as John pulled another chair over to the desk. While Brad was not looking, John grabbed his right shoulder and muffled his groan.

They decided to have a best of seven "world series" in their usual manner, by dumping all the cards into a paper bag and then each pulling out twenty-five players at random; those twenty-five would comprise the roster each would have to utilize and manage, good or bad. Brad mixed them thoroughly in the bag before they took turns choosing.

"Maybe they've got a card for you, Dad," he wondered. "We should get the 1934 set and see."

John laughed in appreciation of his son's admiration. "How about we get a bite to eat first?" the father suggested.

"Okay. Can we have pizza?"

"Sure."

They set the game down and made their way across the parking lot to the Knotty Pine restaurant. Across Route 50, the large sign of the First National Bank caught Brad's eye; it had a digital clock that alternated the time and temperature. It currently read 97 degrees. "How can any place be this hot at dinnertime? It's almost six o'clock!" Brad marveled, having known only the relative cool of Chicago area evenings until now.

His father just smiled and didn't respond. As with some of Brad's questions about the coal mine, he did not have an answer.

The restaurant seats had colorful orange padding, while a hard tile floor stretched all the way back to the kitchen. Nearly as soon as they sat down, John and Brad were met cheerily by one of the several high school-aged girls who worked as servers. Already in love with the nostalgia of his dad's home area after just a couple of hours, Brad shyly grinned at the girl, struck with an immediate crush on her.

"Something to drink?" she greeted them warmly.

"What do you have for soft drinks?" John asked.

"Well, we have Coke, Seven-Up, root beer—and, of course, Ski," mentioning the last item as if it was available anywhere around town.

"What's *Ski*?" John asked.

The girl could not withhold a polite giggle. "You're not from around here, are you? They started making it down the street a couple years ago, and now everyone's drinking it." Trying to think of a description, the girl tapped her pencil against her lips. "I guess I'd say it's like Mountain Dew, except fruitier."

"Sounds good. I'll have one of those." John replied. He looked over at Brad and then back at the waitress. "Is there a lot of sugar?"

"Not a whole bunch," the girl answered, trying not to be completely untruthful.

Brad was anxious to try it.

"And what to eat?" the girl asked.

"The pork tenderloin sounds good," John said, scanning the menu, "but we're going to have a pizza. Medium sausage and cheese."

When the girl had departed, John and Brad noticed a television high in the corner of the bar. John walked over and spoke to the server working in that area. "How about the Cardinals game?" he requested.

Out of his old habit from George's in Beckemeyer, John took advantage of an abandoned newspaper on the bar. The front page told of plans for a new downtown sports stadium in St. Louis to replace Sportsman's Park, which had been known as Busch Stadium for the past ten years after the Anheuser-Busch Company had purchased the team.

The bartender found the game quickly. The Cards were playing under the lights in Cincinnati at Crosley Field. When John noticed the identity of the opposing team, he inched a little closer to the television.

Long after they had emptied the pizza pan, John and Brad were still watching the entire game together. The Reds hustling rookie second baseman had caught John's attention, as the dust and grime covering his uniform reminded John of his teammates on the Gas House Gang for that one day back in 1934. The television announcer mentioned that the rookie was a hometown boy from the West Side of Cincinnati, having been signed by a scout named Ralph "Buzz" Boyle.

With two out in the top of the ninth, the Cardinals were losing 6–3 to the Reds. As the last hope for Redbirds, an aging player named Stan Musial was sent up by manager Johnny Keane to pinch-hit for Cardinals pitcher Ed Bauta. Musial had gotten his first shot in the majors seven years after John had received his own, as both men were summoned to St. Louis at the end of a season in September, and now Musial was in his final campaign, twenty-two years later, with more hits than anyone in the history of the National League.

Brad and John were stunned when the great Musial was called out on strikes by home plate umpire Doug Harvey to end the game.

"That's okay," John said to his son. "If you want to emulate any ball-player, emulate Musial. He always works hard, and he takes pride in his work being done well."

BIBLIOGRAPHY

Feldmann, D. *Dizzy and the Gas House Gang.* Jefferson, NC: McFarland and Company, 2000.

Feldmann, D. *El Birdos.* Jefferson, NC: McFarland and Company, 2007.

Fleming, G.H. *The Dizziest* Season. New York: William Morrow and Company, 1984.

Goodwin, D. K. *No Ordinary Time.* New York: Simon and Schuster, 1994.

Gregory, R. *Diz: The Story of Dizzy Dean and Baseball during the Great Depression.* New York: Penguin Books, 1992.

Halberstam, D. *October 1964.* New York: Villard Books, 1994.

Hartley, R. and Kenney, D. *Death Underground: The Centralia and West Frankfort Mine Disasters.* Carbondale: Southern Illinois University Press, 2006.

O'Neill, D. *Sportsman's Park: The Players, the Fans, and the Game.* Chesterfield, MO: Mathis Jones Communications, 2007.

Schoendienst, R., and Rains, R. *Red: A Baseball Life.* Champaign, IL: Sports Publishing, 1998.

Newspapers Utilized

Belleville (IL) News Democrat
Brooklyn Eagle
Brooklyn Herald
Brooklyn Times-Union
Chicago Tribune
Cincinnati Enquirer
New York Daily Mirror
New York Evening Journal
New York Sun

New York Times
New York World-Telegram
Philadelphia Evening Bulletin
Pittsburgh Post-Gazette
Pittsburgh Sun-Telegraph
St. Louis Globe-Democrat
St. Louis Post-Dispatch
St. Louis Star-Times
The Sporting News

ABOUT THE AUTHOR

Doug Feldmann is a professor at Northern Kentucky University and a former scout for the Cincinnati Reds, Seattle Mariners, and San Diego Padres. Seven years after a collegiate career at Northern Illinois University, he played for the Beckemeyer Eagles in the Clinton County League from 1999 to 2001—the hometown of his father, John, who played professional baseball in the Chicago Cubs and Chicago White Sox organizations.

Doug is the author of twelve other books about some of the most beloved teams and figures in sports history. He lives in the Cincinnati area with his wife Angie, their son John, and their dog Dizzy. More information on Doug and his books is available at dougfeldmannbooks.com and on Twitter @D_FeldmannBooks.

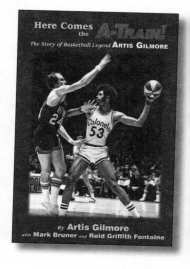
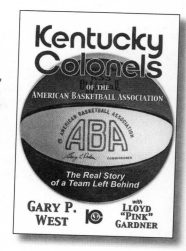

UnCorked!
Kentucky Sports Legend Corky Withrow
By Sherrill Williams and Charles Thurman

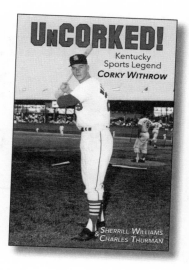

UnCorked! is the true story of two-sport legend Corky Withrow of Central City, Kentucky, one of the greatest high school basketball players in the Commonwealth who went on to play professional baseball with the St. Louis Cardinals.

Authors Sherrill Williams and Charles Thurman take the reader on a journey to 1950s Kentucky, where small town high school basketball was king and Corky was known as one of the best. The book describes, in detail, the hard-nosed, hard fought battles on the court and the thrilling action of the nation's second most successful program in wins.

The book also presents Corky's time in professional baseball, including his struggles in the minor leagues and his time in the big show playing alongside St. Louis great, Stan Musial.

With *UnCorked!*, readers will gain an appreciation for the hard work, and raw talent, of one of the state's best athletes of all time and member of the Kentucky High School Basketball Hall of Fame—Corky Withrow.

6x9, 288 pages, $24.95
ISBN: 978-1-942613-32-9

Clinton County, Illinois
A Pictorial History

Clinton County, Illinois – A Pictorial History chronicles the history of Clinton County and its communities from the 1800s through today. Included are over 600 historic (many never-before-published) photographs of life in Clinton County, including its families, businesses, buildings and homes, churches, schools and more.

8½x11, 144 pages, $39.95
ISBN: 978-1-942613-16-9

See More Great Books

at

WWW.ACCLAIMPRESS.COM